Copyright © 2017 by Sean Redenbaugh

Paintings on cover by world renowned artist Leonid Afremov.
Check out his amazing work at https://afremov.com/

Printed by Ingram Spark / Lightning Source
Printed in the United States of America
2017 First Edition

First Printing, 2017
ISBN 978-0-692-85082-4

Acknowledgements

    The second time around, I have found that much of the process of writing a novel has been easier than the first time through. Knowing you've done something before can often prove to be the only motivation needed in such tasks. However, inevitably there may come a time when prior accomplishment isn't enough to fuel the next one. It is in these times outside sources are needed to give you a little… push.

    For me, I don't have to look far for a push. At my side, offering endless amounts of idea-bouncing, you-can-do-its, and keep-up-the-good-works, is my loving and supporting wife Amanda. She is always there for me, always proud of me, and always willing to give me encouragement.

    And although he will never understand his true merit, I must also thank my ever-faithful and patient dachshund Spades, who throughout most of the writing, spent long nights either curled up at my feet under my writing desk, or sleeping next to my laptop in a chair until the wee hours of morning.

    I would also like to thank my family for everything they do. They have always been supportive of my efforts to follow my passions.

    There are also five people who served as my editing squad on this book that I would like to thank: Barb Redenbaugh, Shannon Farnsworth, Karl Mayer, Gina Adams, & Ryan King (instagram.com/vayouking). They were my first line of defense for finding errors, detecting plot holes, and giving me great feedback to create the best possible book I could. Thank you all for taking the time to read with discerning eyes.

I would also like to thank Leonid Afremov for permission to use his beautiful artwork for the cover. See copyright page for info.

Lastly, I want to thank all those who read this, who have decided to invest a little slice of their life in my story.

SALIMA FALLS

CHAPTER ONE

Raging Green Eyes

Eight, Zero, Eight, Three... Winston's fingers aimed carefully this time. He had to dial the number for the restaurant three times before he got it right, which wasn't uncommon. The phone at his desk sat a bit too far away from him due to the short cable that connected it to the jack in the wall via a little hole in the back of his desk. He tried to pull it closer over and over for the first few weeks he was here, but eventually gave up. The guy who oversaw setting up the computers and phones here at JLM Software said he was out of the longer cables the day Winston first got here. That was five years ago last week.

During those five agonizing years, Winston had learned a few things. One being that the phone guy on average set up about four or five new workstations a week to accommodate the ever-rotating sales staff which occupied the sixth floor of this building, somewhere on the south side of Dunsport. It seems nobody lasted here. In fact, Winston currently held the third highest seniority among the sales staff, though it wasn't something he bragged about, for fear it might trigger them to make amends for their oversight, and give him his walking papers right away. He glanced over at the cheap plaque they gave him last week for making it to five years, which hung slightly crooked on the wall. He kept meaning to fix it but never could remember at the precise time he was walking by it.

Another thing he learned was that no matter how many times you asked the phone guy who worked for this company, he would never remember to bring you a longer cord for your phone when he finally got some in. Winston often thought about going to the nearest electronics store after work and buying his own, but he couldn't get himself to spend his own six dollars knowing it was something the company should provide. So, he just did nothing and got used to it the way many people do with the mundane inconveniences in their lives. They grow passive, and complacent in their lot, however amazing or lackluster it might turn out to be.

And finally, Winston learned that for the most part he hated this job. Software sales wasn't something he had any passion for, or any real talent, for that matter. But the money was good, and that seemed to justify it in some way. The hours of his life apparently had a price, and sometimes he was ashamed at the negotiated rate at which he sold them. But with all it took from him, it gave him a few things too. It was these things he was thinking of today as he punched in the numbers on the phone over and over.

His life was a middle-class life, somewhere in the upper half of society. The part of middle class where you live in a two thousand square foot house in the fifth nicest neighborhood in the city. The part where a few sushi rolls and a twenty-dollar bottle of wine is a special occasion and not the norm. The part where vacations consist of a weekend away and not two weeks in Europe. Where a four-year-old charcoal-colored BMW gives you pride, and makes you feel like you made it in life. Where shopping is done out of need or holiday, and not out of boredom.

But all the downs in Winston's job and life only made the ups seem that much more palatable. And today was an "UP" day by all accounts. The sun was shining strongly, both in his office, and on his life. Today was a day when he felt like he had more than he did, when he felt lucky to have what he had. You see, the best part of his life was home waiting anxiously for him. He could picture her sitting by the window, looking down the road for his BMW, with a beautiful smile on her face. She was the most gorgeous girl Winston had ever laid eyes on, and the prized joy of his life. She was the reason he could brush off all the mundane inconveniences. She was the reason he took this job that he did not enjoy, and she was the reason he was ok with all of it. Her name was Caroline, and today was her birthday.

Winston and Caroline had met almost three years ago at a cookout hosted by a mutual friend of theirs who was breaking in their new house with friends, beer, and a fire. Images of that night flashed through his head. He remembered sitting by the fire, nursing his beer, watching the flames flicker on the silver can that spun in his fingers, and wondering what he was going to do with this life of his. It was then, lost in thought, that he looked up and saw her walking across the yard. Through the flames, she almost seemed to be a mirage, entering his life in slow motion. She wore a white flower in her blond hair which waved in the night air, which had just begun to cool. Her yellow V-neck shirt had thin straps that hung loosely on her shoulders, and rippled slightly in the breeze. They were introduced by a friend, and the rest of the night became a blur for Winston. He got lost watching the flames dance in the reflection of her eyes as they talked and laughed for hours in front of the fire.

Looking back, he knew immediately that someday he would marry her, yet it still took over two years for him to get from the mirage by the fire that night to a bent knee and a ring in the sand in front of her. They had only been married three short months as of this morning, yet he could hardly picture what his life was like before she came along. Without her, he knew this would feel like a crummy dead-end job, where he wasted his life away on dollars he could live without, while fluorescent lights tried to suck out his soul from above, and his computer screensaver displayed dreams of far off wonders he may never see.

But knowing he had Caroline made it all worth it. It made this tiny room seem like the throne room of a king, this building like his own personal castle, and his work seem important and noble. These useless dollars now had a use for him. They made it possible to have two thousand square feet of middle class life with a beautiful woman whom he adored. They made sushi and twenty-dollar bottles of wine on special occasions such as her birthday possible. Yes, today was most certainly and "UP" day for Winston.

Thus explains the excitement and nervous anticipation that rushed through his body on this late afternoon. He was supposed to leave work an hour ago when a client of his called with a last-minute request. He almost didn't answer the phone, too anxious for sushi and smiles, but his numbers were lower than normal this month, and he knew he could use the extra money, especially with his surprise for Caroline coming up. That phone call led to an extra hour of work, and it was the reason he was still in his office right now, and not already sitting at the restaurant with his beautiful new bride.

Nowadays, he often thought about that phone call, and how simply answering it had changed his life completely.

Tonight was the night he had planned on surprising Caroline with a weekend away in the mountains. They would spend two nights in a warm and cozy log cabin that overlooked five hundred acres of the most pristine wildlife within a day's drive of Dunsport. After taking her out for sushi, they would come back home to a nice glass of their favorite red wine, and he would tell her to pack a bag. He could barely wait to see the look on her face when he told her. She had no idea. The cabin was already booked, and they would be leaving in the morning. He could almost smell the trees now, could almost hear the quiet of the wilderness and the roll of the flames in the fireplace, flickering as they had that night he first laid eyes on her.

And he needed some time away with her. He had been so obsessed with his sales numbers at work and working late hours, that they had hardly had time for each other these three months. He was focused on getting them a little stability, and he realized lately he might have been overdoing it. He had vowed to change his priorities after being handed that cheap plaque, and tonight was the beginning. He was going to start putting her first again. He was going to start truly experiencing life with her, and not care so much about his monthly numbers. A weekend away in the mountains was going to be a great start. He smiled thinking about it.

And it was more this excitement and anticipation than the short phone cable that explained why it took him three tries to dial the number for the restaurant. His fingers were fidgety, and as he waited for the call to connect. He spun the bottle of wine on his desk in circles with his other hand. The Celtic cross etched in the dark glass reflected the light in the room along with the gold leaf foil covering the cork as he spun it.

He had stopped to pick up the wine and flowers on his lunch break today, a smart decision considering he was about to miss the sushi reservation, and would have had no time later.

"Hello, you've reached Asuka Gari, how may I help you?"

Winston was hard in thought about Caroline, and was startled by the girl's bubbly nature. "Uh…yes… I was…. could… Sorry, let me start again. I had a reservation for five-thirty tonight for two, and we are running a bit later than we had planned. I was wondering if I could move that to six-thirty?"

"Awe, no problem sir. I'm sorry to hear that, I'll see what I can do you for. Could you tell me the name on the reservation please?"

"Caroline… or Winston… I'm not sure, probably one of those two." He knew it was under Caroline, but he always felt awkward when someone called him sir, and sometimes this made him talk in circles, or try to make himself sound younger or dumber than he was. It was stupid and he knew it, and the irony wasn't lost on him.

"Oh yes, I see it now. I'll just go ahead and take that off for you. Let me see what else we have." Winston could hear the clicking of keys on her computer. "We do have an opening for two at six ten. I'm sorry but that's the only slot I have between now and ten o'clock tonight. We seem to be quite busy tonight. It must be the weather." Winston looked out the window in his office and remembered shopping for flowers at lunch. He agreed it was an exceptional day. The sun was shining and it was the perfect temperature, without a cloud in the sky. "I hope that works for you. Do you want me to put your name down?"

Winston looked at the clock on his computer. Six ten. If he left right this second, he might have just enough time to stop at home and get Caroline before heading to the restaurant. "Yes, I'll take it."

"Great! I have you down then, we will see you at ten after six!"

"Thanks for your help." Winston knew it would be close. He immediately hung up the phone and powered off his computer. After one last peek at the clock, he grabbed the bottle of wine on his desk and spun around. He quickly picked up the bouquet of flowers on the table behind him. He stood up, pushed his chair under his desk and headed for the door, and just as he got there, his boss popped around the corner.

"Winston. How come I haven't seen the details on that Booker upgrade proposal yet?" His tone was harsh and his gaze was penetrating. And he had a forceful way of standing in front of employees, slightly too close, as a way of making them feel uncomfortable and intimidated. This was the manner in which he stood in front of Winston now. He was the owner of this company, and the kind of boss that everyone dreaded, and tried to avoid. They all seemed to be waiting for him to retire, but this business was his only passion, and they knew he never would. Winston got good at avoiding him, and the misery that came from talking to him. He would never ask personal questions or show the slightest care of his employees' lives outside of work. He considered their spouses, children, prior commitments, medical problems, appointments, and illnesses all nuisances that took them away from their duties to him. Winston and his coworkers often joked about being robots under his control. Few had ever seen his office on the tenth floor, and they all surmised it was filled with screens and cameras and computers and buttons for monitoring and controlling his flock of robots. Winston hated him, and he was sure the feeling was mutual.

"The numbers have been crunched, I just have to put some final touches on the last page. I can have it printed and in your mailbox first thing Monday morn…." The last syllable was still in his throat when he was cut off.

"Monday is no good! I want to look it over this weekend. Have it in my mailbox before you leave. Don't disappoint me Winston." He turned to walk away before Winston could even get a sound out to explain his plans with Caroline and the cabin. He knew the words would do little good anyway. He had to fulfill his robot duty, or he knew his job and his middle-class lifestyle would be in jeopardy come Monday. So, he set the flowers and wine on his desk with a heavy thump and quickly punched the power key on his computer again. He pounded his fist on his desk as he waited for it to boot, seemingly slower than usual, as he debated dialing the restaurant for the fourth time.

Eleven minutes later he was angrily shoving the paperwork in his boss's mailbox, mumbling something under his breath about an ungrateful bastard. He dodged the usual chatterboxes on the way to the elevator. Betsy, with her never-ending stream of funny cat pictures, had her face in a piece of chocolate cake leftover from last week's party. He sprinted by as she looked up with her mouth too full to stop him. He then avoided eye contact with Dan, who undoubtedly had another nauseating story about his son achieving some feat in middle school sports that has apparently never been done before.

Winston turned the corner after the last cubicle and took a right towards the hallway. He saw two women enter an open elevator door ahead of him. They were accountants from the second floor who ventured up to the sixth every Friday on some mission for numbers, heading back to their domain of equations and turtleneck sweaters. He had never been to the second floor, but based on these two specimens, he always imagined it as a dimly lit place, with too many snacks and too little heat, filled with the sound of keyboards and slow music. They were deep in conversation about some lifetime show when the doors started to shut, with Winston still twenty feet away.

"I'm coming. Hold on." He was still holding the wine bottle in one hand and the flowers in the other, and neither accountant seemed to notice him. "Hey! Hold the elevator!" One woman turned her head towards him as the other kept on blabbering about the show. The doors touched each other just as he reached them. He elbowed the button frantically, but it was too late. The elevator was already descending. He looked up at the numbers above the other car. Four… Three… Figures… It was headed down too. He kicked the elevator door in frustration and darted for the stairs instead. He looked at his watch. He knew if they were more than a few minutes late they would give away his table. He raced down the stairwell, taking steps two at a time, until he reached the ground floor, sweating, and even more ticked off. It seemed some unseen force was trying to ruin his perfect plans.

After zipping through the maze of people in the lobby, taking the back entrance to the parking lot in the rear of the building, and finding his four-year-old charcoal colored BMW, Winston set the wine and flowers on the empty passenger seat beside him and fired up the engine. As he slammed the door and backed out of his parking space, he picked up his phone and held down the round button on the front. "Call Caroline." The phone responded with its robotic, yet feminine voice. "Calling Caroline." Winston pulled out of the parking lot onto Baker Street, dodging the familiar potholes that the city had long forgotten about, until that sweet voice on the other end met his ears.

"Hey there, are you almost home?" She spoke with a relaxed, carefree tone, no doubt feeling none of the stress that was pumping through Winston's veins now.

"Sorry. I just left, actually. My jerk of a boss dumped something on me right as I was walking out the door. I swear he does it just to get to me. I would have been home by now!"

"It's fine, I'm ready to go. Just sitting here by the window enjoying the sunlight. Isn't it beautiful outside?" She closed her eyes and Winston could sense she was smiling on the other end, as he braked for the red light in front of him.

"It would be nicer if I didn't get stopped by every damn light in the city!"

"You don't need to talk like that Winston, it's Friday. You let your job affect you too much and I don't like it when you get like this."

"I'm sorry. I'll try to calm down." Winston merged onto the two-lane highway that ran just around the edge of the city and led to their little slice of suburbia. "I called the restaurant and changed the reservation to ten after six." He looked at the clock on his dashboard. It's six already, so we will be a little late. Hopefully they don't give our table away. They seemed busy tonight."

"I'm ready to go, where are you exactly?"

"I'm close to the Jefferson boulevard exit, so I'll be there in five minutes at the most."

"Okay, I'll grab my purse and lock up the house and wait for you on the sidewalk. It's so perfect outside! You can just swing by and pick me up. I'm sure we will be fine. I can't wait to see you!"

Winston stepped on the gas a little harder, even more anxious to see her now that he could hear her voice again. "Me too. See you soon. I Lo…" Before the words finished leaving his mouth, he noticed the sign for Jefferson Boulevard out of the corner of his eye at the last second. In his haste, he had no time to check his mirrors and simply swerved into the exit lane without looking. His tires squealed on the fresh pavement and his phone fell from his hand and down the gap between the seat and the console, hanging up on Caroline. The wine and flowers jostled in the seat next to him.

Another car was just to the right and slightly behind Winston's. The driver was forced to slam on the brakes as Winston's car swerved in front of him, narrowly missing the front left fender. Winston gritted his teeth as he watched the other car sliding behind him. The tires locked up and slid on the pavement, leaving long black streaks in the sunlight, as smoke drifted into the air from the melted rubber. Winston had no time to stop and apologize, and simply kept going, as the other driver slammed on the gas, throwing rocks in the air with his sticky tires, a dark black object among a cloud of dust.

A mile or so down the road, Winston saw the other car in his rear-view mirror. It was coming up on him fast and he watched until it closed the gap and was directly behind him, maybe five feet from the bumper. Winston saw the man waving his hand wildly out his driver side window, flashing obscene gestures and pointing madly at him. By the mumbled words that made it to Winston's car, he could tell the man was screaming furiously at him, though he couldn't make out what he was saying. It was no doubt vulgar and filled with fury, like his actions. The sun was at a harsh angle, and cast a dark shadow across the car in his rear-view mirror, hiding most of the menacing figure chasing him. Winston could only see the man's eyes. The sunlight seemed to focus on them with precision, just as they focused back on Winston. Their eyes locked on each other with a magnetism that seemed to drag time with it.

Their gaze was only broken by the movement of the other car. The driver whipped into the passing lane and slammed on the gas. Shifting his view to the mirror outside his window, Winston saw the black car moving up beside him. He pressed the gas harder to keep the lead, but the other car was faster. There was nothing he could do but watch as the black mass roared up next to him. Winston tried to keep his focus ahead of him, but something inside him just had to look at the other driver. He turned his head as the man honked and waved his finger at Winston, filling the air with even more words of hate as he inched over in his lane until the cars were mere inches apart. Once again the man's face seemed to be perpetually in shadow and he could only see those fiery green eyes locking in on him.

The car flew ahead of Winston in the fast lane and he saw the familiar blue and white logo on the rear. It was also a BMW, much like Winston's, but newer and as black as the night. It shined with a newly washed gleam that reflected the sunlight directly into Winston's eyes as it swerved into the right lane ahead of him, barely missing his front bumper. Winston held his hand up to shield the glare but failed to see the other car's brake lights with the sunbeams in his eyes and smoke pouring from the exhaust. He noticed far too late that the gap between the cars was suddenly vanishing. Before he even got his foot on the brake, his car slammed with a resounding crash into the rear of the black car in front of him. Winston saw the wine bottle and flowers in the seat next to him fly through the air into the dashboard in slow motion. There was an explosion of glass and red liquid that mixed with the flowers and seemed to hang in the air and glisten in the sunlight. For the smallest of instances, Winston stared at it like it was some sort of abstract suspended still life.

A moment later, after the cars parted again, he realized the consequences of it all. His mood returned to the anger filled fumes of earlier. His car was now damaged for sure, and his night was wrecked. It was bad enough that he was late for what was supposed to be the best night in a long time. It was bad enough that his boss treated him like crap. That he hated his job and answered the phone when he shouldn't have. That he missed the sushi reservation once, and might again. But now the wine and flowers he had so lovingly picked out for his perfect Caroline were lying in a jumbled massacre on the passenger floor. It seemed to symbolize his failure to create even one perfect weekend, let alone an entire life. Things often didn't go his way, and many times he blamed those around him. Today wasn't his fault, it was the fault of his boss, the fault of his client, the fault of two turtleneck-wearing accountants, and most recently, the fault of one black-BMW-driving jerk with a bad attitude in front of him. His own anger welled up, and he pounded his foot on the gas again.

His car moaned like an injured lion, ignoring the pain for one final chase, one final hunt. He flew up to the other car again with fury and moved into the passing lane. The other driver glared back at him with those pulsating green eyes and swerved along with him, keeping Winston behind him. Back and forth they went from one lane to another, cursing and gesturing wildly at each other, locked into a battle of will and determination, like a Matador and a bull.

At one point Winston managed to pull nearly even with the black BMW on the right, but his tires slipped off the road and he nearly lost control. In his rage, he hadn't noticed that he was approaching his house on the right. The other driver had laughter in his eyes as Winston recovered and neared him again. Winston got in the left lane, knowing the other driver would follow suit. He got as close as he could to the other car, leaving just enough room to escape, knowing the other driver would likely brake again. He watched the rear lights in front of him closely, waiting for them to light up, for that perfect moment to pass.

Suddenly, the other driver tapped his brakes, and as soon as the red light shined into Winston's raging eyes, he jerked the wheel to the right and hit the gas, barely scraping his bumper again on the other car. The other driver seemed to know exactly what Winston had planned, and in an instant, he had hit the gas and flew into the right lane, cutting him off again. Winston braked just in time to avoid sliding off the road again, and the other driver stared back at him in his rear-view mirror. Their eyes were locked in a heated glare, as both cars slowly drifted to the right in unison, filling the air with dust and rocks and malice.

What happened next happened in utter slow motion for Winston. Time seemed to slow all energy and motion to a crawl, but had no effect on thought or agony. He was helpless to watch machine and metal, dust and rock, flying through the air and skidding along the ground. Helpless to change the direction of force and inevitability as their cars continued to slide farther off the road. Helpless as their eyes never blinked or left each other's stare among the chaos around them. Hate had formed a direct line between Winston's eyes and those raging green eyes in the mirror looking back at him. Drops of sweat were frozen still on their way down his face. The stare was intense, unbroken by the noise and motion of the cars, until out of the corner of his eye, Winston noticed something bright and white.

In the endless and torturous stop motion of that moment, Winston blinked and turned his eyes toward the white object ahead. As the seconds ticked by, each felt like a minute, but this new sight changed everything. It made those minutes turn into hours… to years. The white object was about thirty feet away and standing just off the sidewalk. It was Caroline.

She was standing with her eyes closed, silent and happy in her own world of joy. A world which consisted only of the white dogwoods that lined the street, along with the beautiful green grass under her feet, and the warm rays of sunlight that touched her. She was wearing a beautiful white summer dress that billowed slightly in the breeze. Winston could only watch as the sun held her in its embrace, lifting her up in majesty like a shiny pearl among dark waters. In her hand, she held a small bundle of the flowers she had pulled from the tree, and she held them up to her nose to take in the wonderful smells of early summer. She had one of these flowers in her hair, which gleamed like silk in the sunlight.

It has been said that a person's life flashes before his or her eyes during the worst seconds of their life. But this isn't entirely true. It's not their whole life that flashes before them. It's only the best parts. The parts that the soul wants to relive one last time. For Winston, these seconds were the worst seconds of his life. He felt all at once the thousand days of happiness he had shared with Caroline between the flickering flames of the fire that night and the screeching bellows of tires in this instant. He felt the taste of their first kiss. The softness and warmth of the first time he touched her skin. He saw the look on her face when he took her to see the new baby elephant at the zoo last year. He saw the tears in her eyes the night he got on one knee on the beach in Costa Rica. He felt the wonderful ache in his heart when she walked down the aisle towards him. He felt the excitement of their first night in their new house. And he wanted more than anything to go back.

He wanted to relive those moments again, all the way up to this day, only with more appreciation this time. And he wanted to go back to the office today. Back when he watched the sunlight pour through his window, and to try again. Caroline was more important than it all, and he knew in this moment what he would do. This time he would leave the phone ringing and his client waiting. He would leave an hour earlier and not be there when his boss stopped by his office. He would leisurely walk past Betsy and look at her latest cat picture with a smile on his face. He would stop and listen to the story about Dan's son and his heroics in last night's game. He would smile into the sunlight as he drove home. He would open his window and take a deep breath of summer air. He wasn't sure how he got to this precise moment in time, but he would go back and forget the other driver and all the rage and anger he was responsible for. Caroline was more important than all of it.

But the sad truth is that moments and seconds and minutes all come in order, one after another. Winston knew he couldn't go back. There was no changing it. He knew only the seconds ahead of him were malleable. Only the minutes and hours he has yet to encounter could be forged into something new. The ones behind him were gone, and the one staring him in the face has long been written by the actions leading up to it. He was just a spectator now. And he could only watch the cruel story of these seconds unfold before him.

The black car in front of him slid onto the sidewalk as Winston lunged his foot for his brake. The driver's green fiery eyes were locked on Winston's as the car slowly entered the grass, unaware of the shining white beauty hopelessly in his path. All Winston could do is close his eyes and slam on the brake pedal as he screamed her name one syllable at a time. "CAR…O….LINE!"

When his car slid to a stop next to the sidewalk, Winston opened his eyes and time returned to its normal selfish hastiness. He could no longer see Caroline, but only the other

car as it righted itself and returned to the road. Winston's door
flung open and he jumped out of his car. He ran to the grass
under the dogwood where Caroline was standing only a
moment ago. She was lying motionless in the grass at his feet
as he screamed her name over and over. He dropped to his
knees next to her and pulled her lifeless body onto his lap,
holding her in his arms. The sweet smells of summer were
gone, and all that filled the air was the pungent smell of
smoking brakes and burnt rubber, mixed with the horrifying
odor of the black car's exhaust. Apologies and tears flowed
down from Winston like a waterfall onto her face. He shook
her and cried, begging her to wake and say she was all right.
His veins boiled with fear and sadness, anger and fury,
hopelessness and despair, yet he could only watch with a dark
heart as the other car sped away, taking his life and love with
it.

ONE YEAR LATER

CHAPTER TWO
Darkness and Rain

The clouds hung low above Dunsport, thick and bulky, adding to the darkness of the night. It was like a blanket laying over the city, holding in the stench, keeping out the stars and moon that were surely out there somewhere. It was cold for this time of year, and the rain was still coming down, as it had been for days. It seemed the rain never stopped in this god-forsaken city. At best, it would slow to a drizzle, misting the face of any poor soul that dared it. Winston's windshield wipers scraped across the glass with a harsh sound, which seemed to be their main duty now, as they did little about the rain.

Dunsport was an old city, marked by crumbling brick at every street corner, and decade old potholes in the roads that have long been forgotten by the powers that be. Winston's tire crashed into a deep puddle, rocking the car, and shooting water ten feet in the air. The empty glass bottles rolling around on the floorboard rattled against each other. Maybe he didn't see it because of the rain, or maybe he simply didn't care.

There were, of course, parts of the city that had a new shine and glisten on them, but every time Winston drove past a new building, or a bright new neon sign, he thought that it was like putting pearl earrings on an old lady. It did little to cover the age and weariness. And the potholes in the roads and the stench in the air persisted.

Winston's car pulled up to a run-down apartment building in a part of the city he used to avoid. He stopped on a painted number next to the sidewalk that matched the number on his door, and stared out the window at the rain. He hated every square inch of that building, if not the entire city. After one last gulp, he tossed the bottle in his hand to the floor with the rest of the empty ones.

When he was back in his middle class suburban life, he used to drive past ugly buildings such as this and wonder what kind of people lived there, and what sort of things happened along the way in their lives to lead to their paltry existence. Now he was one of them, and he knew firsthand the kinds of horrors and disappointments that life can throw at you when you least expect it.

He reached for some newspapers and a bottle in a brown paper bag that were lying on the passenger seat, and then stepped out into the rain. It was coming down steadily now, and he tucked the newspaper under his arm inside his coat. He had been drinking for a while already, and the world was slightly swirling around him. He closed his eyes and could feel the drops hitting his face, and hear them bouncing off the black leather at his shoulders. He didn't bother to hasten his steps as he walked past the front of the car in the rain, still dented from that fateful night a year ago. The bent metal reflected the light from the streetlights above. The sight of it pained him less and less over the last year, but on this night especially, it stabbed at him even harder than usual. He leisurely walked up the broken sidewalk to his apartment, letting the rain soak him and chill his skin.

Inside his apartment, Winston stepped over the garbage and clothes that littered the floor between the door and countertop bar. He slid his arm across the bar, knocking aside old food boxes and empty bottles of beer, some of which fell to the sink or floor in a crash. He dropped the newspaper and bag onto the bar and sat down harshly on a stool. He pulled the bottle of wine from the bag and tossed the soggy paper to the floor. He sat there in silence, spinning the bottle of wine on the bar top in circles with his hand. A Celtic cross was etched into the dark glass and gold leaf foil covered the cork. As it spun, it caught the light from the street lamp outside that was coming through the window, and reflected it into Winston's eyes.

The phone on the counter rang loudly, breaking the silence, yet Winston never flinched, as if he didn't even notice it. He simply reached for the corkscrew and began opening the bottle of wine like it was the only thing on earth. After a few rings, the phone beeped and then he heard his own voice on the box next to it.

"Not here. Leave a message." His voice was unwelcoming and emotionless.

Beeeeeep.

"Winston, this is Raheem, your favorite landlord. Listen, it's the eighth of the month already, and we still haven't received your rent check. This is now the fourth month in a row, and to be honest, I'm getting a little tired of talking to your answering machine. Please drop off the money at the office by tomorrow, and I'll waive the late fee this time. I'll be expecting it. Later."

Click.

Winston set the cork aside and lifted the entire bottle up to this mouth. Several gulps later, he slammed the bottle back onto the counter with a thud. Red wine dripped down from his lips to his chin, and fell to his lap. The sudden rush of alcohol brought warmth to his insides, and he noticed the red light blinking on the phone, indicating there was a message. He hit the play button and slid the newspaper over in front of him as he listened.

Beeeeeep.

"Winston, this is Mark, your boss. Look, I've tried working with you but things have gotten out of control. Today was the third day in a row you haven't shown up. And when you do show up, you come in smelling like booze." Winston grabbed a marker from the cup on the counter and stared at the newspaper intently, as if he wasn't even listening to his boss's words. "Terry is tired of covering for you, and I'm tired of making these calls. I have to let you go. Don't bother coming in on Monday. I'll have accounting put your last check in the mail. Sorry it had to come to this."

Click.

Winston never flinched or looked away from the newspaper, as he was listening. The news of his firing had no effect on him. He simply pulled out the car dealership ads and slowly flipped through them, scanning them carefully. He had become numb to the world. Not finding what he wanted, he crumpled up the papers and threw them at the wall. Next, he turned to the classified section and began searching those.

The phone rang loudly again, as he took another drink from the bottle. Still he didn't bother to pick it up. After the beep, another familiar voice called out to him.

"Winston! Pick up man, if you are there, it's me, Marlow." Winston flipped another page in the newspaper with indifference to the pleas. "Come out with us tonight man, let's have fun for once... Hello?" Winston managed to turn his head towards the answering machine. A small part of him wanted to answer and listen, but a bigger part of him wanted to rip the cord from the wall and throw the machine against the wall. "Hello," Marlow continued. "Are you really not there? I bet you are sitting there listening to me right now." Marlow knew him well. "Ok, but I'm going to keep calling until you answer, I swear."

After the click, Winston walked over to the answering machine. He was reaching for the plug in the back when it rang again. His hand paused and he listened, until Marlow's voice shot out at him again.

"Winston. Marlow again as promised. I..."

Winston picked the receiver up and held it to his ear. "What do you want?" His voice was dull and a little mumbled.

"Hey buddy, I knew you were home. Just listen to me man, I think you should come out with some of us tonight."

"I'm not going out." Winston replied dryly. He walked back over and sat in front of the newspaper and continued his search.

"Come on man, Marc and Cindy and some others are headed over to Side Pocket to shoot some pool and have a few drinks."

"Not interested." Winston took another drink from the bottle and picked up the marker.

"Look buddy, I know it's Caroline's birthday. I know you're probably planning on drinking yourself into oblivion, but I think you need something different. I think you need to come out with us, have a few laughs, and try not to think about it for just one night. What do you say?"

Winston spotted something in the paper and picked it up closer to his eyes. A smirk crossed his face and he circled the ad in red. "I'm busy."

Marlow was getting frustrated. "What could you possibly be busy with? You already sound half drunk. I can come over and pick you up if you need me to. You just need to get out and get your mind off it. All you do is dwell on the past. You need to let me help you, man, I'm your best friend."

"There's nothing you can do to help me man. I just have to keep looking."

"Looking for what? Don't tell me you are still out there trying to hunt down that damn car, man. It's been a year! You are wasting your tim…"

"What do you know about it!" Winston shot back at him with alcohol-fueled anger. "He could be out there in the city right now! He needs to know what he did. He needs to know what he did to my life. Time is all I have left."

Marlow eased his tone a bit. "Sorry man, I don't mean to upset you. I just think you need to do something fun for a change and try to forget what happened and move on."

Calm returned to Winston's voice. He was still wearing his wedding ring after all this time. He spun it on his finger. "Of all nights to forget about it, this ain't it. Look… I have to go."

"You don't even know what the man looks like, or the license plate number. I know you always say you would recognize his eyes, but it's pointless." When Marlow mentioned the man's eyes Winston closed his own and could see those fiery green orbs staring back at him again in the rear-view mirror of the black car. "He could be a thousand miles away by now," Marlow continued. "He could have sold the car, or wrecked it, or traded it in on something else. Hell, the car could have been melted down by now and turned into beer cans for all you know." There was a pause and then Marlow started again. "Caroline would have wanted…"

Click.

Winston could take no more. He hung up on Marlow before he even finished his sentence. He tore the ad from the page in the newspaper and shoved it in his jacket pocket along with his car keys. He snatched up the bottle of wine from the counter, shoved the cork back in the hole, and headed for the door. He was halfway out when he heard the phone ringing again, mixed with the pounding of the rain on the sidewalk outside. The door shut behind him with a thud as he stepped out into the rain.

CHAPTER THREE

The Red "E"

Winston was sitting in his car outside his apartment, still fuming from his conversation with Marlow. "What does he know about it!" he said to himself, as the water poured down from his hair onto his face, and gathered in his stubble. He wiped his eyes with the backside of his hand, and took a sizeable swig from the bottle of wine before replacing the cork and tossing it into the passenger seat. The driving rain was pelting the windshield and car from all angles it seemed. He could barely see what was outside.

He looked up at the tiny worn photo that was sticking out from his visor, pulled it down, and held it in his hand. It was a photo of him and Caroline, from less than a week before the accident. More rain dripped into his eyes, and he smeared it away. He propped the picture against the dash and grabbed for the wine again.

"I'll find him baby, I swear. I won't rest until I face the man who took you from me. I promised you that much." The tears in his eyes mixed with the rainwater and fell to his lap. He took another large gulp from the bottle, and red liquid ran out of the corner of his mouth and dripped down his chin. "I'm going to look him in the eyes and…"

Winston paused and looked at his own eyes in the mirror. He didn't know what he would do if he ever got to face the man in the black car, but he was afraid of what he might do.

He looked back at Caroline's face in the photo, and ran his finger along her hair and down her cheek. His finger and hand were both shaking. "I miss you so much." Emotional and pain-filled screams raged inside the car, which would have been heard a block away if not for the rain. A dog barked somewhere off in the distance. "I'm so sorry," Winston said through the tears. He wiped his eyes, put the photo away, and pulled the crumpled piece of paper from the classified ads out of his pocket. He stared at the heading in bold letters.

FOR SALE: Black BMW: 2010 3-Series

He looked at the picture of the black car and suddenly visions of the man's fiery green eyes came to him. Quick flashes like tiny lightning storms jolted his vision; the car, the eyes, the smoke, the swerving, the sliding, the impact. Fury brewed in his mind as he reluctantly relived the moments, as he had done a thousand times since that day.

Winston checked the address on the paper, then turned on his windshield wipers, and slammed the car into gear. In an instant, he was racing down the rainy avenue, and the inside of his car was filled with orange light each time he passed under the streetlights above. The alcohol was racing through his veins as fast as he was racing through the city, and his eyes were intensely focused on the yellow centerline. His vision was blurred and each passing car seemed like six. The windshield wipers seemed to mosey back and forth in slow motion. Sometimes his blinks felt like several seconds, yet when he opened his eyes it was if he hadn't moved at all. And he would think about those eyes staring back at him in the rear-view mirror until he missed a turn and had to double back. Eventually he pulled onto the street listed on the paper in his lap.

Winston checked the number over and over as his car slowly crept along the quiet suburban street. Fourteen Twenty-Six. He recited the house numbers aloud as he rolled past them slowly. "fourteen eight, fourteen ten, fourteen twelve…" His eyes lit up when he spotted the black BMW sitting innocently outside a cozy little house that looked like every other house on the street. He pulled over and parked his car in sight of the house to get a better look. He shut off his headlights and looked intently through the rain, examining the car in small intervals as the wipers cleared away the rain. This could be it.

He read the address again on the paper. One, Four, Two, Six. He could see the numbers mounted on the house in black lettering, shining in the porch light. He needed no confirmation after seeing the car, but still said the numbers aloud. "One, Four, Two, Six."

The world was now beginning to spin faster and faster as the alcohol permeated his system. Winston took one final look at the picture of Caroline and reached for the bottle of wine beside him. Just as he was about to finish off the last few gulps and debate his next course of action, the front door to the house suddenly opened.

Winston quickly pulled the bottle away from his mouth and leaned forward until his face was only inches from the glass. He watched closely as a man stepped out and hurriedly ran through the rain and hopped in the car. Winston's eyes widened, but try as he might, he wasn't close enough, sober enough, or seeing clearly enough to recognize the man or his eyes.

He saw the black car's lights turn on and heard the engine fire up. As it backed out of the driveway, Winston sunk back in his chair trying not to be seen, until the car took off ahead of him. He waited a few seconds before turning on his lights and shifting into drive. He followed the other car through several turns and down roads he had never driven before. He tried to be inconspicuous, fighting both his urge to simply slam into the other car, and his slowly failing motor skills. Flashes of the first time he hit the back of the other car filled his mind, and he only snapped out of it when the brake lights in front of him glistened off the beads of rain on his windshield.

They had arrived at a small pub on the outskirts of the city. Winston looked around him at the buildings outside. He had never been here, or at least not that he remembered. The black car pulled into the small parking lot next to the pub, and Winston pulled his car over to the opposite side of the street. He quickly killed the engine and lights on his car and watched as the man left the black car and hastily walked into the pub through the rain. He looked carefully at the man, taking in everything from his unzipped brown leather jacket to his boots that splashed in the rain as he jogged to the door. The neon lights of the bar were bright on the outside of the building, leaving a faint red glow all around. The pub had one of those hipster names like Eclipse or Elixir. Winston could only see the large letter "E" glowing bright red from his car.

When the man was safely inside the door, Winston took one final look at the photo in the visor, then gulped down the last of the bottle of wine and threw the empty bottle to the floorboard in a crash. He opened his door and stumbled out onto the street, losing his balance and nearly falling before righting himself. The rain poured down on his face as he looked up at the streetlight. His keys were still in the ignition, and the driver door was still partially open behind him. Just as he reached the other side of the street, a car flew by, inches from his back. The tires crashed through a puddle of water, sending a wave of water in Winston's direction. He turned towards the car just as the wall of water crashed into his face, knocking him backwards and soaking him completely.

He fell to the sidewalk and landed with a splash on the wet concrete. He screamed belligerently into the night towards the car as it sped away. He pounded his fist into the sidewalk in anger, bloodying his hand.

Sitting in the red glow that was cast by the large red "E" above him, he looked up at the sign. "Emanation". The letter N flickered on and off in the night and cast blinking shadows all around him. He managed to get to his feet, and stumbled down the sidewalk to the entrance to the bar's parking lot. From there he spotted the black car and toddled gingerly towards it, stopping about ten feet behind it.

He had been in this situation before… standing in front of a car that may or may not have been responsible for the downward spiral in his life. It had been a year since Caroline's death, and he spent most of his free time looking for this car. In fact, he used to be quite diligent about the whole process. He collected car sales ads and classifieds, he printed out internet ads matching the car in his area, he had notebooks filled with VIN numbers, license plate numbers, drawings of stickers and decals, anything unique about each car. He got quite good at researching vehicle collision and accident reports. He took pictures of the drivers and wrote down addresses. Yet as his search continued to fail in giving him the answers he was looking for, he widened the search more and more, and found more and more solace in the bottle. He was becoming hopeless and reckless, a lethal combination. He knew he couldn't keep going on like this, but it was all he had. It was his only motivation to live… that eventually he would find the man responsible, and face him. Then, and only then, could he move on.

But tonight was different. He felt something in the air, as if the last year was meant to lead him to this place… on this night. It seemed so perfect. Tonight was the anniversary of her death. Something was different tonight… something more intense, more tangible, more promising. Something was different about Winston too, and about this car. As he stood behind the car, the moonlight glistened off the wet metal directly into his eyes, the same way the sun had done so a year ago. Flashes of the sun in his eyes, and the fire in the other man's eyes crowded his vision.

Winston ran his hand along the rear bumper and taillights, breaking up the droplets and letting them run down the car. The light sparkled off something hanging from the rear-view mirror, grabbing his attention. He squinted his eyes and wiped the rain temporarily from his face, but he couldn't tell what it was. He stepped around to the driver's side and leaned into the window, cupping his hands above his eyes and pressing his forehead against the glass. He could see some sort of metal medallion in the shape of a ring hanging from the mirror. The surface looked scaly and weird, like a snake in the shape of a ring, with its own tail in his mouth. Something about it was intriguing to Winston, as if he had seen it before. He kept his eyes on it and walked to the front of the car to get another angle.

When he stood in front of the car, the sight of the headlights and wheels aimed directly at him brought tears to his eyes. He knew this is what it must have looked like to Caroline for a split second, if she ever saw it coming at all. He ran his finger around the blue and white circle of the logo, tracing the edges of the colors as he thought about that night.

"I told you I'd find him Caroline." Winston turned his furious gaze upon the entrance to the pub, and the bright neon red "E" above it. He looked at the blood on his fist from slamming it into the sidewalk. "I feel it. This is the car. I found him. I know it. It ends tonight, one way or another…"

CHAPTER FOUR

Approaching White Light

Winston walked across the parking lot to the front door of the pub. The doors were large and heavy, and hard to open, especially in his current condition. He missed the handle the first time he reached for it, but when he finally opened the doors he was greeted by familiar smells and sounds. The air was filled with the scent of fried food, spilled alcohol, and mumbled conversations, all competing with the low thump of the music coming from the far back corner of the room. A lone guitarist was pounding the strings and belting out his lyrics with force. "I'm waking up to ash and dust, I wipe my brow and I sweat my rust, I'm breathing in the chemicals… yeah."

Several people saw Winston enter and cringed at the sight of him. His hair was soaked and unwashed for days. Beads of water dripped off his beard. His hand was bloody, and he reeked of alcohol and dirty wet clothes. His eyes were red and puffy, and filled with rage.

Winston scanned the crowd for the man he saw walk in. He took a few steps and bumped into a man leaning in to whisper into a young woman's ear. The man spilled a few drops of his beer on the girl's blouse. "Hey, watch where you're going jerk!" The man pushed Winston's shoulder and caused him to knock over a chair. Winston turned and looked into the man's eyes. He immediately knew it wasn't who he came for and though he wanted to smash a bottle over the man's head, he simply turned away. His would instead add this fuel to the already sizeable fire in his eyes. His right hand curled into a fist.

He walked farther into the pub, and at a small round table near the right wall, Winston saw the man in the brown leather jacket and heavy boots. He was sitting and laughing with several other men of similar stature and wealth, happily drinking the cold brew in his hand. Seeing the smiles and happiness on his face only increases the hatred in Winston's heart and eyes. He walked towards the table, and about halfway there, snatched up a full beer that was unattended on one of the tables he passed. He walked up to within a foot of their table and stood there silently, listening to bits and pieces.

"… flight from Atlanta… meetings all day… probably Tuesday or Wednesday of next week…" Soon they all halted their conversation to look up at him when they noticed him standing there.

Winston's gaze was intense, and he stood in silence, looking deep into the man's eyes. Green! Winston felt the rage boil in his veins. "Can I help you?" the man said, in an unappreciated tone. Winston was focused and did not even blink. He said nothing, never breaking eye contact. Time was passing slowly for him. The green-eyed man spoke up again. "Are you stupid or something? I asked you a question. Can I help you?"

After an agonizingly long two seconds, Winston finally spoke up. His eyes never lost their focus on the man. "Is that your black beamer outside?" Winston's words were monotone and dry.

"Yeah, why?", the man said.

"How long have you had it?", Winston continued.

"What's it to you?" The man looked at one of his buddies in disbelief, and let out a chuckle.

Winston had no patience for the man. He needed his answers. This time he spoke slower, with more force. "I said… how long have you had it?"

The man shook his head at Winston. "I don't see why it's any of your business." A couple of his friends were laughing at the odd situation in front of them.

Winston took a step closer until his legs touched the table. "You ever run into anything?"

The man was growing agitated with the stream of questions. "Look, why don't you get lost buddy, we are trying to have some drinks here." He spoke with a confidence of a man who was much larger and more sober than the one in front of him.

Winston raised the beer in his hand to his lips and chugged every last drop, and then slammed the empty bottle down harshly on their table with a bang. He looked even more intensely into the man's eyes. "You ever run into anybody?" He stressed the word body, emphasizing it slowly so the man was sure to hear it.

The man sat his beer down and stood up. He was a few inches taller than Winston first thought, and due to Winston's diet of mostly alcohol and potato chips, about twenty or thirty pounds heavier than he was. The man stepped around the table and stood face to face with Winston. "I'm going to tell you one last time. Get your drunk ass out of my face and leave me

and my friends alone, or you're going to get yourself hurt."
Two of the man's friends also stood up and looked directly at
Winston. A few people at the surrounding tables stood and
took a step away, nervous about what might happen next. He
broke his stare with the man and peered around him. It seemed
to Winston that about half the bar now had their eyes on him.
Winston knew he was entirely too drunk and outnumbered at
the moment, and with his only good decision of the night, he
took a step back. "That's right…", the man continued. "Just
keep walking."

Winston turned and slowly made his way to the door as
the man yelled across the room. "And stay away from my
car!" Winston grabbed another unattended beer on the way
and heaved open the door. He stepped back out into the rain,
disappointed in himself. He wasn't sure what he wanted to
happen when he came face to the face with the man, but this
wasn't it. Tears ran down his face. He lifted his head to the
rain and let the drops wash them away.

Inside, the man sat back down with his friends. "Can
you believe that guy?"

One of his friends took a drink from his beer. "He sure
was obsessed with that car of yours, man."

"I know. I'm not sure what the hell that was all about.
I knew I should have bought the economy car with better gas
mileage. Decided to treat myself a bit."

His friend began to chuckle. "Did you get insurance on
that thing yet? You've only had it what, a couple weeks. He's
probably out there right now messing with it."

Suddenly the laughter left the man's face. "He better
not be." He stood up and grabbed his jacket. "I'm going to go
check on it." The other men anxiously followed after him.

Outside Winston walked back over to the black car. He
wanted to at least write down the VIN number so he could do a

little research later and find out if this was in fact the right car, even though he knew all he needed to know when he looked into the man's eyes. He was standing by the driver door, digging through the pockets in his jacket for a pen, when he heard the man shout from across the parking lot.

"Hey asshole, get away from my car." Winston ignored him and walked around to the front of the car again. He ran his hand along the edge of the hood. "Get your hands off it!" he heard the man scream as he began walking towards Winston in the rain. Winston knelt and examined the front bumper more closely, and he could see that there was a small dent along the right side. The grill had a small hairline crack in it too, as did the headlight casing. It had obviously run into something. Tears began to fill his eyes, and he slammed his fist onto the bumper.

"I knew it!", Winston whispered to himself as he stood, his eyes red with fury. He still held the half empty bottle in his hand. He chugged the rest of it and walked towards the men. When he got to the rear of the car he raised his voice and looked directly at the man in the brown leather jacket. "It was you, wasn't it?" he said, with eyes full of rage.

The man pointed his finger at Winston. "I don't know what you are talking about but if you touch my car again you're going to regret it." Winston was wobbly drunk and leaned back against the car. The bottle made a clink against the metal. The man's eyes lit up with anger. He grabbed Winston by the collar of his jacket and threw him to the ground near the sidewalk. Winston crashed in a puddle and hit the pavement with a thud. Muddy water splashed in his face and the bottle slipped from Winston's grip and rolled a few feet away. One of the other men picked it up.

"You don't even know what you did, do you?" Winston mumbled under his breath.

The man looked down on him. "Go home now, you pathetic drunk, before I call the cops."

Winston laid his face down in the mud. The men began to walk back to the bar when Winston stumbled to his feet. He regained his strength enough to lunge at the man's back and grab him around the neck. He squeezed with all his strength and screamed at the top of his lungs. "You killed her! You killed her!" The rain beat down on them all and one of the other men pulled at Winston's arms, but deep anger gave Winston strength. He held on tight as they struggled to free his hands from the man's neck. The man in the leather jacket choked and gasped for air as his friend who held the empty beer bottle raised it high in the air. He brought it down on Winston's head with a loud explosion of glass. Winston went limp immediately and fell to the ground again. The man in the jacket panted for air and rubbed his neck. When he gathered himself, he turned around and gave a powerful kick to Winston's side. Winston rolled onto the sidewalk, barely conscious. He was lying on his back and bleeding from the side of the head. His wallet had fallen out of his jacket and into a puddle of water a few feet away.

The men looked down at Winston's crumpled body and then looked around them. There was no one around, and two of them simultaneously said, "Let's get out of here." Soon three cars roared past Winston's limp body as it sat soaking and bleeding. The rain poured down on him.

Fading in and out of consciousness, Winston felt the water hitting his face. He could feel the throbbing where the bottle cut him, and could taste the stream of blood that made its way to his mouth. It ends tonight… one way or another. He remembered his words from earlier and wondered if this was indeed the end for him. He saw a bright light. It started small and then grew to fill his vision. He thought of Caroline and mouthed the words "I'm sorry" before passing out, succumbing to the white light that closed in on him.

CHAPTER FIVE

Kerplush, Kerplush

Winston's eyes were closed, but it wouldn't have mattered much if he could open them. The white light was intense and the beam powered through his eyelids as it approached, filling his sight and mind with whiteness, with nothingness.

He couldn't move his body at all, and could barely think. The alcohol and the crushing blast to the head left him motionless, lying on his back on the sidewalk in the pouring rain. He felt only the pain in his head, and the sadness in his heart. He wasn't sure which overwhelmed him more. His mind was unable to hold onto any single thought. Only small flashes of Caroline, the black car, and the man in the leather jacket shot through his head. Yet he lost them just as fast as they came.

As the light got closer and closer to him, sounds began to come back to him. It was the one sense he could focus on. He heard the rain hitting his head and splashing in the puddles all around him. He heard a rumble that grew louder and louder as the light grew brighter and brighter. It was accompanied by the constant whoosh of water, and just when it felt like the light and sound were about to come crashing through his eyes and into his brain, they both suddenly stopped, and a wave of water pounded his face.

Winston was unable to move or open his eyes, so he focused intently on the sounds. He heard the high-pitched creak of metal hinges, and a loud clunk a couple of seconds later. This was followed by a new sound heading straight for him. Kerplush, Kerplush, Kerplush, Kerplush. It was the sound of heavy footsteps plodding through the rain-soaked street, coming closer and closer to him. For a moment, whoever belonged to those footsteps stopped next to Winston, blocking out the light that was shining on him from above. Winston could only listen.

"Ooooh weeee, what a mess do we find ourselves in here?" the voice says. It was deep and strong and powered through the rain. "Yes sir, I'd say I've got quite the mess on my hands right here. Yes sir." Winston felt strangely calmed by the man's strong voice and presence. He wanted to open his eyes and see who it might be, but he couldn't manage it. He wasn't entirely sure he was even awake at this point. "Don't worry though, I'm a get you fixed right up. Yes sir, I know just where I'm a take you, buddy." Winston listened to the voice, and felt a strange peace come over him as the unknown man moved around him, blocking and unblocking the white light of the headlights that flooded his face with light. "Doc'll fix you right up, real nice like. Yes sir."

Winston heard the man walk back to the car on the side closest to him, followed by the creak of another door hinge. Then the footsteps came back to him, along with the mumbling. "...fix you right up, yes sir." Winston felt the man kneel next to him. His voice lowered and was even slower and more calming. "Don't you worry buddy, I'm a take you to the doc. Doc always knows what to do. This might work out just fine for him. Yes sir." Winston felt the man's hands reach down and lift him with ease off the wet concrete sidewalk. The rain was still coming down on his face, and as he was being carried, he could see the shadows changing on the back of his eyelids from the headlights below him and the streetlights above him.

Winston felt himself being laid onto the bench seat in the back of a vehicle, and heard the clunk of the door shutting. A few seconds later he heard the man get in the driver's seat and shut his door as well. The car popped into gear and took off, rocking Winston back and forth in the back. He didn't care at this point where he was being taken. The weight of the entire night, the alcohol, the throbbing wound on his head, all seemed to be falling on him at once. He was exhausted, both mentally and physically. Part of him wanted the car to just drive off a cliff and end this nightmare he had lived for a year. He tried to push those thoughts out of his head and think about Caroline. The sound of the rain pinging off the metal roof of the car, along with the occasional mumbling of the driver, began to lull him in and out of sleep, and he finally passed out entirely to visions of her standing around the fire the night he first met her.

Winston woke some time later when the car hit a rather sizeable bump in the road. He felt the car turn several times along the way, and listened to the driver, still talking to himself.

"Need to fix that road, yes sir. No need for bumps like that."

The darkness on the other side of his closed eyelids told him it was still night outside. He could still hear rain hitting the roof of the car. Lying on his back, he managed to crack open one of his eyes and look out the window of the car. They were no longer in the city, and all he could see was black sky. He was glad to have his senses back, until he felt the pain in his head. It was sharp and pounding, surging down his neck. He also felt his side aching from the strong kick he received.

"Quite a mess you are, yes sir. But no worries. I'm a taking you to Doc's… just what you need." Winston thought maybe the man noticed his eyes were open, but he could see the driver was still just talking to himself. His voice was deep and smooth and comforting to Winston. He moved his head slightly to get a better look at the man behind the wheel. He couldn't see his face, but certain things stood out. He was a black man, probably in his sixties Winston guessed, but still large and strong as an ox. He remembered how easily the man picked him up off the sidewalk, as if he were only a child. He could see the man's large hands on the steering wheel, which, by comparison, appeared smaller than a normal wheel. He was wearing a black beret that hung slightly off center to the right side of his head.

Winston felt the car braking and himself rocking forward in the back seat. He heard the driver whistling a little tune, and then they turned off the main road. He listened carefully to the sounds of rocks bouncing around and hitting the bottom of the car. When he looked up and out the window he could see the faint glow of corn stalks drifting by outside, rather close to the car. He lifted his chin and saw the same scene out the window next to him. They were on some sort of narrow gravel road, lined on both sides by cornfields that formed walls just inches outside the car.

Suddenly, the rain abruptly stopped, and he could begin to see stars peeking through the darkness of the sky above him. The car slowed and turned once more onto a smooth road. Winston could see the corn stalks disappear as they left the gravel road, and heard the quiet, soothing sound of rubber on dry pavement underneath him. Soon they slowed to a stop and Winston could see a few large magnolia trees outside the window, glowing from the light of the moon.

"Doc's gonna be mighty interested in this one. He's in a right mess I say. Yes sir. Might work out just fine." Winston hears the driver get out and shut his door, then hears footsteps make their way around to the other side of the car. He knew they had arrived at whatever destination they were headed to, but it sure didn't look like a hospital. The slightest bit of fear, mixed with indifference, crept in on him. The door opened at Winston's feet and unsure of the situation, he suddenly shut his eyes and pretended to be asleep again. That soothing voice though calmed his nerves. Something about it made him feel like he was exactly where he was supposed to be. "Come on buddy, I'm a get you someplace comfy to lay down and rest. You're a right mess. Yes sir."

Winston felt those large strong hands lift him out of the car with ease and shut the door behind him. The air was warm, and the night seemed almost perfect, quiet, and still. Winston dared to crack his eyes just a bit and peek out of the tiny slit. The driver walked slowly but smoothly up to the front door of a small, quaint little house and pressed the doorbell with a free finger. After a few seconds, the door slowly opened, and Winston shut his eyes again.

"Well, hello there, Carter. What do we have here?" The doc's voice was kind and gentle, full of care and hope. He seemed to be almost expecting them.

"He's a right mess. Yes sir. Found him lying in the rain on the sidewalk, head all busted up and bleeding. Got himself into a mess, I'd say. Figured you would fix him right up. Hope it's not too late for you Doc."

"Not at all Carter. I was just reading. You did the right thing. Sounds like the guy had a rough night. Go ahead and lay him down right over there." The doc stepped aside and gestured to the couch. He shut the door behind him and walked to the closet in the hallway to grab a blanket and a pillow. He set the pillow on one end of the couch, and Carter gently laid Winston down, and then pulled the beret off his head. When Winston's head hit the soft pillow, all the pain and anger and sadness left his body. He listened to their voices and was at peace for the first time in a while, as he sank deeper into the cozy couch.

"Why don't you leave him here for the night Carter. It's late, and I'd like to take a look at that nasty cut on his head. He could use a good night's sleep too, by the looks of him." Doc unfolded the blanket and covered Winston from neck to foot. "How about you swing back by the diner tomorrow around lunchtime and pick him up there?"

"Yes sir, that sounds mighty fine. I'll let you git to your work." Carter walked towards the door, and when he got there, he turned back to the doc with a big smile on his face. "See you fellas tomorrow then." Winston cracked his eyes just enough to see Carter place the beret back on his head and step outside into the warm, crisp night air. As he shut the door behind him, Winston let his eyelids fall back into place, and immediately fell asleep.

CHAPTER SIX

Liquid Sunlight

When Winston woke late the next morning, it was to the sound of running water in the next room and the clanging of pots and pans in the sink. Bright sunlight was streaming through the window above him and seemed to be aiming directly for his face. The previous night was still a bit blurry, but the pounding inside of his head was a reminder of the alcohol at least. The sounds of the dishes pierced his ears and fed the throbbing. He shed the blanket and stretched his legs out along the couch. His body felt as if it had been rolled down a steep hill and at the bottom was only a wall.

He slowly sat up on the couch and tossed the blanket that was covering him aside. He took a deep breath and felt pain in his side as his chest expanded. He touched his hand to it and pulled back in pain. When he lifted the shirt he was wearing, he saw a nasty purple and black bruise that stretched from the bottom of his rib cage to the underside of his arm.

He stood and ran his fingers through his hair, where they encountered a bandage and some tape on one side. When he pressed on it he winced in pain, just as he had done with his side. The shooting pain down his neck served as an instant reminder of the events the night before. Suddenly, the bottle of wine, the classified ad, the black car, the bright red neon sign, and most of all the man in the leather jacket, came crashing back from his memory. He looked down at the red mark on his fist, and remembered punching the sidewalk in anger. "I had him," he whispered to himself. His memory got foggy after that. He remembered something about being taken to a doctor, but wasn't sure where he was.

He looked around the place and knew he had never been here before. This wasn't a hospital, or an emergency room, or even a low rent clinic in the seedy parts of Dunsport. This is someone's house. It was small but nice and orderly, clean, and warm. It was the sort of house that might be the subject of a photo in a magazine. In front of him was a beautiful yet simple stone fireplace outlined by a wooden mantle. The wood floors were aged but still full of character and strength. They squeaked a couple of times as he stepped towards the wonderful smells coming from the kitchen.

As he rounded the corner he saw an older man in perhaps his sixties putting dishes into the dishwasher. The man turned when he heard his footsteps and greeted Winston with an impossibly large smile across his face. He was wearing freshly ironed beige dress pants with perfect seams on the sides, a buttoned short sleeve plaid shirt with a thin tie, and shiny black shoes that perhaps were just buffed and waxed.

"Hey, look who's finally up. I take it you slept well?" Winston simply nodded. In fact, it was the best sleep he could remember. The man walked over to Winston and held out his hand. "It's nice to finally meet you. You can call me Doc, everyone else seems to around here. I guess that's what happens when you've been the only doctor in a small town for as long as anyone can remember." His eyes were full of kindness and hope, and the way he smiled at Winston eased his nerves. "I'm afraid I still don't know your name though."

As they shook hands Winston cleared his throat and managed to offer a very scratchy and modest "Winston." He cleared his throat again as the doc pulled out a chair from under the kitchen table.

"Well, Winston, why don't you have a seat. I was just cleaning up after making some breakfast for you. I figured you needed some nourishment after your… rough night. It has been keeping warm in the oven, waiting for you to wake. Let me go grab it." He slipped his hands inside a couple of oven mitts and pulled a hot plate out of the oven. He walked it to Winston and sat it in front of him, along with a fork and a napkin. "Eggs, bacon, sausage, and toast. I hope that is to your liking."

Winston simply nodded again, trying to force a smile. His head still pounded with the beat of his heart. He never had been much of a morning person, even before the accident, but recently he hadn't seen too many mornings at all. It had been so long since he had sat at a formal table and eaten a traditional breakfast, that the smells were mesmerizing to him. It was as if they were relics of a past life or memories from his childhood. He closed his eyes and took a deep breath through his nose.

The doc went to the fridge and returned with a large glass of orange juice that he sat on the table next to Winston's food. "Here's some fresh orange juice from Greta's. She runs a small grocery in town and sells oranges there from her own trees on the other side of town. Along with the best fresh squeezed orange juice you'll ever have. She can't keep up with all the people in town clamoring for it. Nice lady too." Doc smiled his comforting grin. "Oh, and I almost forgot..." He reached into his front shirt pocket and pulled out two small white pills and laid them on the table. "These are for the pain. You came here with quite the bump on your head, and a sizeable gash to go with it."

Winston reached up and felt the bandage on his head again.

"Now don't go messing with it." The doc said in a playful tone. "I sewed up the cut. Eight stitches in all. But it will be quite sore for a few days or more, I'm afraid." He patted Winston on the shoulder. "But you'll be just fine. No lasting damage I'm happy to say." The doc turned around and opened the closet door adjacent to the kitchen.

Winston pulled his hand away from the bandage. "Doc," he said. "I don't know what to say… but…"

The doc smiled when Winston spoke and cut him off as he hesitated. "No worries Winston, it's what I do. We'll talk more about it later, okay." He turned around, holding a top hat in his hand from the closet. "For now, just eat your breakfast and take your pills." Winston downed the pills as the doc wished and took a big drink of the orange juice.

"Mmmmm, you weren't kidding, this is really good," he said, as he looked curiously at the glass filled with the most brilliant orange, as if he were drinking liquid sunlight.

"Best around, I'd stake my reputation on it." The doc picked up some papers on the counter and put them inside his briefcase. He paused and looked deep into Winston's eyes. "I think you'll find there are many things in this town worth your time."

Winston took a few bites of egg as the doc picked up his briefcase and tucked his hat under his arm. "Now listen, I have to head into the office for a while, but feel free to grab yourself a hot shower. Just make sure you don't get those stitches wet, ok?" Winston agreed and then wondered about his clothes as the doc spoke up again. "I almost forgot. I had my helper come over and help take care of you last night. She cleaned you up and changed your clothes. They were soaked and filthy, so she threw them in the wash last night, and I put them in the dryer a little while ago. They are in the room at the end of the hall next to the bathroom. Your jacket and shoes are in the closet just off the kitchen. I hope what you're wearing isn't too uncomfortable."

"It's fine," Winston said. He looked down at his current outfit. He hadn't noticed until now, but he was wearing red and white plaid pajama pants and a white t-shirt with a pocket on the left chest. The thought of someone undressing him and cleaning him up in the condition he was in last night made him turn red a little. He got an embarrassed look on his face. "She?"

The doc chuckled slightly at his embarrassment. "It was late but she was a doll and didn't mind helping," the doc said. "Your own clothes should be dry by the time you get out of the shower." He took a few steps towards the door as Winston tried to process all that was happening. He had so many questions, but couldn't seem to get any words out. How will I get home? What nurse? Where am I? When the doc got to the door he turned around.

"I almost forgot, after Carter dropped you off last night I told him to pick you up today at the diner a bit before lunch. It's only a few blocks down the road on the left. Can't miss it." The doc pointed in the direction of the diner. "So, after you finish your breakfast and your shower, you might want to wait for him there. Besides, it's beautiful outside, and a little walk in the sunshine will do you some good I think."

"Carter?" Winston was managing only one word at a time, trying to fill in the gaps in his memory.

"Yeah, he'll be in his cab again, the same one that you rode here in. You can't miss it. He's going into the city afterwards to run some errands for me, and said he would drop you off. I hope that suits you well."

Winston shook his head yes and wondered when he would see the doc again. He still had so many unanswered questions. The doc smiled at him and opened the door. "Oh, and I noticed the ring on your finger. Feel free to use the phone if you have someone back in the city waiting for you." Winston looked down at his finger and spun the ring with his other hand. She's waiting for me all right, but not in the city.

The doc put one foot outside before turning back to Winston. "You can take that bandage off tonight, but I'll need to see you in a week to take the stitches out." He looked at his watch. "You have a little over an hour until Carter shows up, so take your time." He looked up at Winston and flashed that warm smile one more time. "Sorry, but I have to run. It was nice to meet you, Winston." He placed the hat on his head, doffed at Winston, then shut the door, and was gone.

After Winston finished his breakfast and Greta's delicious orange juice, the small blue pills seemed to kick in, and his head stopped pounding and his side stopped aching. He stood in the shower for a long time, thinking of all the things he wished he had said to the doc, and the questions he wished he had asked him about the nurse and Carter and many other things. Afterwards, he found his clothes, got dressed, and folded the blanket on the couch. He looked around one last time and then stepped outside into the sunlight.

CHAPTER SEVEN

Dreamy Little Town

The sunlight was blinding. Winston held his hand up to his face as he stood outside the doc's house, waiting for his eyes to adjust. The sun penetrated his clothes and his skin, warming his insides and melting away his pain. It was the first time in what felt like months that he felt this warm and dry. It seemed to Winston that it was always raining in Dunsport. And it was dirty rain… cold rain… rain that chilled you to the bone no matter what the temperature was outside. But here, outside the city, however far away he was, in whatever little town he was in, it was absolutely perfect.

He felt an energy he hadn't had in a long time coursing through his warm veins. He smiled slightly, and just as he opened his eyes, a newspaper came flying through the air and landed at his feet. He looked up and saw a paperboy on a bicycle riding by on the street waving his hand at Winston.

"Have a good day!" the boy shouted as he continued down the sidewalk. Winston picked up the paper and read the bold letters at the top. The Salima Standard. Winston opened the door behind him and tossed the paper back inside the house. When he turned around, he raised his head to the sunlight and closed his eyes. He took a deep breath and filled his nose with the wonderful smells in the air. He looked around at the overwhelming sights and sounds around him.

To his left, a row of poplars appeared to mark the edge of a field, forming a wall that reached high in the air, which felt protective and vigil. Honeysuckle plants grew at the bases of the poplars, where their small white flowers grew by the thousands, mixing their sweet smell in the air with the musky scent of the poplars.

The walkway in front of him led a short way to the street, and was lined with orange Rhododendron that held the promise of a long summer. Winston walked slowly down the sidewalk to the edge of the street, where two large magnolia trees had grown to a massive size. Wisteria vines had climbed partway up the trunks, connecting to each other overhead, forming an aromatic archway that announced the entrance to the doc's house. Winston looked up and marveled at all he saw. The purple flowers hung like clusters of grapes all around him.

As he reached the street he turned back around to look at Doc's house behind him. It was small and quaint, nestled into the landscape as if it grew from the earth a thousand years ago. The front door was warm and inviting from here, and the brick façade of the house seemed to glow a bright red in the sunlight. He took a few steps away from the house onto the sidewalk that lined the street. He listened to the magnolia leaves as they crunched under his feet and smelled the white trumpet flowers above his head.

From here, Winston could see down the street of this dreamy little town. It looked like an oil painting of some cozy main street pulled from the past or plucked out of a book and placed before him. Little brick buildings lined the boulevard on either side, with their doors opened to greet the passers-by on the sidewalks. In the middle of the two sides of the boulevard was a ten-foot wide stretch of perfectly manicured grass that rolled out like a smooth green ribbon down the middle of the street. Every hundred feet or so, another magnolia tree majestically stood on the ribbon, shading large portions of the sidewalk below. As Winston walked in and out of these shadows, he looked up at the little light poles that were placed evenly between the trees in the middle. Each one had three curved arms which pointed upwards towards the sky and held torches, marching in unison with the trees, alternating down the street and around the corner up the hill.

Winston stopped for a second and looked around. Here and there he saw people walking on the sidewalks, sitting on benches, sipping their late morning coffee, reading a book, or digesting today's copy of the Salima Standard. Some were cruising slowly by in their cars, chatting away the beautiful summer day, and still others were moseying along on bicycles. They all, however, had one glaring commonality. They were all smiling from ear to ear, as happy as a lark, without a care in the world.

Winston, baffled at the jovial nature of everyone in sight, continued in the direction the doc had pointed out earlier. A car went by and the driver smiled at Winston and gave him a little wave as he went. Winston simply nodded. He often didn't know how to respond to kindness, especially the kindness of strangers, and this was overwhelming to him. "Have a good day," he heard as he passed someone who was sitting on a bench along the road. Another nod and Winston kept walking.

A wonderful smell filled the air and he closed his eyes to take it all in, as he walked passed the entrance to a small boutique bookstore. Suddenly, a happy couple walked out of the door and accidentally bumped into Winston. "My apologies," said the gentleman. "It is a lovely day out though, isn't it?" Winston agreed and watched as they scurried off, giggling as they went.

The weather was astoundingly perfect here. Winston looked up to the sky, which was a brilliantly perfect shade of azure, without a cloud in sight. The sun was warm and crisp, and excited the skin as the rays penetrated it, yet the air was still refreshingly cool and dry. The temperature was ideal, with the slightest of breezes, and even the trees seemed to be spreading their arms as if to gather as much of the early summer as they could.

Just past the bookstore, Winston came upon the source of the wonderful smells in the air. It was a small bakery with an old time feel. The aromas of fresh bread and pastries streamed out of the open door and onto the sidewalk where Winston paused. Inside, he saw a portly fellow covered above the waste in white flour, working hard on some delectable creation. The man noticed that Winston's attention was grabbed by the scents of his work and called out to him. "Good morning! Want to try a fresh bagel?"

"No thanks," Winston replied graciously.

"Then how about a muffin? Or perhaps a croissant?"

"I have to be somewhere," Winston explained. "Could you tell me where the diner is?"

The man pointed down the street a bit. "Absolutely, just keep going that way about a block and then cross the street. You can't miss it."

"Thanks," said Winston. He heard the man continue talking as he walked away.

"You take care and come back again real soon!"

Winston rolled his eyes as the man waved at his back through the glass window at the front of the store. A block later, a little more up the hill, Winston stopped to look around, trying to catch a sight of the city, so he could get an idea of where he had been taken. He could not see any far-off buildings, or anything that would give him a clue to where it was. It was different here. The weather was better, the people were nicer, and for all he knew, it felt like he could be a thousand miles away.

As he looked around, he spotted the diner across the street from an old looking hardware store. Above the door hung large vintage lettering that read "Mrs. Powell's Diner." The letters were faded and some of the covers were broken. He could tell that at one time in the past, however long ago it might have been, the letters were lit from behind. As he crossed the street, Winston looked up and tried to imagine how it might have looked in its heyday, bright and new.

When he reached the other sidewalk on the other side, he saw an A-framed chalkboard sign sitting just outside the diner door with writing on both sides. At the top, in handwritten fancy lettering, it said "Today's Lunch Specials." Below that was a small list of familiar comfort foods, also written by hand. "Tuna melt on wheat with potato salad and chips. Grilled pesto chicken sandwich and garlic bread sticks. Broccoli cheddar soup and wedge salad." All along the border of the sign, someone had drawn intricate little flowers and bees and butterflies in colored chalk.

As Winston stood there and followed the buzzing trails of the bees in chalk, two elderly ladies exited the diner right in front of him, engulfed in their stories and rumors. One lady, deep in laughter, backed into Winston, and apologized profusely.

"Oh, I'm sorry dear!" she said as she swiveled around.

"Don't mind her, she's as blind as a bat, and about as smart too," said one of her friends, as she placed a hand on Winston's arm. The group broke up in laughter again.

"Well aren't you a handsome devil!" said a third lady. "Gladys, get your hands off that nice young man for goodness sakes."

The oldest of the women stepped over to Winston, and in the gentlest of voices said "I'm very sorry about this group of imbeciles dear, you have a nice lunch. I recommend the tuna melt." She winked at him and smacked Gladys' hand from his arm.

Winston gave a sheepish gesture and sunk towards the door as the group of ladies watched him, still laughing and carrying on, haggling the one who bumped into him and the one who touched his arm. "… like you've never seen a young man before… just go grabbing young men on the streets... planning on taking him home or what... can't take you girls anywhere I swear…" Winston could still hear the laughter even after he had entered the diner. No doubt they would use this little incident for months as a source of humor among the group. He shook his head to himself, growing weary of all the cheer in this town, and stepped inside.

CHAPTER EIGHT
A Flower in the Shadows

Predictably the hostess waiting for him inside the diner was bubbling with excitement when he approached. "Welcome to Mrs. Powell's!" As Winston stepped up to her podium she noticed the bandage on his head. "Well look at you. Looks like someone bumped his head!"

Winston touched the bandage, having forgotten about it. "I'm ok, I just… fell down yesterday."

The hostess shook her head back and forth with a smile on her face and pursed her lips. "Well you should be more careful mister. You got to take care of your head, it's the only one you got!" She giggled profusely at her own joke. Winston did not join in her delight. He simply stared at her until she continued. "So, would you like a booth or a table?"

"Booth is fine," Winston said with a lack of emotion that she probably wasn't used to in this town. "Preferably by the window if you have one. I'm waiting for a cab driver to show up."

The hostess's eyebrows raised and her smile grew even larger. "You must be talking about old Carter. Isn't he the nicest man?"

"You know him?" asked Winston.

She gave him a look of disbelief as if he had just asked the dumbest question she had ever heard. "You're kidding, right? Everyone knows Carter around here." She motioned for him to sit when they reached a booth in the back corner along the window. "Here you go, you should be able to see from here. If I catch him first, I'll let you know."

"Thanks," Winston said as he slid into the booth.

"Will anyone else be joining you?"

"Just me," he said.

The hostess made a pouty face like she was sad for him to be eating alone. She handed him a menu."

"No thanks," said Winston. "I already ate. I'll just have a coffee. Black. No cream. No sugar."

She pulled back the menu and looked at him as if he were the most peculiar person she had ever met. "One plain black coffee coming right up."

Winston was relieved when she walked away. He just wanted to sit alone for a while and not talk to another overly enthusiastic person. He wanted to sulk over the utter failure of the night before. He wanted to wallow in his own misery, away from all the joy that surrounded him. And so, after his coffee arrived, he sat, looking out the window in anticipation of Carter's cab, knowing he had nothing to return home to, but also that he didn't fit in here in this town. He needed his tall buildings, his dirty streets, his rain, and his mud. He had become those things, and they had become all that he had.

As he looked out the window, he saw the group of older ladies that he had bumped into earlier. They were on the other side of the street, just leaving a small shop. They were still laughing and carrying on. He took another sip of his coffee and looked around the diner. There were quite a lot of people crammed into this small place. Nearly every table was occupied except the one or two nearest to his corner, which Winston was thankful for. The whole room seemed to have a seating pattern to it. There were two or three younger couples having a cold soda and holding hands at tables in the center. Along the back wall, there were booths filled with groups of older men or women socializing over brunch. The wall opposite the windows was filled with business professionals, doctors, and such, going over the latest deal or procedure. In fact, Winston realized he was the only person in the whole place who was alone.

　　　　A few times, as he scanned the room, he made eye contact with someone at another table, and the result was always the same. They smiled graciously at him and gave him the friendliest of nods with their head. Winston always looked away immediately as if he hadn't noticed, and took another drink of his coffee. Behind the counter, across the room, he saw the cook, whistling as he flipped another omelet. The hostess was back in her element, excitedly waiting for another patron to greet as they walked through the door. Nauseating, thought Winston.

　　　　It was in the middle of this thought that he saw another young woman walk out from the back room and begin cleaning the drink cooler over by the salad bar across the room. She had long dark brown hair, a slender build, and a purposeful walk. She wasn't wearing the same bib or smock that the waitresses and hostess wore. She was dressed casually in dress slacks and a buttoned blouse, and seemed to slide in and out of the background, lost in her own world. As her eyes stared at the task in front of her, Winston could tell her mind was elsewhere. She had a blank, emotionless look on her face, and was the only person that Winston had seen the whole time he had been in this town who didn't have a grinning smile on their face at all times. He recognized the look in her eyes. There was something about it that reminded him of himself.

As she finished one chore and moved on to the next, she did so in a very methodic, robotic way, showing zero enthusiasm. Winston was drawn to her and watched her every move. When she went back into the back room out of view, he watched the opening intently for her return. A few moments later, she walked to the front of the diner with a jug of water, and began watering the plants that lined the front windows near the entrance. On her way past, one of the waitresses walked up to her and asked her an inaudible question. She simply nodded her head, and the waitress walked away smiling.

This town and all the sunny faces bored Winston, but there was something overpoweringly mysterious and magnetic about this girl. She had a sad and beautiful look to her, like a flower in the shadows, waiting for the sunlight to reach her so she could bloom. She seemed to move in slow motion as she walked behind the scenes, unnoticed by anyone but him. There was a stark difference in her movements and emotions from the rest of the townsfolk. Winston knew it well. He often felt like he was a spectator to his own life, watching it crumble around him, unable or unwilling to participate in it.

He focused on her intently and tried to catch a glimpse of her eyes. And as if she felt his gaze from across the room suddenly, she glanced over at him for a split second. Their eyes only met for the tiniest of moments, but it was enough to notice her eyes were the same color of deep brown as her hair. They were beautiful, and sad. In that micro-fraction of a second, before Winston could look away or down at his coffee, she dropped the glass pitcher she was holding. It crashed to the floor and the diner erupted with the noise of glass shattering. It seemed everyone in the place jumped in their seat and spun around to look, except Winston. He simply stared in wonder at this new girl. She knelt to pick up the pieces, and Winston caught a look of embarrassment on her face. He was zeroed in on her every move, oblivious to anything else around him. A nearby voice began to penetrate his focus.

"Hello?... Excuse me." His waitress snapped her fingers in front of his face.

Winston snapped out of his trance and saw her standing next to his table.

"Hey there. Thought you fell asleep on me." Winston looked up at her face, obviously happy with her little joke. "Would you like me to top off your coffee?" she said with a cheerful voice.

"Sure," Winston replied while attempting to look around her at the other girl.

"Whatcha thinking about anyways?" she said.

Winston nodded towards the other girl. "Just wondering who that is."

The waitress turned and looked at the girl still picking up the glass pieces. "Oh, that's Emma. Nice girl. Doesn't talk much though. Just sort of does her own thing." Winston kept watching as Emma grabbed a broom and began sweeping up any pieces she might have missed. "You sure you don't want a snack while you are waiting?"

"I'm fine, thanks. Just bring my bill when you are ready." Winston reached into his jacket pocket for his wallet but felt nothing. He patted the other pockets and then reached into the pockets on the inside, but still came up empty.

The waitress smiled at him. "Doc said this one is on him. Said to tell you not to worry about it. Guess it's your lucky day." She looked out the window. "And what a beautiful day it is!"

Just as she said those words, Winston noticed a cab pull up along the sidewalk outside the diner. On the side was a logo that appeared to be a laurel wreath, overlaid with gold letters that read "Apollo." The sun glistened off the letters into Winston's eyes as he thanked the waitress and stood up. He walked towards the door and looked around the diner, but didn't see Emma anywhere. "Have a great day!" the bubbly hostess said as he walked past. He stepped out into the sunshine again and quickly walked over to the cab and hopped in the back.

As soon as the door shut he heard Carter's familiar voice. "Hey buddy. Look at you… all dried up and clean. I knew the doc would fix you right up. Yes sir, I did." Winston ignored him and looked back at the diner, trying to get one last glimpse of Emma through the glass, as Carter continued talking. He watched for several seconds until he heard Carter's voice much louder. "Hey buddy, we ain't making no more stops except yours. You can sit up front if you'd like."

"That's alright. I'm just fine back here," Winston said as he continued to look at the diner. The sun was shining on the windows, and through the beams, he saw Emma come to the front and began wiping the glass on the door. Winston seemed to ignore Carter as he focused on Emma.

Carter turned around and lowered his head so he could see out of Winston's window. "Oh, I see what has grabbed your eye. Yes, I do. Mighty fine girl, that Emma." Carter fired up the engine as Winston kept looking. He heard Carter continue to mumble as the car began to roll away. "Yes sir. Mighty fine…"

CHAPTER NINE

A Long String of Todays

After the diner was out of sight, Winston turned around and faced forward in the cab. He nestled down into the seat a little and stretched his legs as far as the space would allow. He felt tired, both mentally and physically, but it was more than just the night before and the bar. The entire year had taken quite a toll on him, and he knew he was starting to reach a breaking point, if he hadn't already. He wondered how long he could keep up this life.

He faced forward towards the front of the cab, and looked at Carter. He couldn't remember much about his previous experience with him, but when he saw it again, he did remember the beret that Carter wore on his head. And he remembered those huge hands that picked him up ever so easily.

Carter noticed Winston's attention change, and reached his right hand behind him over his shoulder, and offered it to him. "I guess we haven't met. Not formally anyways."

Winston shook his hand and looked into Carter's eyes. "Winston." One word was all he gave. He wasn't sure what else to say, and he felt a hint of embarrassment when he remembered the way Carter had seen him for the first time.

"Nice to meet you Winston. Name's Carter… but I'm sure you figured that out by now." Carter waited to release his hand until he finished talking. He smiled and Winston could see the gentleness in his eyes. But there was something else there. His gaze was long and penetrating, and the way he looked at him made him feel as if he knew already everything about him. "If I do say so myself, you sure do look like a new man today Mr. Winston. Not like the man I saw last night, no sir. My eyes tell me that was a different guy altogether. And boy did that guy look like he had a bad night! Yes sir. Bad night!"

Winston looked away and stared out the window. "Bad year," he said quietly, but still loud enough for Carter to hear. Then he whispered it again to himself as he watched the buildings of the town go by. "Bad year…"

Carter watched attentively in the rear-view mirror. "Well, Doc fixed you up real nice, just like I said he would. Yes sir. I knew old Doc would know what to do. He always does."

Winston faced the front again and took a deep breath. "So… Carter is it… Listen, thanks for picking me up yesterday. I'm not sure how the night might have ended if you weren't there when you were. I could have drowned in a puddle or got ran over if it weren't for you. In fact, I might not even be here right now. So… thanks again." He looked down and wondered to himself if on some level that might not have been the better alternative. At least I might have gotten to see Caroline again, he thought. If that's how it all worked.

"You're very welcome, Winston. Although, I tend to think it's best not to waste time on might-haves and could-haves. I reckon that kind of thinking might drive a man insane, if he were to spend too much time on it." Carter winked at him in the rear-view mirror. "Just be happy you are here. That's what I always say. Yes sir. Life ain't nothing but a long string of todays. Remember that my good man. No tomorrows, no yesterdays, just a long string of todays, lined up all nice and pretty for you." Carter kept his eyes on Winston, and before Winston knew it, they were on a narrow road leaving the town. "Now what you do with them," Carter continued. "Well… that's up to you. So the question you have to ask yourself is, what do I do with mine?"

Winston thought about Carter's words as they left the town. The corn stalks flew by a few feet from the window. "Maybe you're right Carter… maybe you're right." Winston nodded his head slightly over and over in agreement as he looked at the reflection of the bandage on his head in the window.

After about a mile, Winston turned and looked out the back window. The road was so narrow, and the corn stalks so high and close, that off in the distance the road seemed to simply close up and turn in to a thick wall of corn. He kept watching until he heard Carter mumbling something to himself in the front. "…guess we still have a ways to go…"

Winston flipped around and faced the front again. "I would also like you to thank the doc for me. I never really got the chance. He just sort of left me this morning, before I could get my bearings straight or my words out."

"Yeah he tends to do that. Old Doc's a fine man. Busy as a bee that guy, but a fine man he is." He turned off the narrow road, leaving the corn, and drove onto a larger highway of some sort. "I'll be sure to tell him you said as much. You can bet on that. Yes sir."

"So, you say we have a ways to go before we get to the city? How far away are we anyhow?"

"Oh, it's not terribly far. We'll be there pretty soon," Carter said. "I suppose you want me to take you back to where I found you?"

"I guess so," Winston said. "I left my car outside the pub along the street somewhere. Shouldn't be too hard to find." Suddenly, Winston realized he didn't know where his keys were. He patted the pockets of his jacket and listened for jingles, then dug deep into each pocket, finding nothing. Then he remembered a few more details of last night. "Shit, I think I left the keys in the car. In fact, I might have even left the door open." Winston slumped in his seat and sighed.

"Ooooh, that man on the sidewalk had himself a night I tell you!"

Winston looked up at the ceiling of the car above him and closed his eyes. "Mind if I ask you a question, Mr. Winston?"

"Sure, why not," Winston said. He shook his head back and forth, unsurprised at the idiotic circumstances he put himself in, although it seemed to be happening more these days.

"How does a man get himself into a mess like that?"

Winston looked out the window again, off into the distance. "Let's just say I have some… business to finish… a wrong that I need to right." How can it ever be right again?

The rest of the way to the city was traveled in silence. Winston didn't bother following the roads. He was lost in thought, and heard Carter mumble to himself from time to time. The sun began to dance in and out of the clouds and flicker through the window onto Winston's face. By the time they rounded a corner and Winston noticed the edges of the city, the sun had been hidden completely. It was overcast in the city, but not raining for once. He sat forward and looked out the front windshield for the first time since they left.

"Glad to see you interested in where you are going Winston. Seems to me you spend too much time looking out the back window. Can't see anything but where you've been that way. And you're a sure bet to miss something pretty good in front of you." Winston just kept watching without saying a word. "But what do I know, I'm just an old cabbie."

As they turned down the street where the pub was, Winston recognized the red letter "E" glowing on the side of the brick building. He had flashes of the night before, and remembered looking up at it through the rain. He rubbed his fist where it was still red from smashing into the sidewalk. Carter drove slowly up to the entrance, and stopped the cab next to where he picked Winston up on the sidewalk.

"I remember walking across the street," Winston said. He looked at the line of cars along the sidewalk opposite where they were and pointed. "Right around there is where I parked it. I'm sure of it." He looked up and down the street again. There was no sign of his car anywhere. "Looks like it's gone. Damn, I knew it."

"I'm sure it will turn up. The things we lose seem to come back to us eventually if we want them badly enough," Carter said.

"This is a car, not a pair of socks. I doubt it will just… turn up." He sighed and sunk again in the seat. "I better call the police." Then he realized he didn't have his phone either. "Shit. My phone was in the car, I think." He closed his eyes and lowered his head, wondering what else could go wrong.

Carter turned to look back at Winston. "Listen. I'm sure it'll all work itself out in due time. Most things do. I'll just take you back to your place for now. Where do you live anyways?"

"Village East and a hundred and fourteenth," Winston said sheepishly.

"Alrighty then." Carter pulled back onto the street and headed deeper into the city. Winston's mind was in a haze as the myriad streets and buildings passed by outside the cab. He looked down and thought about Caroline and what Carter had said about things we've lost coming back to us. If only that were true…

Winston was still looking down when the cab slowed to a stop. He looked up and saw the apartment building he called home. A small part of him was embarrassed, but the bigger part of him didn't care what anyone thought. They hadn't been through what he had been through. They hadn't felt the disappointment he had. They hadn't lost Caroline. What did they know.

"You take care of yourself now, Mr. Winston, ok?"

"I'll try. Thanks again Carter. My wallet is missing too, but I bet I have some cash laying around inside somewhere. Let me run in and get some for you. How much do I owe you?"

"Don't worry about it. I was headed to the city for Doc anyways, whether you tagged along or not. You were no extra burden."

"You guys have done too much for me already," said Winston. He stepped out of the car and leaned in one more time to look at Carter. "It won't take me a second to run in." He shut the door and stepped onto the sidewalk, taking a few steps towards the building before he heard Carter's voice through the open passenger window.

"Just remember what I said Winston. Todays are all we've got, my man. Leave the yesterdays behind and keep your eyes in front of you."

Winston turned back. "Just wait here, I'll be right back." He ran up the sidewalk and opened his door. Luckily, these days he never locked it. He had nothing of value anymore anyways, at least not valuable to him. As the door shut behind him, he rummaged through the mess of empty bottles on the table, then through a pile of old newspapers on the counter, then through a mound of dirty clothes on the couch. He finally found some cash laying on the TV stand, next to a bottle of whiskey and a bag of stale chips. He stuffed it in his pocket and headed for the door.

When he swung the door open, he was surprised to see Marlow standing just on the other side. "Whoa, where did you come from?" He tried looking over Marlow's shoulder for Carter's cab.

"Nice to see you too buddy, long time no see" said Marlow. He paused and waited for a second. "Nice to see you too... how are you doing... come right in... these are all acceptable greetings when you haven't seen your friend in a few weeks," he said jokingly as Winston kept looking around him, making no eye contact. "What are you doing anyways?"

"Wait right here, I have to do something really quick." Winston grabbed the cash from his pocket and stepped past Marlow. He stopped after a few steps and stood on the sidewalk, looking in both directions. Carter and his cab were gone.

Marlow saw him holding the crumpled cash in his hand. "What is that money for? And who are you looking for?"

"This money was for the cab driver that brought me home just now. I told him to wait right there."

Marlow looked at him incredulously. "I never saw a cab when I walked up, or a driver. Not on the sidewalk or on the street. I think you are losing it man."

"Well it was here two minutes ago!" Winston snapped back.

Marlow kept his disbelieving glare focused on Winston as he stood looking down the street in both directions. Then he noticed the bandage on the side of Winston's head.

"Whoa, what happened to your head buddy? You fall in the shower?" Marlow smiled and used a joking tone, trying to make light of the situation. He knew everything Winston was going through and was well aware of his erratic behavior lately.

Winston gave up on the search for Carter and walked back past Marlow into the apartment. "I guess he took off as soon as I went inside. I told him to wait."

"Whatever you say man," Marlow said. "And why would you take a cab. Where is your car?"

Winston hesitated to answer. He knew every answer would lead to more questions, and he wasn't sure if he had the energy for it all right now. "It either got towed or stolen last night. At some bar called Emanation, or something like that."

Marlow shook his head in disapproval. "So, you blew off your friends last night to go to a bar on the edge of the city? Dude, you can't keep doing this. Whatever you think you are accomplishing, it's a waste of time. And do I even want to know what happened to your head?"

Winston looked at him with a serious look on his face. He wasn't sure how Marlow would take this next sentence, but he hoped he would be on his side this time. He talked low and slow. "I think I found him last night."

"Who?"

"Him! The man. The black car. Him, that's who!"
Winston couldn't understand why it seemed he was the only
person who cared or thought about the other driver. This man
and his car had been the center of Winston's life for a year
now, but no one seemed to share in his concern or misery.

Marlow shook his head and put his hand up as if to say
he didn't want to hear anymore, but Winston continued. "I
followed him to that bar. I found him and followed him."

Marlow pursed his lips and lowered his hands. "And
then what?" He was still shaking his head when Winston
answered.

"He didn't like me so much."

"I can see that," said Marlow, motioning to his
bandaged head.

"I think one of his friends hit me with a bottle or
something. It gets a bit fuzzy after that."

Marlow stopped shaking his head. The look on his face
turned to one of concern for his friend. "Yeah, I'd say it might
have gotten fuzzy." He matched Winston's serious tone. "You
could have been killed, man." Marlow's concern for his friend
often turned to anger when Winston did something stupid, but
this time he was more fearful than angry. Winston looked
down, and for the second time today, he thought about the
possibility of his own death. Marlow continued in a lighter
tone. "Look man, I'm hungry. It's past lunch already, you
want to go grab some pizza? You can tell me all about last
night, and we can figure out what to do about your car. Okay
man?" There was a pause. Winston was still looking down in
thought. He looked up. With no car, no wallet, and no phone,
perhaps it would be wise not to push away his only remaining
friend. He decided for once to give in and listen.

"Sure," he said. "I haven't had lunch yet either."

Marlow pat him on the back and they walked out the door together.

CHAPTER TEN

Always a Story

Marlow drove a beat-up pickup truck, eleven years old but still chugging along. The passenger door creaked loudly when Winston opened it, and he often had to slam it violently for the latch to catch. Marlow never cared about cars the way Winston did, and saw them only as transportation. That's why when Winston brought home his BMW a few years back, grinning wildly at his new status symbol, Marlow could only see a monthly payment larger than he would ever have wanted himself. He smiled and acted like he was impressed at the time, but really, he saw no point.

"Still driving this hunk of junk?" Winston said, as he slammed the door shut beside him.

"As long as the wheels keep turning," replied Marlow. He handed his phone to Winston. "Here, you can use my phone. Call around and see if you can find your car." Winston took the phone and without saying a word and started searching for towing companies, calling them one by one.

By the time Marlow pulled into the parking lot at the restaurant fifteen minutes later, Winston was on his fifth or sixth call. "No, I don't have my license plate number memorized… do you know yours?... can't you just tell me if you have any charcoal colored BMWs on the lot?... two thousand ten… yes I'll hold… ok forget about it…"

"Not having any luck?" Marlow said with a grin as he turned the ignition off.

"These idiots think everyone has their license plate number memorized."

"Nine, Eight, I, Zero, Two, U," said Marlow with no hesitation. Winston looked at him in disbelief. "What, you don't know yours?" Marlow asked with a jabbing tone. Winston just shook his head and handed the phone back to him. They both got out of the truck in unison. It was cloudy, and without the sun, quite a bit cooler than it was this morning. When he saw the building, Winston realized he had never been here before. "Buenitos?"

"Yeah," Marlow replied. "I've been wanting to try this place. I've heard they have awesome Italian style pizza." As he opened the restaurant door for Winston, he hoped Winston wouldn't figure out that he chose this place on purpose, knowing that it would have no memories of Caroline attached to it. He had learned from experience that it was a good idea not to visit their old hangouts, and Winston seemed to be in a decent enough mood. No need to spoil it so soon.

After finding a booth off to the side and ordering food and drinks, Marlow stared across at Winston, looking again at the bandage on his head. "So, let's have it." Winston looked back at him and then down at the table, wondering where to start.

"Last night, after you called, I headed out. The rain was coming down pretty hard. I'm not sure where at this point, but I went to a house. Got the address from the paper." He stopped talking when the waiter brought two drinks and sat them on the table. Marlow was already shaking his head, as Winston thought about the house. Damn, the paper with the address was in my car too. He wondered how he would find the house again. After the waiter walked away, Winston continued. "When I got there, he was leaving, so I followed him to that bar."

"Yeah, I got that much figured out," Marlow interrupted. "You jumped some guy and got beat up in the process. It was stupid if you ask me, but I know you don't care. You only care about drinking yourself into a frenzy, and then going out looking for trouble. And sooner or later trouble always finds you. Or you bring it on yourself. Either way, this time you ended up hurt. But you could have gotten yourself killed."

"That's not all," Winston jumped in. He chose to ignore Marlow's rant. "I checked the car out. The front was dented."

"Yeah, so what. He could have bumped into a mailbox for all you know. And I see you're still wearing that damned ring. You know what I said about that."

Winston knew he was going to be skeptical. He looked Marlow directly in the eye. "I know it was him! I could feel it..." He looked down at the table again and spun the ring on his finger. After a pause, he said "...and I lost him. But I found him once, I can find him again."

"Don't tell me you are still going on with this… nonsense."

"Nonsense? How could you say that to me?" Winston looked away from Marlow. He wondered why it always seemed that everyone else just forgot about Caroline. Doesn't anyone else care about what happened to her? He was becoming more and more alone in his misery, as he watched his friends just move on from the thought of her. But he couldn't move on.

Around the restaurant, he watched all the happy people eating, and tried to remember what that felt like to laugh and joke, and share a meal. He never got excited about anything anymore, let alone food. So, when their pizza came to the table, he simply began eating in silence, avoiding Marlow's eyes and questions. Ten minutes of silence went by as they ate without speaking.

When the food was all gone and the table was cleared, Marlow lowered his tone and continued. "Alright, so you think you found him, is that it? And you say your car was stolen at the bar? So how did you get home if your car was stolen?"

Winston swirled the ice in his glass with his straw. "That's the rest of the story," he continued calmly. He spoke slowly as he looked off into the distance, trying to picture it all again. "I didn't go home that night." Marlow raised his brows. "Some cabbie picked me up. He took me to this small town outside the city. He kept mumbling about a doc the whole time. I was sort of out of it." Marlow smirked as if to say obviously, but Winston was staring off into the distance. "That's who took care of my head," Winston continued. "I was out cold until this morning. Woke up at that doc's house. Never got his name. He seemed like a real nice man though. Even made me breakfast."

Marlow rubbed his chin and looked at Winston with obvious skepticism. "And what town did you say you woke up in?"

Winston took another gulp from his soda, knowing Marlow wouldn't like his answer. "I'm… not sure actually. I never saw a sign, and it didn't cross my mind to ask anyone. Anyways, that same cab driver picked me up today at the diner there, and brought me home. That's who I was looking for when you showed up. I lost my wallet last night too, and so I went inside to find some cash for him. I opened the door and you were standing there. He was gone." Winston could see that Marlow was hesitant to believe him. "I know it sounds a little fishy, but I'm telling you, it happened just as I said it happened."

Marlow nodded his head slightly. "So, did you get the name of the cab driver? The cab company at least?"

"Why?"

"Well maybe your wallet fell out in the back seat. Maybe he turned it in. We could give them a call."

"I didn't get the name of the company," Winston answered. Marlow looked down at the table and shook his head. "The driver said his name was Carter though," Winston continued. "I do remember that at least. Also, there was some sort of logo on the side of the car. It was like… a laurel wreath… with gold lettering. I think it said..." Winston stared up at the ceiling, searching for the word he saw that morning. "Apollo! That was it. In gold letters. I remember now. He must have pulled away right before you walked up this morning."

"Must have," replied Marlow. "Wait a minute," he said, trying to lighten the mood. "You don't have your wallet?" He smiled. "So, you're saying lunch is on me I guess?"

Winston slid to the edge of the booth. He smiled for once. "Hey, it was your idea anyways," he said as he stood up. He pulled out the money in his pocket he was going to give Carter. "Here you go. These four dollars are all I got. I'm heading to the bathroom."

"Hey," Marlow said just after he turned to go. "You better call the police and report your stolen car." He reached into his pocket and pulled out some change. "And the cab company too. Call information, they can give you the number. My phone's battery is getting low, but I saw a payphone just outside." He pointed in the direction of the payphone and held out the change to Winston. "I'll take care of the check while you're gone." Winston took the coins and walked away.

Marlow could see the edge of the payphone out of one of the restaurant windows across the room. After the waiter brought the check, he waited for Winston to leave the bathroom and walk outside. Once he saw him put the phone to his ear, he pulled out his cell phone and began looking for information about the cab company. He could find no reference to "Apollo" in any cab company list or Internet search. He shook his head back and forth, as if to confirm his own disbelief.

He finished paying the bill about the same time he saw Winston hang up the phone outside, and met him at the door on the way out. "So how did it go?" he asked, as they walked to Marlow's truck.

"I filed the report," Winston replied. "So far it hasn't turned up. They said they would call if they find it. I gave them your number."

"You call the cab company?" Marlow asked.

Winston opened the passenger door and hopped in. After Marlow got in and started the truck, he answered. "No, I called my insurance company. Turns out I don't have a rental car option on my policy. So, I'm out of luck it seems, until they find my car."

Marlow looked at him with concern again. "Maybe it will do you good to spend a few days at home, staying out of trouble." He kept talking as he pulled out of the parking lot, knowing Winston hated hearing the tough advice. Winston gave no response. He just ignored Marlow and stared out the side window.

"I'm worried about you man," Marlow hesitantly said. "I… I think it's time you started worrying about the future instead of the past. Maybe talk to your therapist again. I know you haven't gone in months." He looked at Winston and could see that his words were sparking anger in him, but he knew he had to keep going. "And you might not want to hear this, but I think you need to forget about the wreck and move on."

Winston turned his head and looked at Marlow with disgust. "I'll never forget." His voice was dark and chilling.

"It's making you crazy man."

"I'm not crazy!"

"I wouldn't be too sure about that."

"What are you talking about?" Winston glared at him.

Marlow didn't care anymore if Winston got angry with him. "I looked up that cab company at the restaurant. I'm your friend, man. Be straight with me."

"What is that supposed to mean?" Winston snapped.

Marlow pulled into a parking lot and stopped the truck. "It doesn't exist. That's what I'm talking about. There's no Apollo cab company, or any company for that matter called Apollo. Not in this city, anyways. You're losing your grip man."

"You think I made up that story? Why in the world would I do that?"

"I'm not sure what I think anymore, Winston. But there's always a story. I'm tired of stories."

Winston scowled at Marlow. "Maybe they are a new company. Maybe they forgot to register with the city. Maybe they don't have a website. I have no idea!"

"No!" Marlow shrieked. "It doesn't exist! Only in your busted-up head. Probably the same with this doctor… doctor no-name… in the mystery town."

Winston looked out the window and thought about Caroline. "I'm not crazy man," he said without looking at Marlow.

"Then take me there," Marlow calmly said. "Take me to this… town."

Winston hung his head and looked at the floor of the truck.

"Well…," Marlow said impatiently. "Lead the way."

Winston sighed. "I don't know where it is." He looked at Marlow, who was shaking his head. "I told you I was barely conscious the whole way there."

Marlow didn't say a word. He just started the engine and pulled back onto the road. They headed in the direction of Winston's apartment. No words were spoken the rest of the way there. When they finally pulled up to the building, Winston reached for the door handle and Marlow finally spoke. "I only say this because you are my friend. You need to forget what happened to Caroline and move on. It was horrible. We all know that. But it's been a year. You need to forgive whoever was responsible. It won't bring her back. It will just ruin the life you have remaining. She would want you to move on. I know it."

Winston opened the door slightly and paused before getting out. He spoke without looking at Marlow. "It never should have happened. It's all my fault. I cannot forgive myself. And I cannot forgive that man. I know that." He stepped out of the car. "My life ended the day Caroline died." He shut the door.

Marlow rolled down the passenger window after the door was shut and shouted to Winston's back. "It doesn't have to be that way you know. Things can change." Winston never looked back. Marlow watched as he slowly walked up the sidewalk to the apartment and closed the door behind him. He stared at the closed door for a few minutes before slowly driving away.

CHAPTER ELEVEN

Chasing Ghosts

When the moon was high in the sky and most of the people of Dunsport were long asleep, Winston found himself walking the streets alone. It had rained earlier in the evening and as he walked, his shoes splashed in the puddles without trying to avoid them. He had been drinking since Marlow left, and the alcohol coursing through his veins muddled his head. His hand clung tightly to a bottle of random brown liquor. It was the second of two bottles he brought with him tonight. When he finished the first one, he threw it at a brick wall outside a closed business just to watch it shatter. He liked breaking things when he was drunk, because it reminded him of himself.

He took a swig as he focused on Marlow's words. *Losing your grip…* He pressed on the bandage on his head until he felt a sting of pain in the wound. *Seems real enough to me!* His mind bounced around inside his head, from thought to thought. *Losing my grip? What does he know? I had the guy in my grip and let him go! It won't happen again!* He took another gulp from the bottle, and felt the burn as it splashed down his throat.

He walked for a long time, down roads he had never been down, past buildings he had never seen. When he passed under a streetlight, he would veer around the orange glow that cast down upon the sidewalk, staying in the shadows whenever he could. He felt safe there, at home in the darkness. He looked up at the moon, which was just a glow behind the clouds in the night sky. The sun would be up soon, he thought. He kicked a rock along the road to pass the time. After he finished the last drop of alcohol in the second bottle, he stood still, swaying like a tree in the breeze.

He closed his eyes and thought about Caroline. Marlow said he drank too much, but Marlow didn't understand. He will never understand. What he didn't realize, was that she was always waiting for him at the bottom of the bottle, with her flowing hair and her eyes…. those eyes. She was among the raindrops that fell on his face. She was in the moon and in the stars. She was everywhere, and yet nowhere.

He looked down and stepped to the edge of the sidewalk. He inched closer until his toes were hanging over the edge. He stopped and stood still. Tears fell down his face as he thought of her. Then he closed his eyes and pretended he was standing on the edge of a tall and rocky cliff. The air was blowing his hair, and he could see the bottom of the canyon far below. With one leap, he could fly for a few moments. He could fly to her. And then he would see Caroline again. He would hold her and…

Lost in his fantasy, standing there with his eyes closed at the edge of the road, he didn't notice a car was quickly approaching. In the middle of his thought, it flew by only inches from his toes. The tires raced through a large puddle of standing water next to the sidewalk, creating a wave of filthy, cold, stagnant rainwater. The wave rose in front of his closed eyes and crashed into and around him, nearly knocking him to the ground. He staggered backward and opened his eyes. He was drenched from head to toe. The dirty water poured down his face and dripped into his open mouth, as he screamed at the car. He hurled the bottle in his hand at the car with all his might as it drove away, only to watch it crash onto the road behind it in an explosion of glass.

It was at this moment, after the glass had all fallen to the ground, that Winston first noticed the car. A Black BMW! He hopped off the sidewalk into the puddle of water that was still sloshing back and forth, and jumped into the middle of the road behind the car. He stared at the taillights for a split second, and began running after the car. Not this time! I'm not letting you get away again, you bastard! He screamed again as loud as he could. "Get back here!" His words echoed off the buildings surrounding the street, and seemed to chase after the car along with him. When the car was about a block in front of him, it had to slow down for a red light, and Winston pressed on even harder, begging his legs to move faster in their drunken state. It was the only car Winston had seen at this time of night and he felt as if he was meant to find it again. It's destiny.

The black car made a right turn and disappeared around the corner ahead. Winston ran with all the energy he could muster and ten or fifteen seconds later when he reached the corner, he stopped and looked to his right and saw the car stopped at the next light, only fifty yards or so away from him. Through his heavy breathing, he managed to yell again. "Hey! Get back here!" He felt a few drops of rain begin to fall on his face as the rain began again, but he was determined to not let the black car get away again. He started running at full speed, hoping the light would stay red long enough to keep the car there, but when he had covered about half the distance between them, the stoplight turned green and the car took off again, straight ahead through the intersection.

Undeterred, he chased after it as the rain pelted his face and blurred his vision. By the time he reached the intersection the car was hundreds of yards away and he knew he was losing it. The stoplight had turned red again, but Winston didn't even notice. His focus was solely on the red taillights of the car ahead of him, and the red glow they left on the wet pavement behind them. He ran with determination and blind rage through the intersection, without stopping to look in either direction. The only direction that mattered was straight ahead, and the car was getting away.

Out of nowhere a yellow car seemed to appear in front of Winston, coming from his left. Running full speed with no time to stop, he slammed into the side of the car near the back door and his body rolled up onto the trunk. The car slammed on its brakes and slid to a stop as Winston fell from the car and crashed onto the wet pavement behind it. Winston sat up and the red brake lights of the yellow car made his face glow a ghastly red that matched the emotion in his eyes. Seemingly unhurt, and fueled by adrenaline and rage, Winston jumped up and pounded his fist on the trunk of the car. "Get out of my way you idiot!"

Through the rain, he noticed a glowing light on top of the car and realized it was a taxi. He quickly opened the rear door and jumped in the back of the car, slamming the door behind him. "Hurry, chase that car!" He pointed to his left at the taillights of the black car. "Don't let him get away! Step on it!"

The driver said nothing. He simply slammed on the gas and swerved left in the middle of the intersection. He sped after the black BMW, which by now looked like only two small red lights in the distance, twinkling in the rain. They seemed to be the only two vehicles out at this time of night, and the darkness was intense, both inside and outside of the cab. The increasingly heavy rain fell loudly on the metal roof, drowning out all other sounds. Winston wiped the water from his face and stared intently out the front windshield, watching every move of the black car.

As fast as the cab was driving, they weren't gaining any ground on the black car. In fact, the other car was getting farther and farther away from Winston's grasp with each bend in the road. *He knows I'm after him.* Winston shouted at the driver in the dark. "You're letting him get away! Hurry up!" The driver hit the gas even harder and took the corners even faster, following the black car at a distance until they were several miles outside the city, yet each time they rounded a corner, the other car seemed to be even farther ahead of them and about to turn again. This continued, as did the panicked urging from Winston, until finally they went around a corner and the car wasn't in sight at all. It was gone. The cab driver slowed the car to a stop on a dirt road, somewhere out in the country.

"What are you doing?" Winston shouted. "Why are you stopping?"

"I can't chase what I can't see, Mr. Winston. Never much cared for chasing ghosts. So, if you can tell me for certain which way he went, then I'll happily go. But I think you'd be guessing at this point." His voice was deep and he motioned for Winston to look out the front windshield. Winston could see there was a fork in the road ahead. Each branch of the fork split off abruptly, and either direction Winston looked, he saw the road twist and turn around another corner. There was no way to know which way the black car went and he knew it. "And I'm quite sure we won't catch him," the driver continued. Not in this car. No sir." The sky was brighter now, and the sun would be up soon. Winston stared at the fork in the road for a few seconds longer, and then sat back in the seat defeated. He slammed both of his fists into the backseat on either side of his legs and stared at the ceiling. I let him get away again!

"He's just a bit too fast for this old car. Yes sir, Mr. Winston. Too fast."

"Wait," Winston said. "How do you know my name?" Then Winston recognized the beret on the driver's head and leaned sideways a bit to take a look at the driver. "Carter? Is that you?" His speech was slightly mumbled.

The light seemed to suddenly reveal Carter on cue, as he shut the car off. "Yes sir, Carter at your service. How's Mr. Winston doing this morning?" They made eye contact in the rear-view mirror and Winston shook his head in bewilderment, wondering how he hadn't noticed it was Carter until now. He thought about the chase and realized he had been so focused on the other car that he hadn't even looked at him once. With no answer from Winston, Carter continued. "By the looks of it, you've had yourself another eventful night Mr. Winston. Yes sir."

"How long have you known it was me? Why didn't you say something earlier?"

Carter smiled at him in the mirror. "Well, I reckon I knew it was you the moment you ran into me, or ran into my car I should say." He let out a little chuckle, but Winston didn't see the humor in it. "Your bandage gave it away. Sorry I didn't say anything earlier. I guess I tend to let people figure things out in their own time. Plus, you didn't seem like you were in the chatting mood. No sir."

Winston's eyes were glassy and red. "Remember when I told you I had some business to finish in the city," he said.

"Well, that black car was the business. That black car was the wrong I intend to right."

        Carter looked at him with concern on his face through the mirror. "Well I'm sorry to hear that Mr. Winston. I apologize my ride here was not up to par. I'm afraid she's getting up there in age, just like me." He let out another small chuckle. "But she's been a good car. Gets me where I need to go at least." He patted the dashboard with his right hand as one might pat a good dog.

        Winston relaxed in his seat again. Something about Carter made him feel at ease. "It's ok, there will be another day." He took a deep breath and let it out slowly. "So anyways, when you dropped me off at my place last night, why did you run off so quickly? I said I would be right back with some money for you. But I came outside two minutes later and you were nowhere to be seen. My friend thought I was a maniac and said he never saw you at all."

        "I had some business of my own in the city, and I told you, Doc covered your fare. Yes sir, mighty fine tipper Doc is. And as far as your friend, well… people tend to see what they want to see I guess."

        Winston leaned forward. "Speaking of the doc," he said. "Did you ever thank him for me? You know, for fixing me up and everything else?"

        "I'm afraid I haven't seen him since then. I do apologize." He could see the disappointment in Winston's face. "But if you are willing, we aren't too far from there and you could tag along while I make a quick stop in town. It's almost morning anyways. I could drop you off at the diner while I take care of my business. Doc is sure to be there by the time we get into town. He likes his coffee in the morning. So, if you aren't in too big of a hurry to get back to the city, you can just thank him yourself while I finish up my run. I'm sure he'd be mighty glad to see you again anyways."

Winston smiled shook his head. "Sure, that'd be fine. I have nowhere to be anyways." He sat back in his seat as Carter started the engine again. The sky was rather light by now, and Winston looked around, unable to tell where exactly they were. Dunsport was nowhere in sight. "How far away is this town?"

"It's not too far." He looked out at the sky. "We should be there shortly after sun up, which won't be long now." He looked back at Winston. "You can just sit back and relax now Mr. Winston. Those eyelids of yours look mighty heavy." Carter turned to the road and chuckled to himself again. "Yes sir, mighty heavy. Might try to rest 'em before it gets too bright out." He put the car into gear and headed down the left fork in the road.

In the back, Winston sank further into his seat and closed his eyelids, which seemed to feel even heavier after he heard Carter's words. He thought about his last visit and said quietly "So what's the name of this town anyways?"

Carter saw in the mirror that Winston would be asleep in no time. "That pretty little slice of heaven is called… Salima Falls."

Winston leaned his head up against the side by the window and said the words aloud to himself. "Salima Falls." He liked the way it sounded. He listened to the tires on the road and dozed off to the sound of Carter mumbling to himself.

CHAPTER TWELVE

Cream and Sugar on the Side

Winston woke to the sound of corn stalks whipping by the car at close range. His eyelids still felt like bricks, and the short nap he managed in the back of the cab was no match for a long night of drinking. His neck ached from the angle at which his head leaned against the car window next to him, or at least that's what he blamed it on. He was certain he remembered the entirety of the night before, but if he was honest with himself, he couldn't be sure. The wound under the bandage ached again now that he was sobering up.

By now, the sun was up and the sky was bright. The rain had apparently stopped during his nap, and from the looks of the clear blue skies outside his window, it wasn't coming back any time soon.

"Hey Carter," Winston said in a rough morning voice. "How long have I been out?"

"Not too long at all Mr. Winston. Not too long at all. But take a look ahead. Your timing couldn't have been any better. No sir. Salima Falls is just ahead."

Winston straightened up in his seat and stretched his neck back and forth. He rubbed his eyes and looked out the front windshield just as they exited the small narrow road that came through the cornfield. As soon as he and Carter entered Salima Falls, Winston remembered the sights and sounds. The colors were brighter here, and the air was crisper. He recognized the doc's house as they drove by. "Hey, there's Doc's house, if I remember right."

"Yes sir, he's been living there as long as I can remember. Nice little place if I do say so myself. Anyways, Mrs. Powell's diner is just a few blocks up ahead. I'll drop you off near there and you can hang out for a bit. I promise I won't be gone long. I'll come pick you up when I'm done. How's that sound?"

Winston nodded his head. "Sounds good." He found himself smiling when he looked at the street that led through town, with the marching magnolia trees running down the middle, alternated by the trident lamps, which were not lit at this time of day. It was early, but the town already seemed to be moving with energy and bustling with people. There were people walking on the sidewalks, laughing and carrying on, a few on bicycles, and the familiar paperboy delivering this morning's edition of the Salima Standard. The gleeful charm that each citizen of this small town exhibited was less nauseating this time for some reason.

Carter pulled up to the old hardware store opposite the diner and stopped the car. "I'll see you after a bit, ok?" Winston agreed, opened the door, and stepped out onto the sidewalk. After Carter drove away, Winston stood motionless, taking in everything around him. He didn't know what time of morning it was, but the weather seemed perfect to him. The sky was blue and bright, and the sun was at a steep angle. The air was warm, yet still cooled the skin as it wafted by, filled with the scent of summer flowers and freshly baked bread. He thought about Marlow's words again, and it felt good to verify his experience the other night. He was here again, back in Salima Falls, and somehow it felt… right. If only Marlow could see this.

The hardware store window in front of him had an old wagon wheel that leaned up against the glass, along with a series of wooden-handled hand tools and old barn signs. For a moment, it reminded Winston of the time when he and Caroline went picking through an old flea market for vintage decorations when they first moved in together. They saw a wagon wheel just like this one and talked about making some sort of towel holder from it. It was memories like this one that often tore him apart at night, when he was halfway through a bottle. But here in the Salima Falls sunlight, he felt the warmth of the rays and could smell the juniper trees on the breeze, and somehow, he managed to not let it overwhelm him. He just took a deep breath and turned towards the diner.

Everything was the same as last time as he approached the door to the diner, everything except today's lunch specials. Winston surprised even himself that he could remember. Tuna melt… chicken pest… wedge salad. This time there was no tuna melt. It had been replaced by a BLT. He took one last look around the street before entering, and wondered if things around here ever changed much at all.

Inside the diner, he was greeted by the same bubbly hostess as last time.

"Well, look who's back. How's that bump on your head doing?" She smiled profusely.

Winston instinctively touched the bandage as she was talking about it. "Alright I guess. I barely notice it actually."

"Well I guess the doc must have fixed you up right nice then."

"I guess so. Speaking of the doc, I'm looking for him. Is he…" Winston looked around the restaurant, scanning for the familiar face. He hadn't spent much time with the doc, but he had an unforgettably easing quality to him that Winston was sure he would recognize. "Never mind," he said. "I found him right over there. I guess I'll just go over and say hi. You think that would be alright?"

"Well of course. Don't be silly." The hostess was full of smiles and made Winston feel at ease. He walked over to the table where the doc was sitting alone, reading the paper, and having a coffee.

"Mind if I join you?"

The doc sat down his coffee, stood up, and extended his hand to Winston. "Well, look who it is. Absolutely, have a seat. I'd like the company actually." They shook hands and Winston sat opposite the doc. "Let me get you a cup of coffee. How do you like it?" He waved over a waitress that seemed to be waiting for his request.

"I usually just get it plain black, but the last time I was here, the waitress looked at me like I was crazy when I told her." The doc seemed amused at his story as the current waitress walked up to the table.

"Dear, can you bring my friend Winston a cup of black coffee? Cream and sugar on the side please. Thank you so much." After she walked away he looked at Winston. "There, now you can drink it however you like and no one is the wiser."

"Brilliant," Winston said with a smile. The doc looked intently at his bandage.

"So how are you doing, Winston? Is that bump on your head giving you any troubles?"

"Actually, it's been great. Haven't even really noticed it. Sometimes I forget about it."

"Well that's great. I think we can take those bandages off now. The cut is closed up and will heal the rest of the way on its own. Those stitches will have to wait until the end of the week though. Scoot over here closer so I can get a better look." The doc patted the chair next to him and Winston nervously obeyed, as the waitress came back and sat a steaming cup of coffee in front of him. Winston thanked her and took a sip as the doc peeled off the bandage on his head. The tape stuck to his hair a bit but came off without any pain.

"Good. It looks like it's started healing up just fine. No sign of any infection. You should be back to your old self in no time." He smiled and patted Winston on the back as a father would pat his son after a fall. Winston took another sip of his coffee.

"Listen Doc, I… I wanted to thank you again for helping me out like you did." He got an embarrassed look on his face and looked away. "I'm afraid I just lost my job though, and my insurance with it. But I want to repay you if I can."

Doc shook his head from side to side. "It was no trouble at all. What kind of doctor would I be if I just let a bleeding man bleed? You don't owe me a thing. Just enjoy your coffee, that's all. Mrs. Powell's has the best coffee in Salima Falls if you ask me."

"But I…" Winston started, before being interrupted.

"No buts," the doc said. "I was happy to have you."

Winston looked down at his coffee. For the first time, he was taking stock of the disarray his life had fallen into. He felt ashamed. "My car was stolen too. And I lost my phone. And my wallet." I lost everything.

"What about a place to stay?" the doc said.

"Still have my apartment…" He nervously stirred his coffee. "…for now, anyways."

"Well it sounds like you have enough problems." You have no idea, thought Winston. "I'm not going to add to it. Call it a favor."

After a few seconds of quiet sulking, Winston put down his spoon. He felt different in this town. He felt a little like his old self. And his old self didn't like handouts. "I appreciate it Doc, I really do, but if you won't let me pay you back, then how about an old-fashioned trade?"

"What do you have in mind?" The doc's face flashed a satisfactory smile, and he seemed interested to hear what Winston had to say. It was almost as if he had expected him to make the offer, like this was what he wanted all along.

"I'm not sure," Winston replied. "Maybe I could wash your car a few times."

"Mrs. Jenkins boy up the street washes my car every Tuesday for two dollars and a soda, I'm afraid."

"Well what about yard work? I haven't mowed a lawn in quite a while but I think I can still manage just fine. I used to really enjoy that." I used to enjoy a lot of things.

"Well, Dave Shumpert is taking care of my yard for me this whole summer actually. He runs a small landscaping company, and this winter when his dog broke his leg, I put a cast on old Stinker. He loves that dog. But I always tell him, if he really loved him, he wouldn't have named him Stinker!" The doc let out quite a laugh and Winston raised his eyebrows.

"I see."

"I had never fixed up a hound before," the doc continued. That's Ms. Willow's job usually. She owns Furry Friends Animal Shelter down the road a bit, but she was out of town visiting relatives down south."

Winston pressed his lips together and moved them to one side. "Hmmmmm. I'm not much help around the house, with cooking or cleaning or laundry. But there's got to be something I can do." He drank some more of his coffee and the doc did as well, as they both looked at each other in thought. Then the doc sat his cup down and smiled.

"I have an idea." His eyes seemed to light up with this new thought. "What do you know about cars?"

"Cars?" Winston seemed skeptical.

"Never mind that, it doesn't matter," the doc said immediately, almost cutting him off. "Anyways, a good friend of mine, Earl, owns an old auto repair shop out on the edge of town. He is alone and he works hard, but he could sure use help with some things up there. It's a lot to handle for one man."

Winston's eyes got big. "I was a software salesman. I don't know anything about cars," he exclaimed.

Doc looked at him like a teacher looking at a kid who wasn't trying. "Surely you can wash windows and fill tires and such, can't you? At the very least you can fetch tools and keep him company. Old Earl is running ragged out there."

"I don't know," Winston said as he was shaking his head.

"If memory serves me right, a month or so ago, Susie Laciak's boy spent his entire spring break this year from school helping Earl out. Lenny, I think was his name. His daddy's a friend of Earl's and Lenny wanted to make a few extra bucks to buy some fancy headphones or something. Fifteen years old but a good hard worker Earl said."

Winston nodded softly while the doc finished talking. "Ok, ok, I get your point. If a fifteen-year-old can do it, I can probably figure it out."

The doc smiled. "That's the spirit! So how about helping him out as a favor to me? And at the end of the week, I promise you will be all healed up. I'll take those stitches out, and you'll be as good as new again. We will call it even. How's that sound?"

Winston smiled back at the doc, knowing he couldn't resist that Salima Falls charm he had. "Alright, you have a deal. Only problem is, like I said earlier, I don't have a car right now. How am I supposed to get here every day?"

"Well, leave that to me. It's no problem at all. Our good buddy Carter makes a run into the city twice a day for me. Once in the morning and once in the evening. You're not too far out of the way I suppose. I'll just have him stop and pick you up in the morning, and he can drop you off in the evening."

Winston marveled at the ease at which Doc seemed to have everything figured out. He always seemed one step ahead of everything. He liked that. "I guess that'll be just fine." He reached out his hand to the doc with a smile on his face. "It's customary to shake when deals are made I think." The doc shook his hand with pleasure, and just as their hands parted, Carter entered the diner and walked up to the table.

"Hey Doc. Nice to see you again." He looked at Winston. "All done Mr. Winston. Sorry to keep you waiting so long. We can head back now, if you want."

The doc stood to greet Carter as he had done with Winston. After shaking his hand, he looked down at Winston. "Winston, why don't you head on out and wait in the cab and I'll fill Carter in on our little deal and take care of the bill."

As Winston neared the door, he hesitated, looking around for Emma again. He hadn't thought about her since the last time he was here, but now that his business with the doc was all wrapped up, he couldn't help but try to catch a glimpse of her again. He scanned the view to the kitchen for her dark hair. The hostess cheerfully took this opportunity to speak again.

"Who ya looking for this time?" She giggled as she said it.

Winston took one last look around, satisfying his curiosity that she wasn't here. "No one in particular. You take care." He shut the door and exited to the sound of the hostess's mumbled voice, no doubt replying with something polite about the weather or the day.

The ride home was rather uneventful. The drinking and lack of sleep were catching up to him, and he had already exhausted the small energy boost he got from the coffee. He could barely stay awake. No more booze for a while…

When he arrived back at his apartment, he quickly thanked Carter and told him he would see him in the morning. Though it was early in the afternoon, he could think of nothing but going to bed, but when he got to his door there was a piece of paper taped to it at eye level. Large black letters at the top spelled out "Eviction Notice." Somewhere down the page in highlighted yellow he saw "10 days." Lovely. He tore it from the door without even reading it and headed inside. He tossed the paper next to the answering machine and saw the blinking red light that greeted him. More bad news probably.

Winston hit the play button and grabbed a beer from the fridge.

Beeeeeep.

"Hey man it's Marlow. Listen, I'll get straight to the point. Jimmy told me they fired you. I'm sorry to hear it man, but I can't say I'm surprised. What are you going to do now? Have you thought about it yet?" Winston lifted the beer and gulped several times until the can was half empty. "Anyway," Marlow continued. "I talked to my boss and he thinks we might be able to find something for you over here, part-time at least. The pay won't be what you are used to, but it's something. It's a fresh start. Anyway, I don't want you to end up on the streets man. But you have to promise me you will start thinking about the future and move on with your life. I'm not going to stick my neck out for you just to have it blow up in my face. He said he wants to meet up later this week and talk to you about a couple options. I'll let you know when and where to be." Winston walked to the window and peeked outside. The clouds were beginning to roll in from the north. "If you don't get your car back by Friday," Marlow continued. "Then I'll come pick you up, ok?" Winston hated when people used questions in a voicemail. It made no sense, and was annoying. "So, get back to me this week if you have any questions, otherwise I'll see you this Friday. Don't leave me hanging on this one Winston."

He finished the beer and tossed it in the trash, which was so full, the can simply bounced off and fell to the floor beside it. He grabbed two more beers from the fridge and stumbled to the couch. He sat and clicked on the TV.

"…chance of rain is nearly eighty percent this…"
Click.
Every damn day I swear.
"…what do you bid on this Showcase Showdown?"
Click.
The usual daytime comfort foods didn't interest him. After two or three more quick channels flips through a parade of endless talk shows, some sort of kids show about animals, and a hesitation to momentarily watch a daytime court judge

berate a helpless lawbreaker, Winston finally stopped when he saw a show about restoring an old car. He thought it might be relevant to his current situation. What do I know about cars, anyways?

Winston finished the second beer soon after the first and tossed it on the floor. After opening the third beer, he nestled onto his side on the couch, sipping it and watching the man on the TV take apart some unknown inner part of an engine. His eyes became heavier and heavier until the half-empty beer fell from his fingers and tipped over on the floor, wetting his carpet as he dozed off to the sounds of words he had never heard.

"In a catalytic converter, the catalyst, in the form of platinum and palladium, is coated onto a ceramic honeycomb or ceramic beads that are housed in a muffler-like package attached to the exhaust pipe. The catalyst helps to convert carbon monoxide into carbon dioxide and it converts..."

CHAPTER THIRTEEN

A Larger Wall Than Most

Fifteen hours later, Winston heard a car honk outside his apartment. He hadn't moved an inch since he crawled onto the couch the day before. It was the most he had slept since Caroline's accident. Over a year ago now. *Wow.* In fact, during the last year he slept an average of three to four hours a night, so this was about a week's worth for him. Morning already? What time is it? He heard another honk and lifted his head. Then suddenly he remembered the deal he'd made with the doc in Salima Falls yesterday. I wonder if that's Carter honking.

Winston managed to stand up and stepped right on the empty beer can he had dropped the night before. He kicked it aside and felt the wet carpet underneath on the bottom of his socks. Great. He rubbed his eyes until they could stay open, and walked to the window overlooking the street. He spread the cheap plastic venetian blinds with his finger and thumb. Outside, he could see the by-now familiar Apollo cab that Carter drove, parked along the sidewalk in front of his door. He opened the front door to his apartment and waved at Carter until he was sure he saw him. He held up two fingers and mouthed the words two minutes. Carter smiled and Winston shut the door and hurried back inside. No time for a shower I guess.

He quickly ripped off his shirt and grabbed a fresh white one from the top drawer in his dresser. It was the last shirt in the drawer and he tossed the one he was wearing into an ever-growing pile in the corner. He did the same with his socks. He couldn't even remember the last time he managed to do laundry or clean the apartment. Those domesticated thoughts seemed pointless to him these days.

He put on his shoes and headed for the door. On the way, he happened to glance at his appearance in the mirror and he barely recognized himself. It had been awhile since he had seen himself in the mirror, and he was dirty, scruffy, and his hair was longer than he liked. He looked older than he remembered. He raised an arm and gave his underarm a quick sniff. His nose scrunched up and he shook his head. I better keep my distance from people today, if possible.

Winston walked quickly down the sidewalk and hopped in the back seat.

"Sorry Carter. I never set an alarm yesterday. I'm not even sure we set a time, did we?" He felt bad about making him wait, but that feeling was short lived.

"Ah it's no problem Mr. Winston. I'm not in any rush, just wanted to make sure you heard me, that's all. I hope my honking didn't disturb any of your fine neighbors."

"In this neighborhood, I'm afraid honking is not the sound that bothers people, if you know what I mean."

Carter nodded his head as if he was sad to hear it. He started up the engine and headed out. "Well, I don't really operate on a strict schedule, so to speak. No sir. But you can expect me about this time each day I would think. I can just honk when I get here and again in a few minutes if I don't see you."

"Sure, that will probably work," Winston said.

As they drove out of the city, Winston was more conscious of the turns Carter was taking, determined to figure out the way to get to this town. After his lunch with Marlow he wanted proof, mostly for Marlow, but a little for himself as well. After about a half hour Winston noticed that all around him were fields. The road turned left then right then left again. It was almost impossible to remember the turns. Every corner looked the same, and every field seemed like the last one. How could I ever find my way?

"This place sure is hard to get to," he said, hoping to get some direction from Carter.

"Yes sir, just a little slice of heaven out in the middle of nowhere."

"I haven't even seen the name Salima Falls on a single sign the whole time we've been driving." Winston looked out the window as Carter turned down another unnamed road that looked suspiciously like the last one they were on. "How do you even know where you are going?"

Carter chucked a bit. "Well I've been back and forth a time or two in my days." He turned again between two fields of corn onto a narrow road that Winston was certain he would have missed if he were driving. He hadn't even seen it by the time Carter turned. "Not too many people know how to get there, and to be honest, the folks in town rather like it that way." He rounded a corner rather hastily again.

"Why is that?" Winston asked.

"Well, I suppose they would rather stay quiet and off the radar I guess. They don't much appreciate the hustle and bustle of the big city. The city is a dark place where people lose themselves, you see."

I know exactly what you mean, Winston thought.

"Salima Falls is a special place, Winston," Carter continued. "Yes sir. It's the kind of place where folks go to be away from all the noise, to calm the waters so to speak, and to find something missing in their lives. It's a peaceful existence, and to them, they don't have much need for anything else."

"So how did you end up there?" Winston asked.

"Well I wouldn't say I ended up anywhere. This isn't the end for me. I just sort of go where I'm needed, and right now the doc needs me, so I belong here."

Winston looked out the window pensively. "I'm not sure if I belong anywhere anymore."

Carter watched Winston in the rear-view mirror. "Well, I tend to believe if you belong somewhere, and you are supposed to be there, then the world just has a way of getting you there. Yes sir, things just sort of happen that are out of your control, with or without you knowing it." Winston felt the power of Carter's words flow slowly and almost visibly throughout the cab. "You just have to have faith that the universe knows what it's doing and you will end up right where you belong."

"How will I know where that is?" Winston asked, without taking his eyes from the fields.

"You don't have to ask or wonder. No sir. You just know, that's how."

While Winston pondered Carter's words, the cab exited the cornfields and arrived in Salima Falls, much like each previous time, with the sun glistening in the perfect blue sky overhead, and the wonderful aromas filling the air around them. Winston closed his eyes and took a deep breath through his nose, letting the effect of the town fully grab him.

As they drove past the diner, he looked out the window intently, hoping to catch a glimpse of Emma as they rolled by, but the sun reflecting off the glass windows kept him from seeing through them. A group of old ladies exited the diner as he looked, and he wondered if they were the same ladies that had bumped into him a few days ago. Out the window, he watched as they passed several quaint shops and businesses. There was a library, an animal shelter, a paint shop, a soda shop, a candy store, a toy store, a woodworking mill, a few small clothing stores dedicated to a particular group of people, and a small grocery store on his side of the car near the corner streetlight.

As they approached the light, it turned red, and Carter slowed the car to a stop next to the grocery store. Winston looked up at the little sign that stuck out perpendicularly from the brick building on a little wrought-iron arm. Winston read the words aloud. "GRETA'S HEALTH FOODS."

"Yes sir," Carter answered. "Ol' Greta's has the best egg salad sandwich money can buy, and the best pickles you ever tasted. Mmmmm, I'll swear by that!"

"I thought she was famous for her orange juice," Winston said in a questioning tone.

"Oh, that orange juice of hers is mighty good too. She grows her own oranges outside of town. I suppose everybody in town has their favorites from Greta's. She's famous for lots of stuff."

As Carter finished his sentence, Winston noticed a girl walk into the grocery carrying an empty burlap sack over her shoulder. She was dressed in blue jean shorts and a black top, with flip-flops on her feet and her deep brown hair pulled back into a ponytail. Though she looked different than the first time he saw her in the diner, Winston recognized her immediately. Emma!

With one quick pull of the door handle and a push of the door, Winston hopped out of the car.

"Hey, where are you going?" Carter asked, as the streetlight turned green again.

Winston leaned into the open passenger window. "Sorry Carter, but I need a few minutes. I'm going to run into the grocery store. I won't be long. Can you wait for me?"

"I suppose I have a couple of minutes," Carter said. "But no more than that. I'll park just around the corner. Don't be too long, I have things to do for the doc."

"Thanks," Winston said, as he turned and headed for the entrance to Greta's.

"Welcome to Greta's!" exclaimed one of the cashiers as he walked in." What is it with this town?

He ignored the cashier and looked all around, but didn't see Emma anywhere. He hurried past a few aisles, looking down each one as he passed, but failed to see her. After he passed the last aisle to the right, he walked into the deli and produce section. On the opposite side, past several large racks of fresh tomatoes, cucumbers, and lettuce, he caught a glimpse of Emma inspecting some strawberries. Her burlap sack seemed to be heavy on her arm, already half full of items. He hid behind a display of flowers and peeked at her through the plants. What will I even say to her?

He watched her for a while as she passed each display, seemingly in slow motion. He saw her pick up a melon and hold it to her nose. A smile formed on his face. She's so beautiful. But he noticed a peculiar thing with her. When others people passed each other in the store, they always smiled and greeted one another in the usual Salima Falls way. But with Emma, she seemed to wander through town unnoticed wherever she went. No one seemed to say anything to her. How could anyone not notice her? She rarely seemed to look up at people either, and seemed to be lost in her own world. *I know the feeling.*

Winston knew he didn't have time to stand here and watch her all day. Carter was probably already wondering if he would be coming out soon. Okay Winston, just go say hi. He stepped out from behind the flowers and headed across the produce section. When he reached Emma, she was staring intently down at some fresh herbs of some kind. Her hair gently swayed as he approached. She put the herbs up to her nose to smell them just as Winston walked up in front of her.

"Oh, I'm sorry, I didn't see you." She seemed startled and stepped aside to let him pass.

"It's ok, I wasn't trying to get around you," Winston said apologetically. "I just wanted to say hi."

"To me?" Emma said.

"Yes, to you. It's Emma, right?" Winston flashed the friendliest smile he had in his repertoire to try to seem less creepy than he knew he was coming off. It was hard to get past the wall girls put up around themselves when meeting new people, and Emma seemed to have built a larger wall than most. Since he could see she was confused, he continued. "You work at Mrs. Powell's diner, right? I saw you the other day when I was there, and I wanted to say hi then, but you seemed pretty busy and I didn't get the chance."

"Yes, I'm at the diner some days." Emma looked down at the herbs in her hand nervously. "I tend to keep busy most of the time." Her eyes wandered around the store, making very little eye contact with Winston. "How did you know my name?"

"Oh, I'm sorry." Winston was embarrassed. "I should have mentioned that. Anyway, my new friend Carter told me your name at the diner the other day when I saw you. He was giving me a ride home and I asked him." He could see her ease up her tension a bit.

"Oh, I know Carter. Great guy. I see him around town all the time. How do you know him?"

Winston hesitated. Let's not go there just yet. "Well, I sort of just ended up in the back of his cab one night and things went from there." Emma was quiet so he continued. Here goes. "Listen, I don't really know anyone in town yet, and this may seem out of the blue, but I was wondering if you wanted to have lunch sometime." The words were out. Now the only thing Winston could do was wait for an answer. The seconds that passed were excruciatingly long. He could tell that she was thinking of a polite way to say no.

"Well, like I told you," she said while looking down at her herbs again. "I'm extremely busy and work three jobs and I tend to keep to myself. I usually just like to eat lunch alone outside somewhere." She paused and Winston could feel his heart sinking a bit. "I'm sure you underst…"

"Absolutely!" he cut her off, just wanting the awkwardness to end. "Look, I'm sorry I even asked. I don't want to disturb you." That was embarrassing. "Well, listen Emma, I don't mean to keep you. I just wanted to introduce myself and tell you my name, since I knew yours." He held out his hand. "My name is Winston."

She took his hand and barely looked him in the eye out of the corner of hers. He smiled and shook her hand. It was soft and dainty, and several seconds seemed to pass before she spoke. "I'm Emma… I mean… you already know that. You just said it… I'm… I'm sorry."

Winston's smile grew even larger. "Nice to meet you Emma." He reluctantly let go of her hand, and just as he was about to walk away, she spoke.

"You look familiar to me." She looked at him closer with both eyes, examining his hair and his face, before shaking her head. "I don't know, maybe I did see you that day in the diner."

"Well, now at least you know what to call me when you see me again. Anyway, I don't mean to keep you from your shopping, and I have somewhere I have to be too." He took a step back away from her towards the door. "But I'll be in town for a week or so, I hope to see you again. Take care." He hurried back out the door and around the corner to Carter's waiting cab.

"Sorry Carter, I happened to bump into someone and so I said hi." He opened the back door and jumped in the back.

Carter looked back at him in the mirror with a skeptical look on his face. "And how's Ms. Emma doing?"

"Fine, I guess. Although she did say she recognized me from some..." Winston stopped mid-sentence and returned Carter's skeptical look into the mirror. "Wait a minute, I never said who I bumped into, how did you know it was her?" Winston looked around to see if she was in sight. "Did you follow me in there?"

"No need to follow you Mr. Winston. My eyes tell me everything I need to know." He chuckled a bit.

"What do you see?" Winston asked in a disbelieving voice.

Carter pulled the cab back onto the road and continued in the direction they were headed. "Well from what I know of you Mr. Winston, you don't seem to be the type of man who needs any last-minute purchases from a health food store. No sir." He chuckled again to himself. "And when you came out of there with no bags and carrying nothing in your hands either, well I knew you must have went in there for something else." Winston looked down at his empty hands and understood. Carter continued. "Plus, when we rolled past the diner back there, I noticed you craning your neck, looking for something. Or someone I should say. So, I pretty much figured."

Winston nodded his head in agreement. "I see your point."

"And to top it off, when you hopped in the back with your empty hands, I noticed you had a big smile on your face too. Only other time I remember seeing you with a smile like that was the first time you saw Ms. Emma."

"Wow, you're good Carter. Can't slip anything by you, I guess." Winston let out a small laugh.

Carter joined with a small laugh of his own. "I should say not, Mr. Winston.... I should say not."

Soon, as they reached the other side of town, just past where the houses came to an end, Carter pulled into the last building in sight. It was a small auto repair shop that seemed to sit just outside of Salima Falls on a dirt lot. The paved road ended at the last house, and there was a hundred feet or so of dirt road that led past the shop and off again around the corner, getting lost among the trees. Another small road joined to the left near the entrance and ran off into the distance.

"Well, we are here," Carter said. "Welcome to Earl's. I'll come get you this afternoon around four o'clock. I'll try to be here around that time, but I can't promise you that, alright?"

"Alright," Winston said as he hopped out the back.

He stood on the dirt lot in the sunlight, taking in his surroundings, as Carter made a loop in his cab and headed back into Salima Falls. He thought about Emma again and smiled the same goofy smile that Carter mentioned earlier. He looked up at the building in front of him. There was a sign in big bold metal letters on the front of the building that read EARL'S AUTO SERVICE & GASOLINE.

CHAPTER FOURTEEN
First Impressions

Winston shielded his eyes from the sun climbing in the sky, and could tell that the sign in front of him that read "EARL'S AUTO SERVICE & GASOLINE" was once a backlit beacon that probably could have been seen from blocks away. But now, however many years later, it was just a bunch of rusted metal block letters. The "E" at the end of "GASOLINE" was dangling at an angle, and the red paint on many of the letters had long worn off.

An awning, roughly large enough for two cars end-to-end, and two side-by-side, came off the building and connected to poles that were anchored in concrete. It created a canopy where cars could be pulled out of the rain or away from the sun. On those poles were two vintage gas pumps that had been out of service for what appeared to be a hundred years to Winston. He tried to envision what it must have looked like in its heyday.

The entire establishment was on a dirt lot, and to the right and left of the main building were a couple of smaller ones and a larger detached garage with huge doors. Several old heaps of rust littered one side of the building, apparently left for dead years ago. There were antique gas pumps everywhere, and rustic signs from long ago advertising everything from cola drinks to long-closed motor oil companies. Hundreds of old rusty tools were lying around or mounted on the outside of the building as decorations. Look at all this junk.

On the opposite side of the lot, Winston saw at least ten newer vehicles lined up. These were apparently the cars that were here for service, and not part of the auto graveyard that he seemed to be in. He walked towards the row of vehicles and stopped when he noticed one with a large dent on the front bumper. It was a yellow convertible that was at least twenty years old, but the dent was a sudden reminder of Caroline's wreck. And it was a reminder of the anger that resided inside of him, not only for the other driver that fateful day, but now a little for himself. He was mad at himself for having been distracted by Emma each time he came to this town. He felt ashamed, as if he was guilty of betrayal. I'm sorry Caroline.

Winston closed his eyes and faced the sun. He let the warmth penetrate his skin and took a few deep breaths to let his feelings of guilt and anger pass. Today was his first day helping Earl, and he needed to be strong today. I can't let every dent be her dent. I can't let every accident be her accident.

He walked under the canopy to the main door that led to what appeared to be the office, and knocked. There was no answer. He opened the door slowly and peeked his head in. "Hello?" There was nothing but silence. He must be out back somewhere. On the opposite side of the office were two doors, one with a window on the left side of the room, and one without a window on the right. Above the one on the left was a sign that read "CAUTION: WORK AHEAD" in black letters on faded yellow metal. It appeared to lead to the main garage behind the office. The one on the right without a window also had a sign that said "KEEP OUT!" Winston wondered what might be hidden behind that door.

He peered through the hazy window in the left door into the large garage on the other side. It was large enough to accommodate at least four vehicles. He marveled at the level of filth everywhere he looked. Everything seemed to be the same greasy color of grayish black, with a little yellow or brown in it. He found out as he opened the door that even the door handles were covered in grease. The door was attached to a spring and shut behind him with a clang.

The door opened immediately in front of the first bay, which was empty. To the right were three more occupied bays. In the first one was an old beat up Cadillac. Next to that was a newer sedan of some sort, and at the far end of the garage was an old beat up pick-up truck that was so covered in filth that the original color was undecipherable. Winston could hear music coming from the far end of the garage near that truck. He must be down there. He walked past open toolboxes, stepped over hoses stretched across the floor, and dodged puddles of oil or grease that seemed to be everywhere.

When he passed the halfway point, the music was loud. He recognized the song playing. It reminded him of his past. It was the same type of music he used to listen to before he met Caroline. It brought back memories of when he was younger, with his whole life in front of him for a change. He moved his lips to the words as they sang out. "Hey, hey, mama, said the way you move. Gonna make you sweat, gonna make you groove…" He moved his arms playing an invisible guitar as he walked around the newer sedan and stopped only when he saw a pair of legs in dirty overalls sticking out from under the truck. The feet were moving to the beat of the song as well. Same taste in music at least.

Winston saw the radio to the right, and since the sound of rock and roll covered the sound of his arrival, he dared to turn if off, supposing it was time to meet his new boss for the week. He stepped over to the radio and turned the volume knob down to a very low setting, not bold enough to simply hit the off button. He immediately heard rumblings coming from under the truck. "…that damn thing, I swear…" Winston walked back to the legs and watched as they squirmed and wiggled out from under the truck, bringing with it an older man in his sixties. "I'm going to throw a brick through you one of these…" The man stopped mid-sentence as he stood and saw Winston. "The sign says ring the bell for service, can't you read?" He stepped past Winston and began digging through a pile of wrenches in a large upright tool chest. "And turn the radio back up on your way out!"

Not a good first impression. "I'm not here for service actually. My name is Winston. The doc sent me. I'm here to work." He extended his hand for a shake. "You must be Earl. I'm sorry I'm late." Earl stopped digging through the toolbox and just stared at Winston without reaching for his hand. He looked Winston up and down in silence, until Winston lowered his hand in embarrassment. Winston wasn't sure what to expect when he agreed to come here, but now that he stood before Earl, he suspected he might have been right in his earlier assumption that he wasn't cut out for this type of work after all.

In the moments of silence that followed, they both scanned each other to gather first impressions. Earl was at least sixty years old, but taller than Winston, and stronger too. He seemed to possess that "old man strength" that came from working with your hands all your life. He was thick and bulky for an older man, and wearing leather overalls on top of a black t-shirt that had several rips. There were pockets in the front of his overalls that held a few pens and wrenches and screw drivers, and his reading glasses hung around his neck from long chains. Earl's head was bald on top, but he still had hair on the sides and back, to go along with his mustache. Something about him made Winston think he might have been a boxer in his younger days. On top of all of that was a layer of grease. Nearly every part of his body had some sort of fluid from a car on it. Winston watched as Earl wiped his hands with a rag and stepped away from the toolbox. He stepped directly in front of Winston, about two feet away. Earl could see Winston was nervous. He noticed the beads of sweat that had formed on Winston's forehead.

Earl was the first to break the silence. "So, tell me Wilson, what kind of work do you do?" He stood with his arms crossed. Winston could tell Earl didn't think much of him yet.

"I, uh... I..." Winston struggled to get the words out with Earl looking so disapprovingly at him.

"Well," Earl interrupted. "That rules out radio broadcaster and motivational speaker. Come on now, get the words out."

"Sorry, Earl sir... sir Earl...er..." Winston closed his eyes, knowing fumbling through another sentence was probably a bad idea.

"Sir Earl? I ain't no English nobleman, Earl will do just fine." Earl smiled. "Now take a deep breath." Winston obliged. "Now, let's simplify this. In five words or less tell me what kind of work you do, Wilson." Earl enunciated each word to give Winston time to think.

"Computer Software Sales," Winston said. "Well I'm not anymore actually. I got fired recently. So technically, I don't do anything right now."

Earl clapped his hands together condescendingly. "Well, Wilson, you can't count to five, but at least you're talking now, hehe."

"It's Winston, by the way, not Wilson." Winston was gaining his confidence back.

"Winston huh?" Earl said. "Like the cigarette. Good name. That'll do just fine." Earl held out his hand to Winston, who shook it and felt the grease squeeze between them. After they let go, he rubbed his fingers and thumb together, feeling how slimy his hands were.

"So, what do you know about cars, Winston?" Earl tossed him the rag and Winston wiped his hand off as he answered.

"Afraid I don't know much about cars," Winston said, with a hint of embarrassment. "I've always worked behind a desk on computers. I never did much manual work. In fact, to be honest, I'm not sure I'm cut out for it."

"Nonsense!" Earl shouted. "Work is built into a man. It's a part of his soul. You're a man, aren't you?" He smacked Winston on the arm. "Technique can be learned, but swinging a hammer, shaping wood and metal, using tools, building things with our bare hands and our own sweat… these things are a part of us, as much as our balls!" Earl took the rag back and wiped the sweat from his bald head. "So I don't want to hear what you can't do or what you don't think you can do. Anything can be learned. So, while you are here in the shop, there will be two types of work. The work you have done, and the work you haven't done yet. Anything you don't know how to do, or any tool you don't know how to use, just ask, and I'll show you. Okay?"

Winston just nodded. *What have I gotten myself into?*

"Good. Now don't worry, I'm not such a hard ass after you get to know me. Just not great at meeting new people, that's all."

Winston felt it was just better to nod along and listen for now.

"Anyway, I have to finish up this truck before lunch. Guy's coming to pick it up, and I told him it would be done. So, I don't have time to piddle around with you this morning. But I'm sure you noticed, I have a thousand things to do around here. Are you ready to work up a sweat?"

"Yes," Winston said, trying not to give Earl anything to nitpick.

"It ain't glamorous, but it's something I've needed done for a long time. Follow me."

Winston wondered what torturous task was waiting for him as he followed Earl out of the garage. Earl dodged the hoses and tools with ease like he probably had a thousand times before. They walked outside and the sun was already climbing in the sky and warm.

"Going to be a hot one today," Earl said.

They entered another garage that appeared to have been unused for many years. The windows were caked with film so bad that they let some light in, but could not be seen through. The door creaked as they entered. As they stepped into the large room, Winston noticed the floor had a quarter inch thick layer of dust on it, mixed with old grease and random junk. A few car parts and tools were scattered about here and there, but mostly the place was empty. Winston guessed it was large enough for at least four or five vehicles. *What is that smell?*

Earl walked over to the wall and grabbed a large push broom off the wall. "Like I said, it ain't glamorous. This used to be the paint shed years ago. Many a ride left here a shiny new color." Winston nodded along, finally able to identify the smell. "I'd like to get this place cleaned up so I can park cars in here while they're waiting on me. Or maybe someday even hire a new guy and start painting cars again like my old man did. Right now, it's just a filthy waste of space." He handed the broom to Winston, and Winston smiled and shook his head. "That's where you come in handy. I don't think you will have a problem figuring out how to use this tool." Earl grinned from ear to ear. "Sweating will do you some good. If you get thirsty, there's a water pump out back of this building. Let it run for a few seconds, and it will be ice cold." He walked past Winston towards the door and said one final thing without even turning around. "And maybe you'll sweat some of that alcohol out of your system." Startled, Winston turned just in time to see Earl's back leaving the paint shed. Winston pulled the neck of his shirt up closer to his nose and smelled it. Then he cupped his hand and breathed into it to smell his breath.

CHAPTER FIFTEEN

Shoeprints in the Snow

After Earl left the paint shed, Winston stood there, looking all around at the filth and years of dirt and dust that had gathered on the floor. He could see clear footprints where he and Earl walked into the room, and where Earl walked to the broom. It almost looked like shoeprints in the snow.

He could see there were dividers along the back wall hanging from the high ceiling down to the floor between each of the bays. They were resting at the back of the tracks that ran along the ceiling all the way to the front bay doors. He walked over to one of the dividers and could tell at one time they might have been white or clear, but now he could see they were covered in thousands of coats of paint mist. He could see individual colored tiny dots of many faded colors.

When he saw black he immediately thought of the black BMW of his nightmares. I never even considered that the car could have been painted. This realization gave him a hopeless feeling. Although he had convinced himself that he found the man responsible once and for all the other night, deep down he suddenly felt a twinkling that there was a possibility he was wrong. If the car was painted a different color, there is no way I will find it, and no way I'll find him.

Winston knew the spiral of darkness that lay ahead if he continued to think about Caroline, so he tried to focus on the task at hand. He was here to pay off a debt. He could have died if Carter and the doc had not cared for him that night, and he owed them his time. So, where do I begin?

The windows were covered in a film which prevented the light from fully illuminating the paint shed, so the room remained slightly dark and the air was stagnant and dusty. He walked over to the door and flipped one of the switches on the wall. He heard a pop at the far end of the room. A single bulb above the far bay had exploded. The glass rained down on the floor. He hesitated before flipping the rest of the switches with his eyes closed. Of the twenty or so overhead lights above the bays, only two had turned on, but there were no more exploding bulbs, to Winston's disappointment. At least the electricity works in here.

Next to the light switches there were three yellow boxes covered in dust that hung on metal cables. Each box had three large red, green, and black buttons, along with masking tape wrapped around it. On the masking tape was writing in black marker covered in dust. He brushed away the dust with his thumb to reveal "Door #1" on the first box. Let's see if these babies will open, I need some fresh air. He looked at the three colored buttons that were unlabeled. Green means go, right? He pressed the green button and nothing happened. Hmmmm. Black maybe? When he pressed the black button, the large door in front of him lurched off the ground with a sharp tug from above, and then slowly rose with the harsh sound of metal bending and warping and scraping after years of sitting.

As the doors rose, they let in a stream of sunlight that washed over the floor. Winston hit the same buttons for the other two doors, amazed that they still worked. In seconds the place was filled with sunlight and fresh air, and the extra light highlighted the amount of work in front of him even more.

Across the room, the sunlight caught a few pieces of shiny metal hanging on the far wall and reflected into his eyes. He stepped to the right so the glare wasn't right in his face, and saw that the objects on the wall were two old bicycles, in need of some care. They looked like they hadn't been ridden in ages. There were also hundreds of old license plates across the top of the wall mounted side by side that stretched all the way around the room in rows. Winston spent some time reading some of the customized lettering on the plates and deciphering the states before he looked back at the broom in his hand. Time to get to it, I guess.

He started nearest to the door and began sweeping the dust from the back wall to the open doors in front, and out into the gravel and dirt. Under the dust he occasionally found a tool or random piece of equipment that he picked up and wondered about its purpose, before tossing it on the shelf in the back. The temperature outside has already risen about fifteen degrees since he woke this morning, and before even twenty minutes passed, sweat was already pouring from his temples and forehead down into his eyes.

He took off his shirt and wiped his face dry nearly every trip from the back to the front, keeping it tucked into the back of his pants for easy access. It hung out the back and swayed when he walked, like the white tail of a deer. About a half hour later, when he had swept nearly half the garage, he stopped and looked back at what he had done with a sense of accomplishment. There was such a visible difference where he had swept that gratification was nearly instant. Under the dust was a concrete floor which, now that it was clean, looked polished and smooth, and even glistened in the sunlight.

Winston smiled as he wiped his eyes. He was enjoying the hard work, actually. He was using muscles he hadn't used in quite a long time, and the ache felt good to him. His body seemed to be excited to be back in use after being so poorly maintained for over a year. He took a break to walk out into the sunlight and stretch his sore muscles. He closed his eyes and let the sunlight warm his face and chest. This isn't so bad, he thought.

An hour or so later he finished the entire floor. He was so wet that it looked like he just jumped into a pool with his pants on. He stood out front, wiping the sweat from his eyes and admiring his work. Would you look at that. It looked like a totally different place than it had a couple of hours ago when he stepped in here for the first time. He had even gone back and swept the first part again, unhappy with his first go at it.

When he stopped sweating finally, he noticed for the first time how thirsty he was. Let's go find this water pump. He walked around the side of the building to the back, where Earl had mentioned he would find the pump. Behind the building, he saw a huge mound of old tires that towered over twenty feet in the air, and spread nearly half the width of the paint shed at the base. There were hundreds of different sizes and widths and tread patters. There must be two thousand tires here! There was also a rather large pile of assorted pieces of wood, haphazardly thrown in a large mound. Why is he saving all this?

In front of the colossal mound of tires, about ten feet from the back of the shed, an old-fashioned water pump sprang up from the ground. It was red and about three feet off the ground on a rusted metal pipe that ran into the ground. There was a bucket on the ground where the water would fall. What is that for? Winston had never used one of these pumps before, and looked at it with a puzzled look on his face. There was a large horizontal handle at the top that clearly was to be used to pump water out of the ground. He lifted the handle and brought it back down. A few drops of brown muddy water drizzled out the front of the pump. I'm supposed to drink this?

Winston kept pumping and with each successive pump the water gushed a little harder and a little clearer. Eventually, he didn't have to pump at all and the water simply poured out. He held his hand under the icy water and when he was satisfied with the color, he cupped his hands together under the flow and leaned over to gulp the water out of them. Wow! He had never tasted fresh water from a well, and he drank like a man who hadn't had water in weeks. When he was done, he put his whole head under the water and stood to let it run down his back and chest. He wiped his face dry with his shirt before shutting the pump off and heading back inside the paint shed fully refreshed.

The sun was not quite directly overhead and Winston knew it wasn't quite midday yet. He found some glass cleaner in an old storage room, along with some rags, and began spraying and wiping down all the windows around him. Maybe they will let some light in now. He worked his way around the perimeter of the shed, wiping down all the windows and doors, and then when he was finished, he began on the back counter and cabinets that ran the entire rear length of the room. He organized all the tools and equipment the best he could and just as he was finishing, he heard clapping to his right.

When Winston turned, he saw Earl walking into the paint shed, clapping his hands together with a large smile on his face. He was covered in grease and appeared to have worked up a large sweat himself. He had a rag throw over his shoulder.

"Well, butter my butt and call me a biscuit," Earl exclaimed. "I never thought it would look like this again!"

Winston burst out laughing as he put the last tool on the back shelf and walked over to Earl. "It wasn't easy."

"Work's never easy, but damn son, you did a hell of a job. How does it feel?"

Winston looked around and felt pride for what he had done. He nodded his head over and over. "Really good actually."

"Amen to that, Winston. Amen to that."

"So, what's the deal with those bicycles over there?" Winston gestured to the other wall across the shed. "Did you used to ride or what?"

Earl strained his eyes and held up his hand to shield the sun. "Oh, those old beauties over there?" He took a few steps towards them. "I haven't even laid eyes on them in years. I forgot they were even in here." He stared at them for several seconds. Winston could tell they brought back memories for Earl. "Yeah, I used to ride when I was a younger man. But those days are long gone." He looked at Winston. "It would take some work to get those babies on the road again. Anyways, I bet you worked up quite an appetite. It's time for lunch, what do you say to a couple of sandwiches and some iced tea?"

"I say bring it on." They both chuckled a bit and walked over to the door. Earl hit the black buttons on each yellow box and the doors began shutting with their familiar screeching and creaking behind them.

"I suppose I have to grease those tracks at some point." Earl said.

Winston followed Earl to the main office door under the canopy that he had entered when he first arrived. Inside, he saw the two doors to the left and right of the counter again, one with windows and one without. He read the sign above the door to the far right with no windows again. "KEEP OUT." Earl quickly crossed the room, threw open the door, and entered. Winston hesitated. He walked to the counter and saw a bell sitting there, and for no reason he could think of other than curiosity, he tapped the bell, letting out a small ring. He heard Earl in the other room yell at him. "Leave that damn bell alone! I hate that thing. Come on in here Winston, what are you waiting for?" Winston kept his eyes on the sign, reading the words over and over as he walked to the door. Let's see what's behind door number two…

CHAPTER SIXTEEN

Wet Behind the Ears

As Winston entered the door that read "KEEP OUT", he was a little surprised at what he saw. Behind "door number two" was a makeshift one-bedroom studio apartment. The walls were metal, and the ceiling was open to the wooden rafters. Above the rafters, he could see a tin sheet-metal roof. In the back was a bed, a couple of dressers, and several wall mounted shelves that rose nearly the entire height of the wall to the ceiling. Separating the "bedroom" from the "living room" was an old ragged recliner with an ottoman in front of it, along with a small table that held an old television. To the left was a countertop and sink, along with a stand-alone stove pushed into the corner next to a refrigerator. The whole room was about the size of a single car garage, and when Winston looked closer, he realized that was exactly what it was at one time. He could still see the garage bay door at the back behind the bed. There was a door to his right, which he could only guess led to a bathroom. Winston hoped there was a shower somewhere in there.

Earl shut the fridge door and turned around, holding two glasses of iced tea. "Welcome to my… humble abode," he said as he handed one of the glasses to Winston. "It's not much, but it has all I need."

"Thanks for the tea. So, you live here at the shop?" Winston looked surprised.

"Well, I like to think the shop is out there beyond these four walls." Earl retrieved a chair that was leaning up against the wall and unfolded it next to the recliner. "But inside here is my home. Now have a seat," he said as he patted his hand on the folding chair. "Kick your feet up and take a break. You were working hard out there today. I bet your feet are chirping loudly at you."

Winston sat down and propped his feet up on the ottoman next to Earl's. He took a sip of his tea and realized how right Earl was. His feet throbbed now that he finally took his weight off them. He let out a loud sigh and laid his head back a bit, closing his eyes. "Yes they are," he said.

Earl went back to the fridge and pulled out some lunchmeat that was of indistinguishable species to Winston, followed by bread, lettuce, and condiments. He grabbed two paper plates from the cabinet to the right of the sink and began assembling the sandwiches.

"Guess I'm not used to all this hard work," Winston continued. "I told you, I'm a software salesman. Well, I was, anyways. I stared at a computer for my paycheck."

Earl handed Winston one of the sandwiches and sat his drink on the little table next to the recliner. He sat down with a plop in the recliner and rolled his eyes at Winston.

"Software? I'm not even sure I know what software is. Sounds like blankets and pillows if you ask me," Earl said with a laugh.

"Just as glamorous, I assure you. It's computer programs and code, that's all," Winston explained. "Boring stuff, really."

"Hell, I didn't know what a computer was until my life was half over. If you ask me they cause nothing but trouble in the world."

Winston looked straight up at the tin roof above. "I bet it sounds like a freight train during a rainstorm in here when you're trying to sleep. How do you manage?"

"Manage?" Earl said. "Son, when you work as long and as hard as I do, you don't have to TRY to sleep. It don't matter what's happening outside." Earl took a bite of his sandwich and smiled at Winston.

"Fair enough," Winston said. "So how did you get into the car repair business anyways?"

"I was born into it," Earl said. "Didn't have much choice in the matter I suppose. Pop owned this place for thirty years before me. Hell, I used to run around the shop as a little boy, dodging cars and playing in the dirt!" Earl stood and walked to the fridge. "Want a refill?" Winston simply nodded.

"Yeah, my earliest memory is sitting on that concrete floor out there next to a tire, watching Pop loosen lug nuts with a torque wrench." He filled his and Winston's cups and then sat back in the chair. "I sat in tires, not highchairs. And I grew up with wrenches in my hands, not action figures." Earl looked around the room, as he thought about his past. "All I've ever known is cars. Never been good at anything else I suppose." A few bites later, Earl's sandwich was gone, and he tossed the plate on the little table.

"So your dad left you this place?"

"Pop died in seventy-nine. I was working for him by then. Small jobs and stuff like you're doing. When I found out I was to inherit the shop, I nearly shit myself. I was only nineteen years old, wet behind the ears. I could do small repairs, but Pop always handled the big stuff. He was a tough old man, all the way to the end." Earl smiled as he thought about his dad. "Luckily there were enough cars laying around here for me to learn on, and enough loyal friends of Pop's to keep the business going until I got on my feet. I probably shortened the life of a few dozen cars before I wasn't green anymore."

"Sounds like it was hard work."

"You bet it was. I worked my tail off. I saw how hard Pop worked for years, and always felt like after he was gone I could still feel him somewhere in the corner of the shop, watching over me, making sure I wasn't dogging it around here. I guess I wanted to show him I could work just as hard as he did, if not harder. I worked too hard I think."

"Did you ever get married?" Winston was nervous about how Earl would react to that question after the words came out. He just focused on his sandwich and listened.

"Yeah, I was married once." Earl paused for a moment and looked down into his tea. He swirled the glass around and watched the ice cubes crash into each other. "Truth be told I spent more time working here at the shop than I ever did with her. All that hard work I was doing to appease Pop didn't impress her too much. Cost me my marriage in the end." He stopped swirling his glass and took a drink. Winston didn't know what to say.

"Suppose I got that from Pop too," Earl said. "Mom left when I was in middle school. She moved back east where her parents lived. I didn't see much of her after that. It was just me and Pop… and the shop. Like father like son I guess.

After my wife left me, I gave her the house and most of the stuff without a fight." Winston looked back at the shelves on the wall filled with boxes. Some were covered in dust. *What did you get?* "Only thing she didn't want any part of was this business. She blamed it for our problems. I got the shop and she got all the rest. I guess that was fitting. So, I threw up a wall in here to close off one of the car bays and brought a bed in. I've lived here ever since. It was supposed to be temporary, until I got my own place. That was over eight years ago."

Winston didn't know what to say. He felt bad for Earl, but knew there was nothing he could do to help. Sitting here listening and keeping his mouth shut was enough, hopefully. Winston wished Marlow understood that sometimes. He finished his sandwich before commenting.

"Sorry man. That stinks. All of it."

Earl nodded his head in agreement. "Sometimes life deals you a shitty hand. We can't all get a full house I suppose. There's always someone at the table with rags. Happened to be me this time around." After a long pause of silence, Earl stood up and pushed his shoulders and elbows back to stretch his chest and back. "But there's no sense getting all worked up about it." He spoke deeper and more masculine, signifying to Winston that the idle talk about the past was over now. "Life goes on. And there's work to be done." He took the tea glasses and plates and walked to the kitchen. "There's always work to be done. Focus on that, I say." Earl tossed the paper plates in a large outdoor rubber trash bin, and set the glasses in the sink.

I thought too much work was the problem. Winston could see the flaw in his logic, but didn't dare question Earl's mantra. He simply followed him back out the door to the main office area. Earl checked the phone to see if anyone left a message.

"What would you think about polishing up Mrs. Davenport's Buick this afternoon. I got the radiator installed this morning and she's ready to go now. Just needs a good cleaning."

"Fine by me," Winston said, happy to get a much easier and simpler project for the second half of the day.

"As a matter of fact," Earl said as he tossed Winston the keys to the car and stepped to the door leading to the main garage. "Pull it around to bay number one and you can work on it in here next to me while I'm finishing up another job. That is, if you don't mind my old timer music on the stereo."

Winston flashed a smile at Earl. "Old timer music? Classic rock is what I call it. Nothing better than some seventies rock if you ask me."

Earl stopped in his tracks when he heard Winston's comment. He looked at Winston in astonishment. Winston could see a father-like pride in his eyes. It was this moment, more than any other moment so far, and for the first time in a year, that Winston actually felt accepted somewhere. Liking the same music was a bond only men could understand, a bond that transcended generations, classes, race, and nearly everything else. And right now, it was like Winston just got invited to the cool kid's party.

"Well then," Earl said with a huge grin on his face. "Bring her around and we'll crank it up. It's the yellow one next to the beat-up Oldsmobile." He continued to smile as he shut the door. Winston headed out to find the car, feeling good about himself for a change.

The rest of the day was spent washing, waxing, vacuuming, and wiping down a yellow car while listening to (and often singing aloud) his favorite songs from the seventies, much to the approval of Earl.

That night, after Carter brought Winston home, and the songs had finally all left his head, he found himself thinking about his talk earlier in the day with Earl in his "apartment." Sometimes life deals you a shitty hand. How true, he thought. He hated how Dunsport always brought back thoughts of Caroline. Every building reaching for the sky, every crack in the old concrete streets, and every raindrop that fell in this god-forsaken city seemed to unite in a common goal, to remind him of the shitty hand that life had dealt him.

One moment you are living the perfect life… Winston picked up an empty bottle on the counter. …and the next thing you know… CRASH! Winston threw the bottle up against the wall, shattering it upon impact. The glass pieces exploded outward in every direction, and the sound of the glass falling to the floor mixed with the sound of the raindrops beating against the window outside.

He walked to the fridge and grabbed a few cold bottles from the top shelf. He sat on the couch, elevated his sore feet, clicked on the TV, and twisted the cap. It was a long day of work, but he didn't mind really. He could only focus on two things right now. Caroline, and the soothing cold liquid that ran down his throat. Life goes on, they say. But how?

CHAPTER SEVENTEEN

The Elusive Rider

Winston woke to the sound of Carter honking his horn again. The morning was much the same as last time. Empty bottles fell to the ground as he stood, and the TV was still on from the night before. He shook off the morning fog, took a quick glance out the window toward the street, and made a mad rush for clothing before heading out the door.

A few apologies later, Carter and Winston were heading out of town.

"The weather seems to be better than it was last night," Winston said, to break the silence.

"Sure does," Carter replied. "Round here it rains at the drop of a hat. Never can tell what's coming up." Carter looked in the rear-view mirror and rolled down the window next to him to let in some fresh air. "From the smell of things, old Earl had you working like a dog yesterday, yes sir!"

Winston smelled under his arms in embarrassment. "Oh, sorry man, I sort of dozed off early last night and forgot to take a shower. Didn't have time this morning either. Never set an alarm. I only woke when I heard your horn a little bit ago."

Carter simply chuckled to himself. By the time they reached Salima Falls, the sky was clear and blue like the day before. The sun was peeking up above the eastern line of trees, hinting at another hot day ahead. Winston waved back at someone on the sidewalk who greeted him. "Probably going to be humid today, after the rain last night," he said, as they drove past the familiar buildings along main street.

"Didn't rain here in Salima Falls," said Carter. "The rain seems to save itself for the city, it seems." As soon as they pulled onto the dirt road and into Earl's lot, Winston felt at ease. He stepped out of the cab and waved goodbye to Carter.

"Smell you later," Carter said as he drove away. Winston never even heard the joke. This was only the second time he had ever set foot at the shop, yet it already felt familiar and welcoming to him. He looked at the sun and stretched his neck. His arms and legs were still sore from the previous day, and he spent a few seconds stretching those too, before he walked over to the main office door.

When he opened the door, he saw Earl, looking over some papers behind the counter with one hand, while eating a donut with the other. He put the papers down when he saw Winston.

"Good morning, Winston. There are donuts in the box over there on the table. Help yourself."

"Thanks," Winston replied. "I could use something to eat. I forgot to grab something last night. Time got away from me, I guess." He grabbed a raspberry-filled donut with white icing and walked over to Earl. He put his elbow on the counter and took a bite of his donut. Earl looked over at him with a questioning look on his face. He crinkled his nose up and sniffed.

"I know, I know," Winston explained. "Carter already told me. No supper… no shower… I had a rough night." He sniffed his underarm again. "Is it really that bad?"

Earl looked at him with disapproval. "It ain't your pits I'm smelling, Winston. It's the booze on your breath."

Winston dropped his arm and finished another ravenous bite of his donut. Here we go again. "I'm of age, if you were wondering. No need to call the excise police on me." He spoke with an arrogance, and a hint of frustration. For the last year, people had told him to lay off or cut back on the drinking, and he was getting tired of it.

Earl focused on Winston. His eyes were intense, but seemed to be filled with pity instead of anger. "Now listen, I'm not going to sit here and tell another man what to do and what not to do when he's on his own time." Winston looked relieved. "I really don't care what you do when you leave here," Earl continued. "But soon I'll be sixty years old, and I've learned a thing or two in my day. Now you can either listen to me or you can turn your head and ignore me, that's up to you. You're a grown man. All I can do is tell you what I know." Winston wiped the look of arrogance off his face and tried to have an open mind. He respected Earl, and after he opened up to him yesterday, he felt obliged to listen again.

"We all have our demons, son." Earl seemed to be looking off into the distance. "Some are in front of us, some are behind us, and some are buried deep inside." He looked directly into Winston's eyes. "Now believe me, I've had my share of demons. You heard about some of them yesterday. But one thing I've learned is that through it all, I've never found any answers in a damned bottle."

Winston looked at the floor. He knew Earl was right, but he didn't know what to do about it.

"The bottle only leads to one place," continued Earl. "And it's a place you don't want to go. Now I was too young and too stupid to change until it was too late." Earl reached out and pat Winston on the back. "I've been exactly where you are right now, you can trust me on that. And I'd cut off my left nut to go back and do things differently." Winston cringed at the visual. "My best advice to you is this. Don't hang on to anything behind you so tightly that you can't reach out and grab what's in front of you."

"Everything is behind me," Winston said.

Earl stepped in front of Winston to face him. "Bullshit. You are young. You have a long life ahead of you, unlike me. I'm just an old fart. Even if you feel like there's nothing ahead that can possibly be as good as what is behind, you can't just bury your head in the sand. There are no answers there. And no answers in a bottle. Trust me on that."

They walked in silence out of the office and into the sunlight. Earl led Winston around to the back of the paint shed that he swept the day before. "I'm sure you've seen the mountain of tires," Earl said.

"Yeah, I saw it." Seven hells.

After Earl explained just how he wanted the pile deconstructed and sorted and organized, he left Winston alone. "See you at lunch," was all he said as he walked away. Winston spent the next four hours pulling tires from the huge pile and sorting them along the back wall of the paint shed. Some were light enough to toss to the ground with ease, and others were heavy enough to injure him if they fell the wrong way. It was hard work, but satisfying to see the giant mountain of tires slowly shrinking with each passing minute.

By the time the sun was high in the sky, and his entire body was covered in sweat and filth from the tires. He had sorted roughly six hundred tires into at least thirty piles. They were stacked neatly on top of each other, four to a pile, in parallel lines that reached out from the shed. His shirt, which he pulled off a while ago, was draped over the water pump. He took it off to wipe the sweat from his eyes and stepped back to assess his progress. Over half way. Not bad. Not bad at all.

Winston turned on the water at the pump and cleaned his face and hands as best as he could. He tossed his shirt over his bare shoulder and headed to the main garage to find Earl. When he wasn't there, he walked to the front of the lot, where he found Earl working on his back under one of the cars that had been jacked up a couple of feet in the air. Winston tapped Earl's boot with his toe as he walked up.

"What do you say Earl?"

Earl's voice echoed from under the car. "I say it's hotter than hell under here, and I'm ready for a drink."

"I was hoping you would say that," replied Winston.

Earl climbed out from under the car with grease on his face and hands. "I could use a little help swapping out this axle after lunch. It's a two-man job. How about you take a break from those tires and give me a hand?"

Winston agreed, feeling good about his promotion from grunt work to assistant. Assistant auto mechanic, he thought. Now that's a title I never thought would land on me. Before he knew it, lunch was over, and he had powered through two sandwiches and a plate of chips, along with two glasses of iced tea.

With full bellies, they walked back to the car, and Earl immediately crawled back under it. "Put your shirt back on and get under here with me," Earl said. Soon Winston was on his back in the dirt, looking up at a mess of car parts he had never seen before. "First time under a car?"

"I think so," Winston replied.

"Man, times sure have changed," Earl said. "People are different these days. I did my first oil change when I was twelve."

Winston was embarrassed about how little he knew about cars, but knew he could turn the tables on Earl rather easily. "Well, I sent my first email when I was six," he retorted. "Do you even have a computer?"

"Pop never needed one, and neither do I," Earl thundered. "Anyway, you made your point." He went on to explain to Winston how he had already removed the wheels and the brake calipers, unbolted the outer tie rod from the steering knuckle, and disconnected the hub from the strut tower. Steering knuckle? Strut tower? He pointed to the place where the old axle was inserted into the transmission.

"Next I have to pry this CV joint out of the transmission socket, then we can pull out the old axle and insert the new one."

"What do you need me to do?" asked Winston, hoping he could handle it.

"Well, I left the pry bar inside the garage, so first thing I need you to do is track that down." I can't screw that up, Winston thought, as he climbed out from underneath the car. "Should be on the shelf above the stereo along the back wall," Earl yelled.

After a few minutes, Winston found the pry bar, and could hear Earl's voice bellowing something impatiently from the other side of the lot. He retrieved the tool from the wall and stepped back out into the sunlight. On the way back, with the cool steel of the pry bar in his hand, Winston took his time and looked to his left. He saw the small dirt road across the street that joined the main street that headed into town. They met about halfway between Earl's shop and where the road became paved again closer to town. The dirt road was lined with trees, and the sunlight was shining down through the leaves.

He saw something moving on the other side of the trees, which caught his eye. He shielded his face from the sun with one hand, and could see a glimpse of someone on a bicycle, periodically popping in and out of view between the trees. When the elusive rider reached the corner, and came into full view, he saw it was a girl. Her hair was blowing in the breeze behind her as she went. He stopped in his tracks. Emma!

CHAPTER EIGHTEEN

Good Fishing Spots

Even at a distance Winston could recognize Emma, as she rode her bicycle around the corner towards Salima Falls. Her hair was blowing in the breeze, and her eyes held an empty stare that seemed to look past everything that was in front of her. She seemed to be in a separate world from everyone else, and Winston could relate. On the front of the bike was a basket that held a paper sack, and the frame was pink and white. He stood there watching her pedal away, oblivious to the fact that Earl had been calling his name for a few seconds now.

Winston's gaze was locked in the direction of Emma as Earl crawled out from under the car behind him. He smelled the air and felt the cool breeze against the sweat on his brow. His concentration remained unbroken as footsteps came towards him in the gravel.

"Got something stuck in your ears Winston?" Earl said, as he wiped the sweat from his forehead. Winston kept his eyes on Emma as she rode farther away down the street towards town.

"I was trying to tell you, I got the CV joint out with a screwdriver, and now I need…" Earl walked up next to Winston and stopped talking when he looked down the street and noticed what was holding his attention.

"Well I see something has your mind occupied at the moment," Earl said.

Winston turned towards Earl with a confused look on his face. "Did you say something?"

Earl shook his head and turned towards the car again. "Forget about it. Come on now, let's get back to work."

Winston watched until Emma disappeared over a hill towards town. There's something about that girl, I swear. He shook his head, wondering why she captivated him so much. Then he followed after Earl.

"Earl," Winston called out with extra pep in his step. "Do you know that girl?"

"That girl?" Earl turned. Winston detected resentment in his voice.

"Yeah, the girl on the bike back there."

"Her name is Emma, son. Show a little respect," Earl snapped.

"I know her name," Winston said. "I just wondered if you knew her."

"Yeah, I know her. Now let's get back to work. I don't have all day to fart around out here."

"How do know her?" Winston asked as they reached the car.

"Everybody knows everybody in Salima Falls," Earl explained. He crawled back under the car. "Why are you so interested in her anyways?"

"I don't know really. I'm just… drawn to her. I guess there's something about her that… intrigues me. She has this… sadness in her eyes." He leaned down to look at Earl under the car. "And she's so beautiful. Can you tell me more about her?"

Earl stopped trying to turn the bolt he was working on. "Goodness, did you ever think maybe she just wants to be left alone?"

"Maybe so." Winston said. He remembered saying that very thing to Marlow a few times about himself. She must be a loner like me. "But," he continued. "She's probably halfway to town by now. You and me talking is not going to bother her." He crawled on his back next to Earl under the car. "I'm curious, that's all. Why does she always ride that bike everywhere, doesn't she have a car?" Earl rolled his eyes. "And why is she always alone?" Earl shook his head, knowing he wasn't going to be able to ignore Winston's persistence. "Does she have a…"

"Okay, okay," Earl interrupted. "I'll tell you what I know. Just stop yapping for a second." Winston shut up. "Now hand me the half-inch socket over there." Winston grabbed the socket, handed it to Earl, and listened intently. "From what I hear," Earl continued. "Emma is what you would call… a loner. She doesn't talk much, and keeps to herself mostly." Earl fit the socket snugly on the bolt and began turning it.

"Why is that?" Winston asked.

"I'm getting to it," Earl said. "Just listen and stop with the questions." Earl focused on another bolt for a few seconds before continuing. "Some years back Emma's mom passed away. It was just the two of them at the time, living in a house about a mile and a half from here. They lived in an old farm house outside of town, down that road over there." Earl pointed in the direction of the dirt lane that Winston saw Emma turn from. "There's an old barn out back, and behind that is Cobb's Creek. It runs through the back of the lot and all the way up near the far end of town. There are some good fishing spots along the banks near there. I'll show you if you are ever interested."

Winston was interested all right, but not about fishing. "So, she comes by here every day? Around that corner over there?"

"Most days she does, I guess," Earl said. "I see her go by from time to time, but I'm usually in the garage or under a car somewhere."

Winston smiled, making a mental note. "What about her dad?" he said.

"He's around." Earl took a deep breath. "But Emma doesn't much want to talk to him anymore I hear."

"You know him?" Winston asked.

"Yeah, I know him," Earl said.

"What's he like?"

"He's a damned fool. A real horse's ass if you ask me."

"Well, no wonder she doesn't want to talk to him," Winston said.

"She sort of turned inward when her mom died," Earl continued. "Built a wall around herself and won't let anyone in."

"I gathered that much when I talked to her," Winston added.

"You talked to her?" Earl seemed surprised and upset.

"Yeah," Winston said. "I bumped into her at the store the other day on my way here. She wasn't real talkative, just like you said." Earl handed Winston the wrench and pointed to a couple of bolts that needed removed before they could take the axle out. "So, she still lives in that house, I take it?"

"Yeah, after her mom died, the house was hers. Some people thought she should sell it and get a place of her own, but she didn't. I suppose she didn't know where to go, or maybe she wasn't ready to move on just yet."

"It's not easy," Winston said.

"She's lived alone there ever since. It's not far, only a few minutes from town. So, I suppose she's never had a need for a car. At least that's what she says. Just rides her bike and keeps to herself."

"Does she have any friends?"

"Not that I know of," Earl said. "Couple of dogs, I think. I've seen 'em run around the fields near here. She's friendly to everyone in town, but I've never seen her do much socializing. Never been a man in her life as far as I know. No one could ever get close to her." Winston could sense the sadness in Earl too, as he told the story.

"Sounds lonely," Winston said.

"I suppose it might be. But then again, some people can be alone and not be lonely. And others can feel all alone in a crowd of people. Only she can say for sure."

Winston shook his head in agreement, knowing there was truth in what Earl was saying. "I saw her working at the diner my first day in Salima Falls," he said.

"Mrs. Powell's diner," Earl said with reminiscence. He hadn't been there in a long time. "It was her mom's diner. She left that to Emma too." Earl finished the last bolt above him. "Now let's pull this axle out." After a few seconds, they were able to work the axle out and lay it behind them. Earl grabbed the new axle next to him and they began the process in reverse. "Easy, don't push too hard on the transmission."

Winston tried to focus on the work in front of him, but his mind kept wandering away to Emma. "So she owns the diner? I had no idea. I thought she just worked there."

"She keeps busy, I hear," Earl said. "She spends a lot of time at the diner, and volunteers down at the animal shelter, and I hear she helps out the doc from time to time too."

"Sounds like she's just filling her time so she doesn't have to think about anything."

"Maybe so," Earl answered. He knew he did the same thing. "But for some people it works I guess." Winston knew Earl was alluding to himself when he said that. "Everyone in town does their best to let her be, but deep down I think they feel bad for her. I know I do."

Earl stopped working and stared off for a few seconds before Winston broke the silence.

"So why does she always ride that bike everywhere?"

Earl seemed to snap out of his thoughts. "Alright, that's enough questions already," he said. "And let her be. Don't you go bugging her, you hear? She's had a rough life and she don't need you bringing it all up again."

"Okay Earl, goodness. No need to bite my head off."

Earl looked at him. "I just want to get this axle swapped out before the sun goes down, and I can't focus with all these questions. Now hand me that wrench, would you," he said, as Winston finished the last of his bolts. "I have one more over here and then I can start putting the hubs and calipers back together."

Winston watched as Earl worked silently for a few minutes. "I guess I'll get back to the tires," he said. "If you have this under control."

"That'll be fine," Earl said. Winston began sliding out sideways from under the car. "Winston," he said before Winston had stood up yet. "I'm going to run into town to get some supplies and test out this new axle after I finish up. You gonna be alright here until Carter comes back to get you?"

"I think so," Winston said. "Got a lot of tires still waiting for me back there."

"Alright then, I'll catch up with you tomorrow then. Hang this back up on your way back, would you?" Earl handed Winston the pry bar.

As Winston walked through the paint shed, he noticed the two old bikes along the back wall again. He walked over to examine them. Overall, they seemed to be in good shape. He squeezed the tires. A little air in the tires, some grease on the chains, and a good cleaning, he thought. He shook the basket on the front and it seemed to be loose.

For the next hour, he sorted tires faster and with more energy than he had before, in an attempt to finish early. When he was finally done, and the mountain of tires that was there at the start of the day had been transformed into several neat rows sorted by size and tread, he walked around to the front of the lot to look for Earl. When he wasn't there, he looked in the office and called out his name. There was no answer. He peeked into Earl's living area and couldn't find him there either. When he was satisfied that he was gone, he went to the main garage and pulled one of the bicycles out from the wall. This should do.

He looked around the garage. There's got to be a pump around here somewhere. Finally, he was able to air up the tires with a hand pump that he found in a cabinet below the shelves. When they were tight with air, he hopped on the bike and pedaled it out onto the dirt lot. The chain squeaked and creaked as it turned, and he returned to the garage. He searched for chain oil, but when he couldn't find any, he just poured a little automotive oil from one of the cans onto the chain as he turned the pedal. His next trip around the lot on the bike was much quieter, which brought a smile to his face. Seems to work just fine. He spent another twenty minutes finding the right wrenches and tightening the handlebar and seat bolts, along with the basket in the front. The brakes needed adjusted and so he twisted the metal screws at the ends of the cables with needle-nose pliers until they were nice and tight. He took it for another spin around the lot. I'm no car mechanic, but I might have a future in bicycle repair.

He grabbed some of the cleaning and polishing supplies that he used on the Buick earlier, and spent the rest of the time before Carter showed up making the bike look as new and as clean as possible. When he heard the familiar honk out front, he rolled the bike into the paint shed and leaned it up against the wall. He walked out front and waved at Carter, glowing with pride from his work.

Winston thought about Emma in silence the whole ride back to the city. Carter seemed to notice and let him be. When he got to his apartment, he called the police station about his car again, but hung up the phone a minute later without any answers. Probably gone forever.

He grabbed a beer from the fridge and sat on a barstool in front of the counter that separated the kitchen from the dining area. He took a drink and let his eyes wander around the room, as he thought about everything Earl said about Emma. His back was sore from lifting all the tires earlier, and his hands were weak. With thoughts of Emma in his head, his eyes eventually landed on a magnet that was stuck to the front of the fridge. It was a magnet that he and Caroline had bought on their first trip together. The colorful beach scene seemed to stare back at him and he immediately felt guilty for thinking about Emma. His mood changed almost instantaneously.

He walked over and pulled the magnet from the fridge. He rubbed the image with his thumb as he held it in his hand. He could see Caroline on the beach, dancing in circles in his memories, as the sun glistened off her bronze skin. That was the day he decided he was going to propose. A tear ran down his face and fell to the kitchen floor.

I'm sorry Caroline. I know I haven't been focused lately. I haven't forgotten about you, I swear. After this week is up, and I'm finished in Salima Falls, I'll find him. I promised you. He returned the magnet to its place, took two more beers from the fridge, and sat on the couch. He turned on the TV and bounced back and forth between thoughts of Emma and Caroline.

CHAPTER NINETEEN

Sunshine and Rainbows

The following morning, Winston woke himself with a panicked scream. He sat up and looked around, into the emptiness of his bedroom, until the white walls surrounding him told him it was just a dream. His heart raced with adrenaline. Holy shit, he thought, as he rubbed his shaking hands on his face in an attempt to get the vision out of his head. He fell back, and his head hit the pillow with a crash.

As he stared above him, the visions of the dream seemed to project onto the white ceiling. He saw himself standing at the corner of Earl's dirt lot, taking a break from the hard work. The sweat glistened off his bare chest and dripped from his forehead in the heat. He wiped his brow with his shirt as he looked out at the road where Emma had rode by on her bike. As she came around the corner this time, he stood still, watching her hair billow softly in the breeze. She was wearing a white sundress with blue flowers and a matching blue flower in her hair.

She turned to him and their eyes locked. Time seemed to slow down, and he watched as a smile slowly formed on her lips. Her skin glistened in the warm sunlight. She raised one hand to wave at him. He smiled back at her and he raised his hand to wave back. They held each other's gaze for a few seconds of bliss. Then, out of the corner of his eye, Winston saw something that caught his attention.

A black car, approaching silently from his left, was coming down the road towards Emma. The smile drained from his face. The car seemed to be the only thing not slowed by the speed of the dream, as it sped towards her. Her head was turned away from the road as she waved at Winston, and she didn't even notice the car coming her way. Winston turned his head slowly towards the car and his vision zoomed in on the mad look in the driver's eyes. The man's head was mostly shielded by shadow, and his hands gripped the steering wheel tightly. He locked eyes on Winston as he approached Emma. Winston tried to shout but couldn't manage a sound. The sunlight sparkled on the shiny black paint of the car. He tried to point, but his arm could only move in slow motion.

Winston looked back at Emma, who was still smiling and slowly waving back at him. She didn't even seem to notice the panic on his face or the inaudible scream he was attempting. Their eyes were locked for what seemed like ten seconds until the car reached her. Helpless, he could only close his eyes a fraction of a second before the black shadow overtook her. At that instant, he woke.

"Noooooo!" His scream from a few moments ago was deafening and seemed to still echo around the room. It wasn't until the hot water from the shower poured down onto his face that he stopped shaking. After a while, the intensity of the dream was replaced by a guilty feeling that slowly crept in on him. This was the first time in over a year that he hadn't dreamt of Caroline, and the first time since he met her that his first thought when he woke wasn't of her. Emma. He pictured her smiling and waving at him again from her bike. He said another silent apology to Caroline, but the thoughts of Emma stayed with him as he dressed and waited for Carter.

"Hey, Carter," Winston said as he climbed into the front seat of the cab.

"How's Mr. Winston this morning?" Carter's voice was deep and welcoming as usual.

"Slept well," Winston replied. "Waking was another matter," he said after a pause.

"Ahhhh, but you did wake," Carter said with a huge smile on his face. "And I'd say that's a wonderful way to start a day. Yes sir!" He started up the car and they took their usual route out of the city.

"I suppose you're right," Winston said. "By the way, I wanted to tell you something else, now that I think of it. I called the police last night and they still have no leads on my car. Sort of ticks me off really. How hard can it be to find a car anyways? They probably haven't even looked. I'll let you know if I hear anything, but it sure looks like I'll be riding with you for the rest of the week."

"Now don't you go fussing about that," Carter said. "It's no burden at all giving you a ride. I don't mind a bit. So don't you worry."

Winston looked at Carter skeptically. "You don't worry about anything, do you Carter?"

"Ain't nothing to worry about in my opinion," Carter answered.

"What about… life?" Winston said. "It's not always sunshine and rainbows out there."

"Life?" Carter laughed out loud. "Well, that's a silly thing to worry about. Life is for living! It's too short to go worrying it away Mr. Winston. Don't waste any time on it. Worrying never changed a thing that ever happened in this world. No sir. Not for the better anyways." As the car left the city, Winston thought about Carter's words.

"If you look out your window," Carter said. "You might notice the sun is shining right now." Winston looked out the window and up at the sky, as Carter continued. "Wouldn't make sense to worry about rain tomorrow, would it? Or to fuss over last week's storm. Why let it keep you from enjoying the sunshine today. You never know, you just might see a rainbow."

"I guess I have a hard time just letting things… come," Winston said. "Or letting them go, for that matter. I guess I just want a say in it."

"Sometimes you get a say about what comes, sometimes you don't," Carter said. "But one thing's for certain. You never get a say about what's done and gone."

"Fair enough," Winston said as they turned down another country road that looked exactly like the previous three. "But either way, I'd like my car back. You might have to draw me a map to Salima Falls though. I've followed along a few times now, and I still don't think I could find it on my own."

Carter laughed again as he made another turn. "Not many can. No sir! Oh, I've told a few folks how to get there in my day." He smiled at Winston. "Yet they rarely can find it on their own." With a wink, he abruptly turned down another field-lined road.

"As far as that car of yours is concerned," he continued. "It will make its way back to you in due time."

"And when do you suppose that is?" Winston said with a little attitude.

"When you are ready, I suppose," Carter said.

"When I'm ready?" Winston turned his head to look at Carter. "What in the world is that supposed to mean? I'm ready now!"

Carter turned down the narrow lane lined with corn stalks. "Maybe you are. Maybe you aren't. Who am I to say? But I tend to think everything happens in the order it is supposed to. And things just seem to turn up when we need them the most. And we often don't have a say in the matter. No sir."

"So all I can do is just wait around and do nothing?" Winston shook his head. Crazy old man.

"Right now, you don't have a car, so you ride with me. When you get it back, I suppose you can drive yourself, if you can find the way." They pulled out of the other side of the field into Salima Falls. "If not, then I'll be around like I always have been."

When they got to Earl's, Winston stepped out and smelled the familiar scents of Salima Falls on the breeze, as Carter circled around and headed back into town. Sunshine and rainbows, he thought. Flawed logic really. Doesn't the rain have to come first for there to be a rainbow?

CHAPTER TWENTY
Perfectly Manicured Lawns

The first half of the workday at the shop seemed to drag on and on for Winston. He spent a couple of hours helping Earl change a radiator in an old Chevrolet truck, and after that, Earl asked him to mow what little grass was out back. His mind, however, wasn't on his work. It was on Emma, and the plan he had made the day before. The bike was all cleaned up and safe and sound in the paint shed next door. Its absence had gone unnoticed as predicted.

As the morning hours trickled slowly by, he found himself thinking more and more about Emma. He wasn't sure if it was Carter's cryptic words or just the otherworldly feeling of this town, but as each hour went by, he felt less and less guilty about it. It was as if the guilt and his life with Caroline didn't exist here in Salima Falls, and remained behind in the city when he came here.

He was, however, certain of one thing. Lunch couldn't arrive fast enough today. Any chance he got, he would peek across the lot to the road where he saw Emma on her bike the day before. He stretched a half hour mowing job into nearly an hour and a half.

When the grass was finally all cut and the sun was fully overhead, Earl came out back where Winston was using a rake to pile up the grass clippings. "What do you say, Winston. Almost done?"

"Yep, just finishing up and ready for a break." Winston quickly finished the pile, leaned the rake up against the back of the paint shed, and wiped the sweat from his forehead.

"How about a cold drink and a sandwich?"

"Actually," Winston said. "I was thinking about heading into town for lunch today."

"Into town?" Earl had a puzzled look on his face.

"Yeah, I thought I'd maybe stop by the diner for a change. Something different. I hear they have great tuna salad. Want to tag along?" As he waited for an answer, he was hoping Earl would say no.

"Nah. Suit yourself," Earl said. "I think I'll get off my feet for a bit." Earl headed into his little apartment and Winston quickly freshened up as best as he could in the bathroom.

"I wanted to show you something before I go," Winston said. "Come here for a minute." Winston led him to the door and they stepped out under the awning. "Wait here, while I go get it." Earl looked puzzled. A few seconds later, Winston rolled the bike out of the door to the paint shed and pushed it over to Earl. He stood in front of him and proudly presented it.

"Instead of walking, I thought I would take this old beauty out for a spin."

When Earl saw the bike, he smiled and reached out to touch it. "Well I'll be a monkey's uncle." He ran his hand along the red crossbar that shined like new for the first time in decades. He felt how sturdy the basket and seat were. "She hasn't looked like this since… well, since I was a young pup like you."

Winston was glad he approved. "I aired up the tires and polished it last night after I finished sorting the rubber out back. I hope you don't mind."

"Mind?" Earl couldn't stop touching the bike. He was smiling from ear to ear. He squeezed the tires and gripped the handlebars. "You did fine work my friend. Brought her back to her glory days. Seeing her like this brings back a lot of memories. What gave you this inspiration?"

"Well, I don't have a car at the moment, and I figured I could sneak into town and grab lunch or look around every once in a while. You know, just to get out of your hair for an hour or so. I'm sure you could use a break from me."

"Hell, you don't bother me. Not too much, anyways." Earl gave him a playful jab to the arm.

"Thanks," Winston said. He felt pride for the first time in a while, and wondered if Earl was starting to enjoy his company. "I guess I'll head out. Want me to bring you back anything?"

"Me?" Earl still couldn't take his eyes off his old bike. "Nah, I got a pickle-loaf sandwich with my name on it inside. You go on ahead." Old people and their pickle-loaf sandwiches! Winston hopped on the bike and pulled out onto the main road to Salima Falls. Earl stood and watched as he rode away towards town. He reminded Earl of a younger version of himself.

Winston looked down the road to where Emma lived as he passed it. The first hundred feet or so was lined on either side with trees and a row of flowers of every conceivable color. The smell was mesmerizing as he passed. He was hoping fate would intervene and Emma would be there at the exact moment he went by, but fate wasn't cooperating today. He strained his eyes in the sun, but couldn't see much farther down the road. About a half mile down, it veered off to the left and a line of trees hid the view.

As he rode into town, moving at the speed of bicycle instead of the speed of car, he was afforded the opportunity to notice things he hadn't before. A small flower shop bloomed in a thousand colors and a hundred scents as he went by. Across from that was a quaint little fire station with a sign that read "Station 119, established 1887." Winston noticed the "e" in "Fire" was flickering on and off, making a slight buzzing sound that faded in and out with the light. There was a group of four or five firemen outside of the large door washing one of the trucks by hand. The red paint glistened in the sunlight.

For ten minutes, he pedaled past dozens of little shops and cute houses with perfectly manicured lawns, until he could see the signs ahead for Greta's on the left and Mrs. Powell's Diner a little ways past that on the right. He rode up onto the sidewalk and came to a stop just outside the door to the diner, where he hopped off and leaned the bike up against the brick wall. He looked through the windows for a glimpse of Emma. I wonder if she's here.

He stepped to the door and opened it for two old ladies about to enter.

"Well, aren't you just the sweetest thing," the younger of the two said.

Winston just smiled back at her. Inside he had mixed emotions. He had been anything but sweet over the course of the last year, and it felt good to be perceived as something other than the bitter and obsessed man he was on the inside, at least before he met Emma. His thoughts went back to her. Emma. For a year, he had a singular motivation. For a year, he saw only darkness in the world. But from the second he set foot in this town and laid eyes on her, it was as if something pierced a small pinhole in the dark sheet hovering all around his life. She was a tiny ray of light that was let into his world, and the more he thought about her or saw her, the light began to flood in. How can it feel so right… and so wrong at the same time?

He stood inside the door for several seconds trying to catch a glimpse of Emma walking through the kitchen or the dining room. I don't have long, before the hostess…

"Well hello there!" Too late. "Want me to get you a table, or are you just going to hang out by the door all day?" Winston sighed and stepped to the podium. He was only planning on staying if Emma was here. He spoke quietly, hoping she would follow suit.

"Actually, I was wondering if Emma was around today?"

She cocked her head and looked at him with obvious confusion on her face. "So, you don't want to sit down?" She was loud and her usual self. Figures. "It's lunch time, you don't want to have a tuna salad sandwich or something? It's our special today. Or how about a cold drink? It looks hot out there." Winston looked around. A couple people were already looking at him.

"I'm looking for Emma," he said even quieter this time. "Is she here?"

The hostess turned towards a waitress that was delivering coffee refills to a nearby table. "Becky… is Emma here today?" Her voice seemed to break the silence of the room. A few more people looked at him curiously.

The waitress thought for a second, and then answered. "What is today? Wednesday? She doesn't come in today. She volunteers down at the animal shelter on Wednesdays and

Thursdays." Winston said thanks to the waitress quickly and was out the door before the hostess could embarrass him any further. He noticed her shaking her head at him through the glass.

Outside he tapped the first person he saw on the shoulder and asked for the directions to the animal shelter. Five seconds and a finger point later, he was back on his bike and zipping down a little side road that branched off the main street. He passed a building that read "SALIMA FALLS POST OFFICE AND BANK" about halfway there. It was small, and if Winston hadn't seen the lettering, he might have thought it was a convenience store or something.

About two blocks after the post office, Winston saw a sign shaped like a paw print on a post outside of what appeared to be a house. Around the outside of the paw, it read "FURRY FRIENDS ANIMAL SHELTER." This must be it. He coasted the bike to a stop beneath the sign and looked at the building. It was a white craftsman style home that had been converted at one point. In the front, there was a large front porch and two pillars that stood next to the steps at the top of the landing. The sidewalk led to the steps and was lined with pink flowers on either side. He got off the bike and walked it up to the front of the house.

To the left, before the stairs began, was another bike. The front tire was wedged in between two vertical wooden posts. There was a basket on the front. This must be Emma's bike. Winston squeezed his own bike in next to hers and rested the front tire between two of the other posts. He looked up at the front door, which was held open by a standing chalkboard sign that had colorfully stenciled letters. "YOUR NEW BEST FRIEND IS WAITING FOR YOU INSIDE…"

Clever, Winston thought as he walked up the steps.

CHAPTER TWENTY-ONE

A Tiny Jolt of Electricity

Winston quietly acknowledged to himself that he had no plan at this point. He knew he was flying by the seat of his pants. Go have lunch at the diner tomorrow and maybe you will see Emma again. That was as far as he had thought it through, though the plan seemed to complete at the time. However, when she wasn't at the diner, he had to improvise.

Now he stood outside the door of the FURRY FRIENDS ANIMAL SHELTER and wondered what exactly he was going to do once he was inside. At the diner, he had hoped to see her casually, as if he was simply there for lunch and just happened to bump into her again. But this was a different story. I guess I'll just act like I'm here to look at some animals.

When he entered, he saw and heard the expected animal shelter sights and sounds. A young girl was behind the counter to his right typing away on a computer. There were shelves lining the wall directly in front of him which held all sorts of dog treats, both for sale and complimentary, along with medicines and grooming supplies. To his left was a hallway that led to the back examination rooms and the kennels. There were also a couple of small rooms past the hallway to the left along the front wall, with windows to the outside. One was filled with kittens, most of which were lounging around on carpeted towers and inside cages. The other had several puppies that were crawling all over each other in piles on the floor. Above it all, he heard the constant sound of an indistinguishable number of other dogs, barking and yapping somewhere in the back.

"Are you here for drop off or pickup?" a voice said from behind the computer screen to his right.

"Oh," Winston replied. "I'm just… looking around." Don't mention Emma, he thought. Keep it casual. Don't make her think you went looking for her.

"So, are you in the market for a new furry friend?" the girl behind the desk said.

"I don't think so, I've never been here and just wanted to check the place out really, see what you have."

"Okay," she said cheerfully. "Feel free to go play with some of our friends over there." She pointed to the two rooms along the front. "They all are looking for a new home. You never know, one might want to go home with you. My name is Sara. If you have any questions, feel free to ask." She smiled at him and then continued typing.

He walked over to the room with the kittens and peered through the window. One was perched on top of the carpeted tower at nearly chest height, just on the other side of the glass. It hissed at him silently through the window. He couldn't hear it, but recognized the familiar signs. It ears were pulled back and its fangs exposed. Easy there. The kitten took a swipe at the glass. I think I'll pass on that room.

He walked a little further and looked into the puppy room. It was filled with wagging tails and smiling puppies. They sure know how to sell themselves, don't they? He opened the door and slipped in, shielding the opening with his foot to prevent escape. Instantly, he was surrounded by puppies climbing over each other to get his attention. "Hey little buddies, calm down now, it's just me." He always talked aloud to dogs when he was meeting them for the first time, assuming it helped them to understand he was no threat. He sat carefully among them on the floor and crossed his legs. He let them crawl all over him in a mad rush for several minutes, until their initial excitement eventually eased up, and they went back to playing amongst themselves again. Now what? I can't wait here all day.

He leaned his back against the wall, and took turns playing tug of war with a few of the rowdier puppies. One cute little brown puppy with blue eyes in the back seemed to be nervously eyeing him from inside his kennel, apparently afraid to come out. "I'm not going to hurt you buddy, you can come out here." The puppy ducked away untrustingly. Winston went back to playing with several of the other dogs. He tossed a ball across the room over and over, and each time a runaway train of puppies chased it down and crashed into the corner, fighting over who got to proudly bring it back to him. After several minutes, the playing seemed to wear out the puppies, and the rowdiness died down. Many of the puppies began to lay down and nap, or nibble on each other's ears. I suppose I should leave soon and try again tomorrow.

When it was mostly calm in the room, the shy brown puppy with blue eyes peeked out from his kennel again at Winston. "Are you finally going to come out and say hi now?" The puppy took one step out of the kennel and looked both ways as if he were crossing the street. He walked slowly around all the other sleeping dogs and sniffed Winston's pants. Winston saw that he was a little bigger and a bit older than the other puppies. "It's okay little man." Winston held his hand out for the puppy to sniff. After a quick sniff, the puppy looked up at Winston with his big blue eyes, and then climbed up onto his lap. He curled up in a ball and nestled cozily between his legs. Winston scratched him behind the ear. "You're a good boy, aren't you?"

Winston looked up and saw Emma watching from the other side of the glass. She smiled at him and slowly opened the door and slipped into the room. Apparently the puppies were used to her frequent visits, because her entrance didn't cause much of a stir among the napping eyes. She sat on the floor next to Winston and rubbed the ears of the nearest puppy.

"I see you've met Buster there."

"Yeah, he just came out."

"I'm impressed," Emma said. "He usually stays in his kennel the whole time people are in here."

"It took a while," Winston replied. "I had to talk him into it."

"He's a good boy." Emma reached over and tussled Buster's ears as he slept on Winston's lap. "So, what brings you in here anyways? Looking for a little guy to take home?"

"Oh, I was just in the neighborhood," Winston lied, hoping she bought his story. "I saw the sign and thought I'd come in and check it out and see what I could find."

"Well, it looks like you found yourself a new friend. Buster's been here for a few months now. He was shy at first, and so he sort of stuck around as people adopted the playful ones. And now people always seem to want to take home the babies. I worry about him." Buster looked up at her with those big blue eyes and seemed to smile. Then he nuzzled deeper into Winston's legs.

"He does seem to like me." Winston pet Buster on the head. He turned to look at Emma. They were sitting with their shoulders nearly touching, and this was the closest he had ever been to her. Her eyes were soft and shy, filled with beauty and reserve. She looked at him and he held her gaze until she nervously looked down at Buster again. Don't make her nervous, you fool. Make a joke or something.

"So, do you work everywhere in Salima Falls?" he said. "I know you said you like to keep busy, but how many jobs can one girl have?"

"I know," she said with a giggle. "You probably think I'm weird or something." She looked down. "I just love animals and knew they needed the help down here. Besides, what else am I going to do with my time?"

Winston understood the meaning that was hiding behind her words. It wasn't that she didn't know what to do with her time. It was that she wanted to bury herself in a task, simply to keep her mind off something. Work was her distraction from reality. Emma was quickly becoming his.

"Well, I could maybe take up a little of your time," Winston said, wondering if he would get the same response as he did at the grocery store. She didn't answer right away, so he continued. "Maybe you could show me around Salima Falls a bit. There's probably a lot I haven't seen yet." Still no response. He tried to decipher the look on her face. She didn't say no yet at least. I guess that's progress. "Maybe you and I could take Buster here on a walk sometime."

At those words, Emma's face changed. She seemed intrigued and excited all of a sudden. "Does that mean you are going to take Buster home?"

"Uh…," Winston hesitated. That's not exactly what I meant. He thought about what to say, but couldn't force the words out. She smiled widely and seemed exited for the first time since he met her. I meant right NOW we could take him for a walk. Winston became lost in her eyes, and her smile seemed to be contagious. And then we would bring him back here when we were done. Seeing the look on her face overwhelmed him, and he didn't want to ruin the moment.

"Perhaps," he said. Her face lit up even more. "You think it's a good idea?"

"It's a wonderful idea! Look how happy he seems! It's perfect!"

Look how happy she looks, is all he could think.

She rubbed the back of Buster's head. "Did you hear that Buster? You are going to have a new home!"

Well, I can't disappoint her now.

"Maybe we could meet somewhere for lunch tomorrow," Winston said.

"You'll need a collar, and a leash, and..." Emma seemed to be talking to herself. He just sat there and marveled at how happy she seemed. He thought she was beautiful before, but now that she was happy and smiling, she seemed almost angelic to him.

"We could grab a quick bite and then walk around the neighborhood and chat."

She ignored him and continued rubbing Buster's ears. "...and some food, and a nametag..." Goodness, how much is this going to cost me? Winston didn't have much money left. He only had what he could find laying around the apartment with him.

Winston noticed Emma seemed to be lost in thought, racking her brain for more needed items.

"Are there any good places around here to eat?"

She didn't offer any suggestions.

"Emma," he said a little bit louder. He put his hand on top of hers and the world froze in place. He felt a tiny jolt of electricity in her skin when he touched it. She immediately snapped out of her thoughts, stopped talking, and looked at him. She felt the warmth of his hand and he could see the slightest bit of panic in her eyes. Is she shaking? He could tell she hadn't been touched in a long time, if ever. Her skin was soft and cool by comparison to his. He gave the top of her hand a quick caress with his thumb as their eyes locked, and then lifted his hand from hers. Not too much. He had her attention at least.

"So, have you been listening to me? What do you think about tomorrow?" Their eyes were locked and he knew she was nervous. She looked down at her hand and felt the coolness return where his hand was.

"I…, I just…"

Oh no, Winston thought. He had seen this before. Please don't say no again.

She took a deep breath and looked up at him.

Here it comes.

When their eyes met, she paused. Something in Winston's eyes calmed her. No one had ever looked at her the way he was looking at her now. She didn't understand what was happening, but she seemed to relax for a moment.

"I think…"

Just do it already!

"I think… that should be ok," she said with a smile.

What?

"I just have to let the girls know up front that I'll be gone for a while."

She said yes?

Winston's face flashed the biggest smile he had worn in over a year. He was the one who was speechless for a change. He didn't want to say the wrong thing and change her mind.

"Café Renaissance is about two blocks from here," she said. "It's a cute little French bistro with these quaint little wrought iron tables outside. They have really good sandwiches too."

"That sounds wonderful," Winston said. "How does twelve-thirty sound?"

"Works for me," she said as she stood up. She reached her hands out for Buster and Winston lifted him up to her. "Now let's go get the paperwork taken care of." She opened the door and they headed to the front desk.

Winston could barely focus as papers were signed and things were handed to him. Luckily, he had the exact number of dollars required, and within minutes, he was walking out the front door past the standing sign again. He was holding a small starter bag of dog food, along with some treats and a leash. Emma was carrying Buster, who was sporting his new red collar. Winston walked over and pulled his bike free and placed the items in the basket.

"You rode a bike?" She looked at the bike strangely as if she recognized it.

"Yeah, I was just up the road a little ways. I think there's room for Buster in the basket, what do you think?"

She walked over and hesitatingly placed him in the basket. There was just enough room. Winston could see the concerned look on her face.

"It's not too far, I'll hold his collar and make sure he's ok. Don't worry."

"Okay," she said, but Winston could tell she wasn't convinced.

"Thanks so much for rescuing him," she said.

"Rescuing?" Winston chuckled a bit at the term. "I don't think I deserve such a heroic term. It's not like I dove into a freezing lake to save him, or fought off a pack of wolves."

"True," she said as she rubbed the top of his head. "But you're still a hero to him."

Winston smiled and nodded.

He turned the bike around and walked it to the road, and then put his leg over the bar. "I promise I'll keep him safe." He patted Buster on the head, who was peering over the edge of the basket in fear.

Winston looked back at Emma. "See you tomorrow, Emma." They exchanged waves and then he sat on the seat. He started down the road with one hand on the handlebar and one hand on Buster. The sun seemed brighter all around him, and the breeze smelled sweeter than ever. Buster sank down in the basket and Winston took his hand off his collar.

"Good boy, Buster." He thought about the look on Emma's face again, and how beautiful she looked when she smiled. "Good boy," he repeated.

CHAPTER TWENTY-TWO

In and Out of Daydreams

As Winston pedaled the bike off the paved road and into the shop's dirt lot, he saw Earl close the hood of a nearby car and wipe the front bumper with a rag. As he neared the car, Earl turned around and tossed the rag over his shoulder.

"Now what do we have here?" Earl said, as he scratched his head. "You go to town for lunch and you come back with a dog? Hope you don't plan on barbecuing that thing."

Winston was still feeling good about seeing Emma. He just looked at Earl with a smile that was so big he was almost laughing.

"You swallow a coat hanger or something?" Earl said. "This town has enough of those damned fools."

"I just feel good, that's all Earl. Don't you ever feel good?" He continued smiling.

Earl looked at him in a way that clearly meant no. "What the heck are you doing with a dog anyhow? I thought you went to the diner." Winston just realized he hadn't eaten at all.

"Oh yeah, I got sidetracked I guess. I happened to ride by the animal shelter and stopped in to check it out. I didn't get a chance to eat, actually."

Earl just shook his head.

"Well, let's go inside and get that little fella some water, he looks scared half to death in that basket." Earl turned and walked inside.

Winston parked the bike against the building and carried Buster and the other items inside to Earl's apartment. When he entered the room, Earl was running some water into a bowl. He placed it on the floor and Winston set Buster and the items down. Buster sniffed the bowl for a few seconds and then started lapping it up.

"So, what are you going to do with a dog, anyhow?" Earl said. "Hell, can you even take care of yourself?" He laughed.

Winston sat on the chair and watched Buster drink his water, as Earl began making a sandwich. "I didn't plan on it. I just went there to see…" Winston's words trailed off. "I mean it just sort of… happened."

Earl walked over and handed Winston a sandwich on a plate and sat down across from him. He tossed an extra piece of bread down for Buster, who sniffed it curiously.

"Pickle loaf," Earl said. "My favorite." Winston looked down at the sandwich in disgust. Pickle loaf? He peeled up the corner of the bread to take a peak, and sniffed it much the same way Buster was doing below him. "With a little ketchup," Earl continued. "Delicious."

Winston unenthusiastically picked up the sandwich and took a bite. Almost instantly, the look of disgust left his face.

He nodded and raised his eyebrows. It was surprisingly good.
He gladly took another bite.

"I told you it was good," Earl said. "Anyhow, I'm no
fool. I know you didn't happen to ride by the shelter. I know
why you went there."

Winston swallowed. "You do?" *It's a small town, all
right.*

"Of course I do. So, tell me something." *Here comes a
lecture.* "How's she doing, anyhow?"

Winston was surprised. Earl wasn't upset. He seemed
curious. "She's ok I guess. I made her smile today for the first
time." Winston paused and was aware that he was beaming.
"That was a first." He took another bite of the sandwich.

Earl rubbed his chin and looked at Winston in deep
thought. Winston wondered what Earl was thinking, as Buster
finished his water, ran over to Earl, and jumped on his leg.
Earl shrugged him off. "Now listen here boy!" Earl said loudly
to Buster. He looked down at him. Buster was wagging his
tail and shining those big blue eyes at Earl. Earl's demeanor
changed immediately. He reached down and rubbed Buster's
head and scratched behind his ears. "Cute little fellow, isn't
he?"

"Yeah," Winston answered. "He's a good boy. His
name is Buster. And I see those puppy dog eyes are hard to
resist for you too."

Earl picked Buster up and set him on his lap. Buster
climbed up and licked Earl right on the nose, and then nestled
in his lap like he had done to Winston. "Buster, huh? Well,
he's friendly, at least."

"I guess the little guy likes you Earl." Earl looked
down at Buster, who lifted his head and seemed to be smiling
back at Earl.

"So where do you plan on keeping this little guy?"

"I hadn't really thought about it," Winston said. "I'm not even sure my apartment allows pets. Although he probably wouldn't want to stay in that dump all day anyways. And I likely won't be there much longer either, now that I think about it."

Buster laid his head down on Earl's lap and sighed. Earl rubbed his head for a few seconds. Winston noticed the change in Earl, and thought he may have glimpsed the smallest smile on his face. He stood and walked to the fridge. "Mind if I grab a Coke or something?" Earl was looking down at Buster and didn't even hear Winston. Winston grabbed a drink out of the fridge and sat back down. Earl was still scratching Buster under the chin, whose eyes were now closed. Both of them seemed to be enjoying it.

"I suppose," Earl started. "He could stay here at the shop until you figure out what you're going to do with him. I don't want him out on the street or something."

Winston smiled. "Well, well," he said. "Old Earl has a heart after all." He reached over and leaned down to rub Buster's head. "What do you say Buster? Want to stay here with Earl for a few days?" Buster never even opened his eyes. He was tired. This was the most excitement he'd had in weeks. "He doesn't seem to have any complaints."

"Well it's settled then," Earl said. "I'd say it's about time we get some work done, what do you say?"

"Sure," Winston said. He stood up and tossed the empty soda can into the trash. "Listen, I forgot to tell you, I'll be heading back into town again tomorrow around the same time."

Earl stood and set Buster back down on the floor. "What now? You planning on bringing back a cat this time?"

Winston chuckled. "No, I made plans with Emma. We are going to have lunch and go for a walk."

Earl gave him the same inquisitive look as earlier. "Is that so?" He seemed to be surprised at the news.

"Yeah," Winston said. "I'm just as shocked as you." He opened the door and they all three headed outside into the sun again. "I'll be gone about an hour or so. I mean, if that's ok with you and all."

"I suppose you're a grown man. You can do whatever you like."

The rest of the day went by in a blur for Winston. He didn't say much, and Earl spent most of his time chatting with Buster. Winston could only think of Emma and their date tomorrow. In and out of daydreams, he helped Earl change the headlights on a town car and swap the hood out on an old truck. The whole time he kept picturing Emma's smile. It flashed in his vision over and over until Carter came to pick him up.

"Had a good day, did we?" said Carter.

"What do you mean?" Winston asked.

"Well, there's a new light in your eyes if I'm not mistaken. Yes sir!"

Winston just smiled at him. "I suppose I did." The whole ride home he tried to picture the conversations he might have with Emma tomorrow. He hadn't been on a first date or felt these types of nerves in years.

When he walked into his apartment later, he saw the red light blinking on the answering machine, and pressed play.

Beeeeeep.

"Winston, it's Marlow. I talked to my boss again. He said Friday works best for him for the meeting. So, I need you here at the office at five o'clock sharp, ok? I talked him into staying a bit late to meet with you. If you don't have a ride, let me know ahead of time and I'll head out early to pick you up. He's a busy man, so doesn't screw this up. Make sure you have your shit together, ok? Nice shirt, slacks, shower, shave… the works. If you play your cards right, you might be able to turn this into something good. You need this, man. You need to turn things around. So, let me know if you need a ride and I'll see you Friday. Later."

After the message ended, Winston picked up the phone and fumbled through a drawer for a Chinese takeout menu. He ordered some Empress Chicken and a couple of egg rolls, and then rummaged around the apartment for some cash. After he found some, he grabbed a beer out of the fridge and walked to his closet to examine his wardrobe options for Friday.

He thought about Emma the rest of the evening until he fell asleep, and for once, he spent a night in Dunsport without Caroline even crossing his mind.

CHAPTER TWENTY-THREE

A Dapper Fellow

Winston woke early and with ease the next morning. He hopped out of bed with a bounce in his step. His first thought was of how Buster slept at Earl's. Part of him felt bad for leaving him on his first night away from the shelter, but now that he looked around his apartment, he was sure it was the right thing to do. There were old pizza boxes everywhere, and bottles of every kind of alcohol scattered all over the floor and tables. He was certain that under the mess there were all kinds of things a dog could get hurt on or sick from. Plus, he would be gone all day and couldn't let him out. It was better that he was at Earl's. At least that way he could see him during the day.

Winston fetched a nice pair of khaki shorts and a button-up shirt from his closet, while he thought about his lunch date with Emma. It wasn't the most appropriate attire for working at a dirty old auto shop, but luckily, he had convinced Earl before he left yesterday to let him have the easy jobs before lunch. He would spend the morning wiping down dashboards and vacuuming interior carpets, trying not to get sweaty or dirty. I'm sure Earl will make me pay for it after I get back with the worst possible chore.

He wet his hair and combed a little styling gel into it, and followed that with a quick shave. When Carter pulled up, Winston was already outside, waiting by the door and enjoying the rare sight of sunlight gracing Dunsport. He opened the door and hopped in the front seat with a smile on his face.

"Well aren't you a dapper fellow today Mr. Winston! Yes sir! By golly, I thought I stopped next to the wrong apartment when I saw you."

Winston just smiled at the jab. "I have a lunch date today, if you must know."

"A lunch date? Well, I'll be. The sun is shining extra bright for you this morning, Mr. Winston. Congratulations are in order I guess."

"Thanks," Winston said. "I look alright?"

"Mighty fine Mr. Winston. Mighty fine. Emma doesn't stand a chance if I do say so myself!"

"Wait, how did you know it was Emma?" Winston said suspiciously. Carter opened his mouth to speak but Winston just continued. "You know what, forget about it. I already know what you will say. Everybody knows everything in Salima Falls. Small town and all." Carter just smiled and started the car.

The sun seemed brighter than normal on the way there. Winston felt like he was finally beginning to learn the way, yet he always seemed to be looking out the window or lost in thought when Carter made the final turn. That last road seemed to elude him every time.

As they drove through town, he watched all the smiling people on their way to breakfast, work, or just morning stroll, and noticed how similar his reflection looked in the window. He seemed to fit right in. Am I becoming one of them?

"Wish me luck," Winston said as he hopped out of the car at Earl's. He watched Carter drive away and turned around to the sound of tiny paws galloping through the dirt. Buster was running across the lot towards him.

"Hey Buster! How's my little buddy today?" Buster jumped on his legs and Winston reached down and rubbed his head. Buster excitedly spun around in circles and then turned to run back to Earl, who had just stepped outside.

"I guess he made it through the night," Winston said. "How was he?"

Earl picked the little guy up and Buster licked his face.

"He's a playful little son of a gun, I tell you," Earl said. "Kept trying to bite my toes through the blanket all night."

Winston walked up and rubbed Buster's head. "Sounds like you two had a good time."

After a cup of coffee and a few more stories about Buster, they got to work. Buster spent the morning running around like a caged lion who had just been released into the jungle. He crawled under the cars and licked Earl's face. "All right, that's enough," Earl would say every few minutes. He got lost among the tires out back and Winston had to go searching for him. He jumped from a toolbox into the back seat of a car Winston had just vacuumed and rolled around all over the freshly clean seat. It was a madhouse all morning, and before Winston knew it, the sun was nearly overhead and Earl was climbing out from under the car.

"What do you say Winston? About time for that date of yours, isn't it?"

Winston climbed out of the front seat of a red Thunderbird and straightened his shirt.

Buster ran up in front of him.

"How do I look?" he asked them both.

Buster cocked his head to the side and looked up at Winston.

"Better than normal," Earl replied. "What time are you meeting her?"

"Twelve thirty."

"Well, there's time to sit down for a few minutes and have a drink, come on." Winston and Buster followed Earl into his room and had a seat around the table. Earl handed Winston a glass of iced tea and poured some water in a bowl for Buster.

"So, what's the big plan for this date anyhow?"

"I'm meeting her at the animal shelter. We are going to some Renaissance place or something."

"Ah Café Renaissance," Earl said with nostalgia in his voice. "Too fancy for a grease hound like me, but a fine choice for two young lads on a date."

Buster jumped into Earl's lap and laid his head between his paws.

"It was her idea, I've never even heard of the pl… oh no!" Winston exclaimed.

Buster raised his head and perked up his ears.

"What?" asked Earl.

Winston looked at the floor, obviously embarrassed. "I'm an idiot. I don't have any money. I used the last of my cash on Buster's stuff yesterday."

"Can't you just use one of them credit cards everyone seems to use nowadays?"

Winston sighed. "My wallet was lost a few days ago."

Earl set Buster on the floor and walked over to an old fashioned safe that sat next to his bed. After a few spins of the combination dial he opened the door and took out a couple of bills. He shut the door and walked back to Winston.

"Here you go," he said as he handed two twenty-dollar bills to Winston.

Buster sniffed the air, hoping it was a treat.

"Are you sure?" Winston hesitated to take the money.

"Yes, I'm sure. I can't have the girl paying for her own first date." He dropped the bills in Winston's lap.

"First date?" Winston looked concerned. "I remember you said she didn't socialize much, but she's never even been on one date?"

"I don't think so, what's the big deal?"

"Well it's a lot of pressure, that's what," replied Winston.

"Oh nonsense!" Earl said. "You young kids and your whining. Your generation does too much thinking and not enough doing. It's simple. You bring her flowers, tell her she's pretty, buy her lunch, and talk to her. It ain't rocket science."

"Flowers. That's a good idea," Winston said. "I saw some flowers just down the road over there. I'll stop and pick some on the way there." He stood and sat his drink on the table. "I better take off then."

Earl and Buster followed as Winston retrieved the bike from the garage. Winston hopped on and pedaled up to them. "Thanks again for the money," he said to Earl. "I owe you." He looked down at Buster. "Now you stay here and be a good boy Buster. I'm going to see your friend Emma. I'll tell her you miss her." Earl picked up Buster and rubbed his ears as they watched Winston pedal away.

Fifteen minutes later Winston was turning down the road to the animal shelter on his bike, with flowers in the front basket and a giant smile on his face. As he approached the Furry Friends sign, he saw Emma sitting on the steps of the shelter. She was wearing a white sundress and her hair was blowing gently in the breeze.

That instant, a vision of Caroline wearing a similar white dress the day of the accident violently flashed in his mind. The shock of it jolted him, and wiped the smile off his face. When his tire left the sidewalk and dropped into the grass, he lost his balance and the bike tipped over. He crashed onto the ground only a few feet from Emma and the bike fell on top of him. The flowers spilled out onto the ground in front of her, and he moaned from the pain. Nice work Winston.

CHAPTER TWENTY-FOUR
French Words

Winston lay on the ground at Emma's feet. His knee was in pain and his face was in the grass. Emma jumped up and ran over to him. "Are you ok?"

"Carol… Emma… I'm sorry, I…" Winston shook his head. Snap out of it you fool. "My tire slipped off the sidewalk back there and I lost control." He looked up into Emma's eyes as she stood over him with a concerned look on her face. Her eyes seemed to calm him. He took a deep breath. "You look incredible."

"Thanks," Emma said shyly. She lifted his bike off him and pushed it over next to hers. Winston got to his feet and brushed off the grass from his shirt. "Not my smoothest entrance," he said.

"Are you sure you are ok?" she said. "Your knee is all scuffed up."

Winston looked down and saw the scrapes on his knee. It was quite painful, but he tried his best to brush it off and act like it didn't hurt. "I'm fine, it's no big deal." He was embarrassed more than he was hurt. He bent down and picked up the flowers one by one. Some of them were smashed and broken, but he did his best to bunch them together in a bouquet, and embarrassingly handed them to Emma in a mangled mess. "These… were for you." Emma took the bouquet and a couple of the broken flowers fell to the ground at her feet. She did her best not to laugh at them. "I'm sorry," Winston said. "I ruined them."

"It's ok," she said. "It was sweet of you to pick them." She pulled one of the white flowers out of the bunch and put it in her hair above her ear.

Winston looked at the flower in her hair and remembered that Caroline also wore a white flower in her hair on that fateful day. His eyes seemed to wonder off for a second and Emma could sense a bit of sadness in his eyes.

"You don't like it, do you?" she said, and reached to pull the flower from her hair.

"No, leave it," Winston said. "Sorry, I was thinking about something else. I like the flower, I really do. And that dress is stunning."

Emma looked down in embarrassment. "I haven't worn this dress in a long time. I wasn't sure..."

"It's perfect," Winston interrupted, as she put the rest of the flowers in the basket on her bike. "What do you say we forget about my little intro here and start over? Want to go get some lunch?"

"Okay," Emma said. "Does it hurt to walk?" she said, as they took a few steps to the sidewalk.

Winston tried to hide the slight limp in his step. "No, I'm fine. It wasn't bad. Let's talk about something else."

"Okay," she said. "So, how's Buster liking his new home," she asked.

"Well, he seems really happy. When I show up he comes running. I think he likes exploring and finding all sorts of crazy stuff to get into.

"That's great!" Emma said. "He was always really sweet, but shy at first."

"Kind of like you," Winston replied. Emma blushed and smiled to herself.

As they rounded a corner, Emma pointed to an old brick cottage. "That house right there is Mrs. Baker's. She used to babysit me when I was a little girl. I remember begging to walk down to the animal shelter with her to play with the puppies."

"So, you've always had a soft spot for animals?"

"I guess so," Emma said. "I used to lay on my back and let the puppies crawl all over me. There's such innocence and kindness in a pet's eyes. You know what I mean?"

Winston couldn't take his eyes off her as they walked. He just listened to her voice and smiled at her, nodding along when necessary.

"You think I'm crazy, don't you?" Emma said.

"No, I don't think you are crazy. And I do know what you mean. I guess that's why they call them puppy dog eyes."

"I guess so," she replied. "Look, there's Café Renaissance just up ahead."

"So, how long have you lived in Salima Falls?" he asked.

"As long as I can remember," she said. "My whole life I guess."

"You like it here?"

"I suppose," she said. "I've never known anywhere else, so I don't have anything to compare it to, but it's fine I guess." They walked up to the café and Emma led them to a quiet corner table outside in the patio area. They sat across from each other and a waitress brought them each a glass of water and a menu.

Winston took a sip of his water. "I've only been here a week, but it seems like a nice place. Kind of surreal actually."

"What do you mean?" she said.

"Well everyone seems so… happy. And it's always sunny and beautiful here."

"Yes, it is," Emma said. "Maybe that's why everyone's so happy."

"Good point. So, do you eat here often? What's good here?"

"I get the Croque Monsieur, usually." She laughed when she saw the confused look on his face. "Don't be scared, it's just a fancy name for a ham and cheese. It comes on a baguette and they use Gruyere cheese, and it's delicious!"

Winston suddenly felt out of place. "Groy ear? I don't think I'm sophisticated enough for this place."

"It's GROO YAIR… and you're fine. Just don't look at the French words. Look at the little subtitles beneath them. Those are in English." When the waitress came, Emma ordered her baguette.

"I'll have a French Dip sandwich and a coke please."

"Ah, that's a specialty of ours," the waitress said. "You'll love it."

"See that wasn't so hard, was it?"

"It was the only one I recognized," Winston said. Emma just smiled at him. "Oh," Winston remembered. "Another thing about this place. Why is it so hard to get here anyways? I can barely figure out the roads. Every time I come it seems like the roads change."

"Yeah, Salima Falls is sort of out in the middle of nowhere I guess. What brings you to town anyways?"

"Well, I had a little accident and I was lucky enough to bump into Carter. He brought me to town about a week ago."

"What kind of accident?"

"Well, I sort of had a nasty cut on my head, but the doc fixed me up and sewed it shut." He turned his head to the side and showed her the stitches that were barely noticeable by now. His hair had grown a bit and hid them from view.

"Oh my god!" Emma exclaimed loudly. "That was you?" She put both hands over her mouth.

Because of her soft-spoken nature, this unexpected outburst surprised Winston and caused him to jump a little in his seat. "What are you talking about?" he asked, with a look of shock on his face.

Emma's voice returned to a whisper, and she mumbled under her breath to herself. "I can't believe I didn't recognize you." She looked away in thought.

"Recognize me where?"

Emma looked back at him nervously. "Remember when we first met at Greta's?" she asked.

When I asked you out and got rejected embarrassingly? Winston thought. "Yeah, I remember." His sour tone went unnoticed.

"Remember when I said I worked three jobs?" she continued.

"Yeah." Where is this going?

"And I said you looked familiar, but I couldn't figure out where I saw you from?"

"Uh huh."

"Well, I finally figured it out," she said.

Winston gave her a questioning look. "You mean you didn't see me at the diner?"

"Nope." There was a moment of silence as Winston looked confused, and Emma smiled at him. "I recognized you from that night Carter brought you to the doc's house."

"I don't understand," Winston said.

"That's one of my three jobs," she explained. "I help Doc sometimes when things come up." Winston started putting the pieces together in his head as she talked. "Mostly cleaning and stuff. Boring things usually, like handing him tools and running after bandages and whatnot. But sometimes, I get to help with his patients if it's after hours or on weekends, or something strange comes up."

Suddenly, Winston remembered his first morning in Salima Falls vividly. He remembered waking with the bandages on his head. He remembered the smell of Doc cooking breakfast in the kitchen. But most pertinent memory to Emma's revelation was how he woke up wearing clothes he had never seen before. His eyes opened wide when he realized what she was saying.

"So, when the doc said he had a nurse come over and undress me, clean me up, and put me in his pajamas…. that was you?" Emma just smiled back at him. He dropped his head immediately into his hands and covered his face with his palms.

"I mean, I'm not a real nurse or anything, but our families go way back and the doc has always been like a second dad to me. He and my dad were always friends. I used to help him out when I was in high school as a part-time job. I've been helping out here and there ever since."

Winston shook his head in his hands.

"Like I said, I like to keep busy," she continued.

"I have never been so embarrassed in my life," Winston mumbled between his fingers with his face still in hiding. He finally raised his head and looked at her with a red face.

"I didn't see anything, if that's what you are wondering," she said.

"That's good to know but it's not what I'm embarrassed about," Winston said. "I'm embarrassed that you saw me in that condition. I was drunk, filthy, beat up… I was a mess." His embarrassment seemed to grow even more. "And I thought my little bike accident earlier was a bad first impression." He put his head in his hands again.

Emma laughed a little, taking enjoyment in his embarrassment. "You were rather messed up when I first saw you. So much so, that I didn't recognize you when I saw you at Greta's."

"Yeah, I had a rough night."

"I'd say. So, what happened to you anyways?"

Where do I begin? Winston looked up at her and hesitated. "If it's all the same to you, I'd rather save that conversation for another time. That is, if you ever want to see me again after today."

Emma just smiled. She liked seeing some insecurity in him. It made her feel better knowing someone out there might be as messed up as she was.

"Didn't you say you were only going to be in town for a week?"

"That's what I promised the doc. After the week is up, I'm not really sure what I'm going to do." Winston looked off into the distance. It was the first time he had let his mind think past the immediate future in a while. "I guess I'll figure it out when I get there."

"So, you are working for the doc?"

"Well, not exactly," Winston replied. "My car and wallet were stolen." He noticed Emma's eyes widen. "It's a long story. Anyways, I didn't have a way to pay him back for stitching me up, so I promised to do him a favor in exchange.

At the end of the week, after I'm fully healed and I'm done helping him out, he will take the stitches out and then we will be even."

"What kind of favor?"

"Well, I offered to work for the doc, but he had nothing for me to do. Then he said he had a friend who owns an auto body shop just outside of town who could use a helper for a week." Emma looked intently at Winston. He could see the fear in her eyes. "So, I'm helping this friend of his, named Earl."

"You are working for Earl at the body shop?" Her eyes were wide and she seemed stressed out.

"Mostly cleaning cars and sorting tires, grunt work really. Buster seems to like it there." Emma was silent. She seemed to be in shock. "In fact, I saw you ride by on your bike a couple of days ago. Do you live near there or something?"

Emma fidgeted in her chair and seemed to want to leave. Winston could tell something was up. Just then the waitress brought their food and set the plates on the table.

Emma looked up at her. "Actually, can I get mine to go? I'm not that hungry after all."

"Sure," the waitress said. She picked the plate back up and shot Winston a concerned look as she walked away.

"Is there something wrong?" Winston said.

"No," Emma said. "I just… just realized I have to get back to the shelter. I forgot I had to give Mrs. Johnson's Sheltie her shots before she picks her up."

Winston knew she was lying and wondered what he might have said. He tried to lighten the mood with a joke. "Do you hate mechanics or something?" She glared at him and seemed to want to leave even more. Winston tried again. "Or maybe you are afraid of cars. You know, come to think of it, I have only seen you riding that bike. Maybe that's it." Winston chuckled at his joke, hoping she would join in.

She looked at him and stood up. He couldn't understand the look on her face. It was as if she was on the verge of tears, just before they fell from her eyes.

"I have to go. I'm sorry," she said.

"Why do you have to go? Did I upset you?"

Emma pushed in her chair and began walking away.

"Wait! Emma! Don't go. I don't know what I said, but I didn't mean it." Emma hurried across the street to the other sidewalk and began jogging away, just as the waitress returned with Emma's to-go box.

"Emma!" he yelled. But she just kept going.

The waitress watched Emma run away with Winston. He looked at her sheepishly and confused.

"I guess you can box mine up too," he said.

"I'm sorry." The waitress gave him a look of empathy and hurried away with his food. When she came back, he paid, and carried the to-go boxes of uneaten food slowly down the sidewalk. What just happened? When he reached the animal shelter, Emma's bike was gone. I don't understand. He looked down the roads in every direction and didn't see her, so he put the meals in the basket of his bike and began the slow and painful ride back to Earl's.

CHAPTER TWENTY-FIVE
A Stolen Sandwich

When Winston finally got back to Earl's, he was a sad sight to behold. Earl stepped out of the office with a cold drink in his hand and watched as Winston slowly pedaled towards him. Winston's head was hung low and there were still a few blades of grass stuck in his hair from the fall earlier. The scrape on his knee had started to bleed again with all the motion from pedaling.

Winston coasted up to the door under the awning, just a couple of feet in front of Earl. He raised his head and looked at Earl, who immediately started laughing. The sound of the laughter caught the attention of Buster, and he came running around the corner as excited as ever. He jumped on Winston's legs in excitement.

"Ouch Buster!" Winston screamed. Buster's claw had accidentally poked the wound from his fall. This caused it to bleed even more, and caused Earl to laugh even harder.

"What's so funny?" Winston asked.

Earl gathered himself.

"I've been on a few dates in my day son. But I never once came back looking like this. Tell me how in the world a man leaves with flowers in his hand for a date, and then comes back busted up like he was in a fight? Ha!"

"I'm glad my pain is a source of humor for you."

"Hehe," Earl continued. "Guess I don't have to ask how it went. I think the grass in your hair and the blood on your leg tells me all I need to know."

Winston hung his head again. "I'm not even sure what happened."

"Well," Earl said. "From the looks of it, I'd say she kicked the crap out of you. Why don't you go put that bike away and get in here and wash that scratch. Come on Buster, let's go."

After Winston put the bike in the garage, he grabbed the two boxes of food and went inside.

"Here you go," he said to Earl as he entered. "We might as well eat these and not let them go to waste." Winston put his sandwich on the counter and grabbed a cloth to wash his wound.

"So, you at least made it to the restaurant I see," Earl said. He sat in his chair and opened the box. "What do we have here?" Buster ran over and stared at him, hoping he would be included in the lunch.

"I can't even pronounce the name of that sandwich," Winston said. "Something French. Grier cheese or something." He threw the paper towel in the trash and sat across from Earl with his box in his lap. Buster spun back and forth between them, watching them both, looking and hoping for fallen crumbs.

"Alright, so let's have it," Earl said. "From flowers to uneaten sandwiches. I'm all ears."

Winston finished his bite of the sandwich as he thought. "Well, the beginning and end of the date were disasters, but I thought the middle part was nice."

Earl chuckled again. "I hate to say it, but there ain't no middle part of a half-hour date!"

Winston bit his lip and shook his head up and down. He could see Earl's point. "Alright, alright, so it was all disaster. Is that better?"

Earl put his palms up to Winston. "Sorry," he said. "I won't interrupt anymore, let's hear it."

Winston dropped a piece of bread for Buster before continuing.

"I sort of had the worst entrance to a date of all time. I saw her on the steps and then lost focus for a second and my tire slipped. I fell off the bike and crashed pretty hard in the grass right in front of her." Earl raised his eyebrows and pursed his lips, trying hard to keep himself from laughing again. "The flowers were all mangled, and my leg was too. After that, we walked to the restaurant. We were talking and it was all going great, and then poof, she got freaked out and left."

"She just walked out on you?" Earl asked.

"Yeah, she got all weird at the table and just stood up and left. Didn't even wait for her food. I'm not even sure what I said."

"You must have said something, bombs don't go off without a light."

"I'm telling you, I didn't say anything."

"Well, what were you talking about?"

Winston took another bite and thought hard about their conversation. "Actually," he said. "Now that I think about it, she got weird right after I told her I worked here. Then I made a joke about her hating mechanics or cars or both. And something about always riding a bike. I'm not sure what all I said, but I don't see why that would upset her."

Earl sat back in his chair. His eyes said he understood, like he might know why she left, but he didn't let on. He only made a joke. "Well Winston, if you ask me, understanding women is like trying to figure out what color the number seven smells like!"

"No kidding," Winston said, as he tossed a larger piece of bread across the room for Buster to chase. It landed next to Earl's bed and slid under the edge. Buster took off sprinting after it, chasing the bread like it was a trespassing rabbit. Winston watched as Buster dove his head under the bed after it. As he backed out, with a mouth full of bread, Buster knocked over a pile of papers and photos that were under the bed, scattering them across the floor.

"Buster!" Winston yelled. "Watch where you are going. Get back here." Earl looked behind him as Buster came running and saw the mess. Winston stood up. "Sorry Earl," he apologized. "I'll clean up after him."

"Now don't worry about it," Earl said. He tried to put his sandwich down and quickly get up, but Winston was already past him. "Just leave those," he said. "It's all right." Buster got in Earl's way as he stood but Winston had already began picking up the pile of photos. As he made a neat stack or two, he seemed to freeze when he noticed Emma was in several of the pictures. He looked closer. There were several pictures of her from when she was a younger girl. He could tell it was her. First day of school. Working inside the diner. High school prom. Her graduation from a distance. Buster ran past Earl. The sandwich that Earl had just sat on the table was hanging over the edge slightly and Buster jumped up and grabbed it, knocking the plate off onto the floor.

Earl spun around when he heard the glass plate hit the floor. "Buster!" Buster was running out the door with a stolen sandwich hanging out of his mouth. Earl picked up the plate and some of the crumbs on the floor, as Winston continued picking up the photos.

He saw one of Earl standing next to a big white car with a huge grin on his face. He held it up to Earl. "Is that your car?"

Earl squinted across the room as he took the dishes to the sink. "Nineteen seventy-two Chevy Vega!"

"Not a bad looking car," Winston said. "For a car that's older than me."

"Haven't seen that car in a while," said Earl. "Now put those down and come back over here."

Winston ignored him and continued flipping through the stack of photos. There were also many of Emma and her mother. He was halfway through the pile when a certain photo made him stop.

What the…

"No way," he said aloud. He stood and turned to Earl, who saw him holding the photo. Winston's face was confused and serious. He held up the photo to Earl. "Why didn't you tell me?" The tone of his voice was different now. Earl just sighed. "Alright, alright. Sit down and I'll explain," he said to Winston.

CHAPTER TWENTY-SIX
The Horse's Ass

Winston handed the photo to Earl on his way by, and sat in the chair with a thump. He didn't take his eyes off Earl. "Why didn't you tell me?"

Earl stared at the picture as he sat. It was a photo of himself and Emma on his fortieth birthday. He was seated at the head of the table, surrounded by friends and family. Emma was six or seven years old and seated on his lap. On the table were gifts from the partygoers. Earl smiled as he held the photo up closer to his eyes. In the picture, he had just finished opening his gift from Emma. It was a coffee mug that said "World's Best Dad" in bold red lettering. He was holding it up and grinning for the camera as Emma kissed his cheek. It was always his favorite photo. He had it next to his bed for years, but eventually it depressed him, and he had to bury it beneath in a pile of photos. He looked up slowly at Winston.

"I haven't seen this picture in a long time."

"Emma is your daughter?" Winston asked. "So, you are the horse's ass?"

"Who said I was a horse's ass?" Earl said.

"You did!" Winston thundered. "You said Emma's dad is a real horse's ass, and that's why she doesn't talk to him much."

Earl nodded. He knew he couldn't keep it from Winston anymore. "She's my baby girl," he said. "She might be all grown up now, but she's still my baby girl. And yes, I suppose I am a horse's ass."

"Why didn't you tell me?" Winston's voice rose a little. "The whole time I've been talking about her and telling you stories, it never crossed your mind to mention that I was talking about your daughter?"

Earl looked Winston straight in the eyes with a cold stare. "Now listen here. I don't have to explain why I do anything to you." Winston felt Earl's penetrating glare. "And don't act like you aren't sitting there with secrets of your own either." He held the picture tightly in his hand and pointed it at Winston. "I might be old, but I'm not stupid. I know a broken man with his own problems when I see one."

Winston realized Earl was right, and changed his tone a little. "Fair enough. I'm sorry." He looked at the pile of pictures on the floor again and back at Earl, after a pause. Buster ran back in, having finished his stolen sandwich, and sniffed around for more. "But I'd still like to hear more about you and Emma. There has to be a story there. Especially if the mere mention of your name can ruin my date with her."

Earl stood for a few seconds, and then tossed the picture back onto the pile next to the bed. He walked past Winston and grabbed two beers from the fridge. He handed one to Winston on the way to his usual chair, then sat and twisted the top off the bottle slowly. He took a long drink, as if trying to buy time, wondering where to start.

"Remember when I told you I was divorced?" Earl didn't wait for an answer. "Well, her name was Rebecca, and she was an angel I tell you. Bona fide angel." Earl looked up at the ceiling. "And boy did she set my world on fire. I didn't know what to do with myself." He smiled.

Winston saw pure joy on Earl's face for the first time, as he talked about his ex-wife.

"Those first two or three years were the best years of my life. At least, I thought they were. Up until she gave birth to Emma. I didn't think it could be any better, but when I held my little girl I knew I was wrong." Earl sat there silently reminiscing to himself for a few seconds before continuing.

"I wanted so hard to be successful, for Pop of course, but also for her. I wanted her to be proud of what I did here at the shop. So, I kept my nose to the grindstone and put in the hours. Looking back, it was all so stupid." Earl looked to the floor. "They would have been proud of me no matter what I did. They didn't care about the shop at all. And I suppose Pop didn't either. Seeing me happy with Rebecca and Emma would have been enough. But I was blind, and let this place consume me. And Rebecca had to have something to do while I was always working, so once Emma was in school, she started her own business too."

"The diner," Winston interjected. He was piecing together the bits he heard from Earl throughout the week. Buster curled up in a ball at his feet and let out a sigh.

Earl nodded his head. "Mrs. Powell's," he continued. "It was named after her mother. I guess all of my hard work rubbed off on her in a way. She put everything she had into that place. I suppose I have to give her credit too. Within a few years, the diner was the go-to place in town. It was all the rage. Young folks went for the soda, old folks for the coffee and homemade pies." Earl got up and went to get a couple more beers from the fridge.

"Between me working here and her running the shop, it didn't take long before we started slowly drifted apart. Those last few years we hardly saw each other as a matter of fact."

"But what about Emma?" Winston said.

Earl sat back down and handed him another beer. "Well, we were as close as can be when she was a child. When she got to high school, that's when Rebecca and I really started to have troubles. I tried not to let it interfere with Emma, but she was really close with her mother by then, and I suppose they formed a bit of a bond over me not being around. It was only natural that her and I drifted apart too. I became the bad guy in the house. And Emma worked at the diner after school with her mom. I didn't see her much either near the end." He took several large gulps of the beer, downing nearly half of it.

"I'm sorry," Winston said. He didn't know what else to say.

"Don't be. It was all my fault. I didn't know how to have a family. Never learned that I guess. All I knew was how to work. I watched Pop and did what he did. And I was too dumb not to make the same mistakes."

"We finally ended it when Emma was fifteen or so. That's when I moved in here. Emma and her mom lived in the house down the dirt road I told you about. They were there for less than a year before Rebecca died."

There was a long pause where Winston wondered if Earl was going to continue, but he wanted to know the whole story. He wanted to know Emma's story. "How did she die?" He waited for Earl to finish his beer before he started again.

"Doc said it was a brain tumor. She died one morning on the way to the diner. It was Doc who found her that morning in the car. She had been driving, and suddenly she just rolled off the road. The car came to a stop after bumping into a tree. When he looked in the window he said she was sitting there with her eyes closed like nothing even happened. He thought she had fallen asleep at first, but he couldn't wake her up."

"Did you know she had a brain tumor?"

"I heard after she was gone that she had gone in a few times for headaches, even while we were together, but she never mentioned any of that to me. I had no idea. She didn't share much with me at that point, the highs or the lows, not that there were many highs."

"Did you see Emma after that?"

"Once or twice, and at the funeral. When Rebecca died, Emma stopped talking to me all together. She blames me for her death. Says it was our divorce that killed her. And the thing is, I'm not sure she's wrong about that. If I had known about the headaches and pain, maybe I would have made sure she got help. If I had been more of a husband, maybe things would have been different for all of us." Winston could see tears forming in Earl's eyes as he told the story. "The stink of it is, I lost both loves of my life at the same time. Rebecca and Emma."

Buster seemed to sense a change in Earl's voice. He walked over slowly and looked up at Earl, who reached down and rubbed him behind his ears. Winston thought he would keep Earl talking so he didn't break down. "So, Emma lived in the house alone after that?"

"She was only sixteen when her mom died, but I was already living here, and she flat out refused to let me come home. Some thought she was too young to live alone, but folks around here felt too sorry for her to do anything about it. And they knew she had grown up fast and had become an independent woman at an early age, so they figured she could handle herself. Plus, the doc said he would check in on her from time to time for me. He let her work part time for him too, as an extra way to keep an eye on her."

Winston seemed to be thinking of something. "So that's why she doesn't drive either," he said. "Because her mom died in the car."

"Emma was home when they towed that car back to the house. She didn't even want to see it. Told them to put it in the barn out back. She never drove it one time after that day, or even got the front end fixed. She said she didn't need it, that the town was so small. But I know better than that. It reminded her too much of the pain she felt when her mom died. That's why she is always riding that bike of hers. People are funny like that. They hang on to those sorts of things. And they have a way of attaching pain to objects, so they don't have to keep it inside. It's easier to just forget. You see, Emma's pain isn't with her anymore. It sits out in that old barn, gathering dust in the form of a car. I guess that works for her."

"What worked for you?"

Earl twirled the empty beer bottle on the table. "You're looking at it. In the beginning, I turned to the bottle. As if that would bring them back. Yet at the time I treated it as if it were my savior. I think you know a thing or two about that." Winston fidgeted in his seat.

"But it couldn't bring them back. Couldn't help me. And it won't help you." Winston looked down. He knew Earl was right. Then he thought about the date he just had with Emma and relived his own comments. *Do you hate mechanics or something? Or maybe you are afraid of cars…*

"I'm an idiot," he said. "I basically taunted her about driving… and about you. No wonder she stormed out on me. She must think I'm the biggest jerk on the planet."

"I don't think so," Earl replied. "I believe that title is reserved for me." He stood from his chair and tossed the bottle into the trashcan by the door as he passed. "You might be second though," he added as he walked out of the room back into the shop. Behind him Buster trotted out with his tail wagging. Apparently, the conversation was over.

CHAPTER TWENTY-SEVEN
The Foolish Man

When Winston arrived back at his apartment in the city that night, he waved to Carter as he drove away into the night, and he stood on the sidewalk next to the street. He looked around at the countless shadowy buildings that surrounded him, and the faded ones that trailed off in the distance behind them into the foggy night. The weight of the city seemed to press in on him and make him claustrophobic. Dunsport was growing more and more foreign to him, and less like home with each passing day that he spent in Salima Falls.

When he stepped inside his door, the place disgusted him. In fact, his whole existence disgusted him. The place stunk of old beer and stale pizza. He thought about what Earl said about being a slave to the bottle. It wasn't going to save him. It couldn't bring Caroline back. It couldn't find his car. It couldn't find the man with the raging green eyes responsible for this life he was currently leading. And it couldn't right the wrong with Emma and make her forgive him.

He knew what he had to do. He rummaged through the cabinets until he found a box of trash bags, and began filling one with all the empty bottles and old pizza boxes that littered the counters and tables. When he filled one bag, he carried it to the sidewalk by the street and sat it down with a clank of glass bottles, then went back inside to start another. He was focused and his eyes were filled with purpose. He moved around the apartment with speed, driven by this new singular desire. All told, he took five trash bags to the curb that night, filled with all the filth that his apartment held for the last several months. He even opened the fridge and threw away the full bottles of various beer and liquor that dwelled there. He found a washcloth and wiped down the counters and tables and then walked around the apartment, picking up all the dirty clothes he could find.

When the place looked like an apartment again, he sat on the couch and closed his eyes. He replayed Earl's story over and over in his head. He wondered if Earl was back at the shop, holding the photograph of Emma on his lap at his birthday party, rubbing it with his fingers and wishing he could go back in time, like Winston often did with items from his past. He couldn't blame Earl if that was indeed his desire. It was the same wish Winston had since the day Caroline died, to go back in time and right the wrongs, and change things. It is a foolish wish, he knew. He knew that it caused more harm than good, but it was unavoidable to feel that way. It was built into a man, the desire to control things and write his own story, to be the conductor of his life. The wise man knows to focus this preoccupation on the present, which will undoubtedly have bearing on the future. But the foolish man dwells where he has no power, on the past. And because of this, he fails to gain control. Only when the past is let go, can a man fully take ownership of his life's direction.

Winston knew deep inside that he was not in control. He was the foolish man. And he was well aware of that fact.

As he sat there, he wondered what Emma was doing. Was she at home quietly reading a book to slip off into an alternative reality? Was she already asleep, dreaming of being with her mother again? Was she lying in bed, thinking about him? He sat there twirling the ring on his finger. He was starting to feel its weight. He slipped it off his finger and set it on the table next to the couch. He rubbed the spot where it had rested for so long. It felt bare and his finger felt smaller. His thoughts slowly returned to Emma as he faded off to sleep.

CHAPTER TWENTY-EIGHT

The Glimmer of a Stream

The air tasted cleaner when Winston woke early Friday morning. Maybe it was the fact that he had rid the place of filth, or maybe it was something else, but he didn't care or question it. He simply stretched his arms and arched his back. He wasn't sure how he felt about today, and had mixed emotions about it. He couldn't believe it had been a week since he first set foot in Salima Falls. It seemed to go by so fast, but at the same time, it felt as if he had known Earl, Emma, Carter, and Doc forever.

Today was his last day of helping Earl at the shop, and then his commitment to Doc would be fulfilled. All that would be left is to have the stitches in his head removed. He ran his fingers under his hair and over the would-be scar. He had almost forgotten about it. And he hadn't thought about the night at the bar where he received the cut again until now either. The flickering neon light and the dented black BMW flashed in his mind, as did the man in the leather jacket. He could feel a small bubble of anger beginning to rise in his mind. For a split second, he debated giving in to the emotion, but then he walked to the window, opened it, and took a deep breath.

Suddenly, thoughts of Emma entered his mind and replaced those of the man at the bar. His anger went away as quickly as it came, as if the two worlds of Salima Falls and Dunsport could not exist at the same time in his mind. He thought of Emma's beautiful eyes and hair, and felt peace wash over him. Then he remembered the awful things he said to her at lunch. He knew he needed to apologize, but was unsure if she would even talk to him again.

Carter had picked him up and made it all the way to Salima Falls before Winston even realized it. He was lost in his own thoughts. It wasn't until he heard the familiar corn whipping against the sides of the car that he even spoke.

"We're here already?"

"Yes sir," Carter replied as they left the field and drove past the doc's house. "Beautiful day today, yes sir. Beautiful day."

"Sorry I've been so quiet these last couple of days," Winston said. "I guess I've just had some things on my mind."

"Hehe, No worries Mr. Winston. I've got sunshine and blue skies to keep me company. May I ask what it is that has you so concerned on a day like this, Mr. Winston?"

Winston looked out the window as they passed the bakery on the right. People were smiling as they walked out, some holding loaves of bread for the day, some just stopping in for a morning bagel on their way to work. "You ever say something so dumb that you don't even know how to say you're sorry?"

"Ahhhh, said something you shouldn't have huh? Many a man has been bitten by that bug, yes sir!" They passed

Mrs. Powell's Diner on the left and Winston turned his head to look. Winston wondered if Emma was already there. Carter peeked to his left and then looked at Winston in the rear-view mirror as he watched the diner. "Well, the way I see it," he continued. "It's your job to say the words and mean them. It's her job to accept the apology, and remember, forgiving is often the hardest part of all."

"But what if she won't even talk to…" Winston started before cutting off his own sentence. "Wait, her? How did you know I was talking about a girl?"

"Hehe," Carter chuckled. "I imagine nearly every time a man says something wrong and has to apologize, it's likely because he said the wrong thing to a girl. Yes sir."

Winston saw a suspicious twinkle in Carter's eyes in the mirror, but he ignored it. "Well, you are right, but like I said, she'll probably avoid me like the plague. I might never get a chance to talk to her again."

Carter seemed to be thinking hard. "That is a tough one, Mr. Winston. A tough one indeed. But I'd keep my eyes open if I were you," he said as they approached Earl's shop. "Opportunity often pops at just the right time, like the man who sees the glimmer of a stream just before he gives up hope and dies from thirst." He smiled at Winston in the mirror and pulled to a stop outside the shop. Winston waved goodbye and headed in to find Earl.

CHAPTER TWENTY-NINE
A House for Buster

It was bittersweet for Winston, standing in front of Earl's shop, knowing this was the last day he was required to be here. This place, in only a week, had started to feel more like his home than that dingy apartment back in Dunsport. The hard work and the sweat and the sunshine had become something he looked forward to. In the city, all he had was darkness, but here he had a purpose, and a reason for getting up in the morning. He had a place to be, a job to do, and a dog with a wagging tail to play with. It all kept his mind off things, and in the back of his thoughts, he knew that after this week was over, he would likely fall back into the darkness of the city life, and the darkness of his pain.

Buster was jumping at his feet before the dust had even settled from Carter's departure. He came running as soon as he heard the car door shut.

"Hey Buster! How have you been buddy?" Buster ran in circles around his feet. "Let's go find old Earl, what do you say?" Just as the words left his mouth Earl stepped out from around the corner of the building. He was already sweating and dirty.

"Not even eight o'clock in the morning and I'm already getting called old. I know how old I am dammit, I don't need your reminders."

Winston looked over at him and smiled. "Now don't get all upset just cause today is my last day. I might think you are going to miss me or something." Winston walked over to him, followed closely by Buster.

"Your last day huh," Earl tried his best to look as if he were unaware. "Oh yeah, that's right. Well, it's about time if you ask me. I haven't had a peaceful day in a week!" Winston could see through his machismo, and knew Earl welcomed the company and would indeed miss him when he was gone. He could see it the first time Buster licked his face. He didn't have anyone close to him anymore. He was lonely.

"Well I wanted to ask you something, now that I think about it," Winston said.

"What's that?" asked Earl.

"Well…" Winston looked down at Buster, who was sitting at Earl's feet. "I was wondering if you could look after Buster here for me, until I figure some things out." Buster cocked his head and looked questioningly up at Winston when he heard his name. "Just for a couple of weeks or so."

Earl knelt down beside Buster. "What do you say little guy, you gonna be alright here with 'Old Earl'?" He rubbed Buster behind the ears. "Yeah, I think he'll be fine here for a bit. Though he better not tear anything up or I'll send Carter to bring you here and clean it up!" Winston smiled. He detected another example of false bravado. He could tell Earl would be happy to have a companion for a while.

Winston knelt down next to Buster too. "You be good, you hear me buddy? I don't want to find out you got into something you shouldn't have." Buster was very excited to have so much attention this morning. He spun in circles as they stood. "So, Earl, what's on the agenda for us today?"

Earl raised his eyebrows. "Well, we don't have any appointments today, and I've already buffed out Mrs. Davies' bumper. Got up early. All we have left is an oil change on that pickup out front." Earl stood there in thought for a second. He looked down at Buster who was smiling up at him, then took a quick step towards the front door to the shop. "Follow me," he said. "I have an idea."

Winston smiled. He liked the pep he was seeing in Earl's steps. "You're the boss," he said, as he followed after him. When they got inside, Earl quickly cleared the table and rustled through some piles of paperwork and boxes. He emerged with a tablet of paper in one hand and a black marker in the other.

"Alright," he said as he flipped to an empty page. "You remember that large pile of scrap wood out back? Next to the tires?"

Winston's enthusiasm drained immediately. Is he serious? "Don't tell me you want that sorted too! I suppose by size and species this time?"

"Now don't get your britches in a bunch," Earl boomed. "Or I just might change my mind." He started drawing on the paper as Winston watched. "Especially after you did such a good job on those tires." Winston watched the lines form what appeared to him to be a house. "No," Earl continued. "I was thinking today we might take it easy and build a house for Buster here, now that he is going to stay for a while. And when you come pick him up in a couple of weeks, you can take it with you." Earl looked down at Buster, who was watching their every move. "What do you say little guy, would you like us to build you your own little house?" Buster wagged his tail in approval.

Winston changed his attitude immediately. "I think that's a great idea!" He looked closer at Earl's drawing and pointed to the front. "What's this for?"

Earl looked at him like he was crazy. "A front porch you dummy! Every house should have a nice front porch! It makes it feel like home. We could get some food and water bowls and make a little spot for them there. And the roof could extend out over the porch too to protect them from falling leaves and rain and stuff."

"Ok, I get it," Winston said. "I think it's a nice touch."

After about ten to fifteen minutes of back and forth on the design, they agreed, and stood back to admire their design. Earl picked Buster up and held him. "What do you think?" Buster cocked his head sideways but offered no other feedback.

"I think he digs it," Winston said.

"Digs it?" Earl looked at Winston as if he were speaking Russian.

"It means he likes… nevermind. Anyway, so how do we get started on this?"

"Think you can handle the oil change on your own?"

Winston looked at Earl curiously. Earl had never trusted him with an auto job on his own, aside from washing. Even if this was as basic as they come, he still felt a bit of pride. "I think so. Just a basic plug pull, right? No cover? We doing a filter too?"

Earl looked at him and nodded. Winston thought for just a second that he saw a hint of pride in Earl's eyes as well. "Yep, just a basic one. You can go ahead and do the filter too. This one takes eight quarts, don't forget. Shouldn't take you but maybe thirty or forty minutes. In the meantime, I'll gather up my chop saw, tape measure, and some tools and see if I can't find some decent wood out of that pile. Just meet me out back when you're done, ok?"

"Sure thing." Winston felt as if he had just graduated. He watched Buster follow Earl out back and then grabbed the toolbox and headed out to the truck in the front.

Exactly thirty minutes later, Winston shut the hood on the pickup truck with a smile on his face. His first oil change and filter replacement went as smooth as silk, and he was even impressed with himself for a change. By the time he got out back, Earl had already gathered a small pile of the best pieces of wood from the pile, and was measuring a piece for cutting. Winston looked at the drawing of the house. There were now dimensions added to the doghouse and random notes around the edges.

"How did it go with the truck," Earl asked, as he drew a pencil line on a board.

"All done. No problems at all." Winston was beaming when Earl looked up at him. Earl simply nodded his head as if this was what he expected.

The next three hours were a whirlwind of sawing, drilling, and hammering. It was the kind of work Winston had grown to love in a short period of time. The smells of sawdust and summer filled his nostrils, and thoughts of Emma occupied his mind as he worked. What will I say to her? How will I find her? I could try the diner and the animal shelter first. If she's not there, where do I look next? Should I ask Earl for directions to her house? I doubt he would agree to that. Maybe Carter or the doc could help me. Or maybe I should just forget about her, she probably won't ever forgive me…

The doghouse was nearly complete before they had taken their first break. It was fun work for a change, and they both reveled in the chance to get their hands on something other than a greasy car. When the last of the roof slats were added, the sun was beating down on them from high in the sky.

"What do you say Winston, time for a drink?"

Winston wiped the sweat from his forehead with his arm. "Sounds great to me," he said. He sat down the hammer next to the box of nails and took a long look at the now built doghouse. "I think we outdid ourselves this time Earl." Buster ran up onto the little wooded porch and peered inside. His tail was wagging back at them. "And Buster seems to approve as well."

Earl nodded his head in agreement. "A coat of paint and something soft to lay on and she'll be good to go. Now lets get out of the sun for a while."

Back inside, Earl grabbed two cold sodas from the fridge and handed one to Winston.

"You know Earl, I had a good time out there today."

Earl simply nodded and popped the tab on his soda. He walked to the fridge to look for something to eat, as Winston sat there with a smile on his face. He grabbed the jelly from the door of the fridge, and then pulled bread and peanut butter from the cabinet next to it. "You want something to eat?" Winston didn't answer. Earl turned to look at him. "Hey!"

"Oh sorry." Winston gave his head a quick shake. "I was daydreaming there for a second. Anyway, what were you s..."

Winston cut off his sentence when he noticed a shiny glare hit him in the eye from outside the window. He squinted his eye and held his hand up to block it. When it went away he walked to the window to see the source.

Rounding the corner of the street was Emma, pushing her bicycle and walking beside it. The glare of the sun was reflecting off the bicycle through the window. It hit him in the eye once again. Winston smiled and leaned into the glass for a better view. Carter's words from earlier came flashing back to him. The man who sees the glimmer…

"Sorry, Earl, I have to run. I'll catch you later, ok?" Winston headed for the door.

"Wait, where are you going?"

Winston was out the door in a flash, but his words made it back to Earl. "Be back soon!"

Earl walked to the window, just in time to see Winston running across the lot to the road, trying to flag down Emma as she walked.

CHAPTER THIRTY

Spirits Lifted

"Emma!" Winston shouted her name across the entrance to the auto shop, as he jogged out to the road. She either didn't hear him or was pretending not to. He wasn't sure, so when he got to the road he shouted again. "Emma!" She turned her head towards him this time, acknowledging him, then turned back on her way, never stopping her pace. She was only about twenty feet away, rounding the corner towards town. He was confused by the look on her face. She didn't look upset with him, only shy. She looked down at the ground as she walked.

When he finally caught up to her, he lowered his voice and touched her shoulder. "Emma." She pulled away from his touch and kept walking. "Look, I just… wanted to say… I'm sorry." He walked after her, slightly behind. The bike served as a barrier between them. "I… I didn't know what I was saying. I totally get it if you don't want to talk to me, but can you just listen at least?" He stopped walking but she kept going. I knew it. I blew it for good.

When she was five or six feet away, he said her name once more, this time in a sheepish, apologetic, yet helpless tone. "Emma." She sensed genuine sadness in his voice, and stopped.

He stepped up to her again. "I swear I didn't mean to upset you the other day." She looked into his eyes and could tell he really meant it.

"I shouldn't have gotten so upset. It's all my fault."

"No, Emma, it's all my fault. At the restaurant, I didn't understand what I said, but now I know. I was an idiot. You were right to leave. I wasn't even sure I'd even get a chance to say I'm sorry. I didn't know if I'd see you again. I'm so glad I saw you walking by." He put his hands on the bike's seat to help steady it for her, and looked down to inspect it. "Speaking of that, I wondered why you were walking your bike into town instead of riding it, but now I see. Got yourself a flat tire. How did that happen?"

"I don't know," she said softly. "I didn't see anything in the road, but it just popped, and I nearly fell off."

"That's weird." Winston had an odd and puzzled look on his face. He looked down the road in both directions like he was looking for someone. More of Carter's words flashed in his mind. *Opportunity often pops at just the right time...* "Really weird actually."

"What's so weird?" Emma asked.

"Just something Carter told me. Almost like he knew we would meet like this today." Emma looked at him with that same puzzled look Winston just had. He wished he hadn't said that. "Just a coincidence probably. Anyway, if you want, we can air up your tire back at the shop really quickly." He could see immediately that Emma didn't want to go any closer to Earl or his shop than she had to.

"That's ok," she said nervously. Her eyes darted around and towards town. "I think I'll just stop by the hardware store and get a new tube. It's on the way, and I don't mind walking. Thank you though."

"Well then let me walk you into town at least?"

"Sure, ok."

Winston gently pulled the bike from her. "Let me take this, I can push it, you just enjoy the walk." The look in her eye showed she appreciated the gesture, and they slowly started their walk into town, as Earl watched from behind the shop window. Neither knew he was watching, or could see him, but if they could have, they would have seen a slight smile form at the corner of his mouth before he turned away to finish up the paint job on the doghouse.

For twenty or thirty seconds, they just walked next to each other without saying a word. They were both enjoying the sun and the smells in the air. Winston eventually looked over at her. "I know our first date didn't go so well, but I really want to make it up to you. I'd like to take you to dinner or something. Do you know any good places to eat? Other than the diner, of course."

She hesitated in answering. "I… I'm not sure about another date," she said. "I don't really…"

Winston prepared for another rejection, and his heart began to break a little more. He cut her off. "I'm sorry, forget it. I shouldn't have asked. I should have known I blew it already."

"I wasn't going to say that," she said. "I was going to say… I don't really like going out on dates in front of a bunch of people, especially with all the eyes in this town. Everyone knows me here, and they will all start to talk if they see me out."

His spirits lifted again. "Oh, well we don't have to go out. That's fine with me. I don't really care what we do. I just want to hang out with you. It's the company that matters, not the location." She blushed when she heard his words. "In fact," he continued. "Maybe we can eat in. I'm not a great cook or anything, but I used to enjoy it." An image of him and Caroline cooking dinner together in their old house flashed in his mind like lightning. She was wearing a yellow kitchen apron and dancing to the song on the radio. With this image in his mind, his foot slipped off the side of the road where it was uneven, and he nearly fell down and dropped the bike on top of him.

"Are you ok?" Emma seemed concerned.

"Yeah, I'm fine. My foot just slipped a little. I'm… sorry… what was I saying again?"

"You said we could cook dinner together instead of going out, which I think is a wonderful idea. You could come over to my house tonight if you want. I get off at seven."

"Yeah, I'd like that," Winston said. "I know you live back that way, but that's as far as I know." He pointed in the direction of Earl's shop behind them.

Emma smiled at him. He was finally certain she had accepted his apology. "Just turn left at the dirt road at the top of the hill. You'll go down about a mile and a half. There's a white house on the left with a front porch swing. I like to sit out there and have my coffee in the morning on weekends and smell the juniper trees. And you can't miss the giant poplar out front. There's an old tire swing hanging from it."

"Sounds like a great place," Winston added. "I can't wait."

After about twenty minutes of idle chat about what they would cook, and what ingredients Emma had and which ones she needed to get at Greta's on her way home, they arrived at

the hardware store. It was directly across from the diner.
Winston remembered the old wagon wheel from the first time
he walked by. It seemed like ages ago. Time had a way of
passing slowly in Salima Falls, and he liked it.

In no time at all, they had a new tube inserted in the tire
and aired up, courtesy of Mr. Burgess, who had run the
hardware store as long as Emma could remember. After an
excited goodbye, Emma walked across the street and Winston
started the long walk back to Earl's shop. It would be well past
noon when he got back, but with the extra pep in his step from
the successful apology, he hardly noticed the walk at all.

Earl could tell by the look on his face when he returned
that things had gone well. He proudly showed Winston the
painted doghouse, which was the same colors as the body shop,
since Earl had used old paint that he found lying around.
Winston agreed that they did a spectacular job building it, and
that Buster would indeed love it. A little later Winston
explained his evening plans, and Earl graciously let Winston
shower and clean up. He gave him an extra toothbrush to use,
and some much-needed clean clothes to wear. The rest of the
evening was an anxious wait for seven o'clock, as they sat
around having a coke and trying to talk about anything except
Emma or the fact that it was Winston's last day here. Winston
and Earl were well versed in the idea of not facing things, so it
was hardly awkward.

Just before seven o'clock arrived, Winston went and
fetched the bicycle he had painstakingly restored. Buster
followed him around, sensing that he was going somewhere.
Earl found an old bottle of wine that was gathering dust and
wiped the glass clean. He walked out to meet Winston before
he left and placed it in the basket on the bike.

"Thanks," Winston said as he looked down at the old
bottle skeptically.

Earl reached his hand out to Winston. "In case I don't see you for a while," he said. "Keep your head on straight."

Winston shook his hand. "Just take care of Buster while I'm gone."

Buster and Earl stood and watched, as Winston disappeared down the long dirt road that led to the old farmhouse where Earl used to live. Once out of sight, Earl turned to head back inside. "Come on Buster, let's get you some food. Your first meal in your new house." Buster followed happily, with his tail wagging from side to side.

CHAPTER THIRTY-ONE

Cascading Electricity

Winston pedaled the bike down the dirt road towards Emma's house. His mind was filled with emotions. He was mostly excited about seeing Emma and spending time alone with her, but this emotion brought with it a small amount of guilt. Salima Falls had a way of making him nearly forget about Caroline and his life in the city. But he never entirely forgot. And whenever his heart leapt for Emma, it also cried a little for Caroline.

He was also nervous, and his heart was racing faster than the bike. He had screwed up the first time so badly, that he didn't expect another chance with Emma. Yet here he was. He couldn't quite pinpoint what it was about her that drew him in so completely, but it was there, whatever it was.

As he approached the house, he recognized the front porch and tire swing hanging from the tree in the front yard. It was exactly how he pictured it when she described it to him. Except now he could see the barn out back that housed her mom's rotting car. She hadn't mentioned it when she described the place. He figured she had tried so hard to forget about that car and that barn, that she hardly even remembered its existence anymore.

He rode down the driveway and came to a stop near the tire swing. He got off the bike and leaned it up against the tree, before grabbing the bottle of wine and walking up the front porch steps. On the porch were two wooden rocking chairs to the left, and a hanging swing to the right, which overlooked the field beside the property. A slight breeze brought smells of harvested corn and juniper trees across the field to him. It was warm outside, and he took a few deep breaths to calm his nerves.

When he stepped up to the door, he saw his reflection, and hoped he didn't look too ridiculous in the clothes Earl had given him earlier. He could hear music playing inside. He patted down a spot of hair that was sticking up from the ride on the bike, and knocked gently on the door. A frenzy of barking inside immediately drowned out the sound of the music, and when Emma opened the door, a large golden retriever and a chocolate brown mastiff greeted him with enthusiasm and overall panic.

"Down Charlie!" She tried to pull the mastiff away with a struggle. "Harley! Go lay down!" On command, the golden retriever walked slowly into the house, but the mastiff was less obedient. Emma smacked Charlie on the rear. He immediately pulled away, but still looked at Winston with excitement. Emma pointed her finger at him and he lowered his ears. "Bad Dog!" she said. He walked inside to join Harley in the other room. "I'm sorry," she said. "They aren't used to company. No one but me is ever here." Somehow Winston wasn't surprised.

He stepped inside and shut the door behind him. The door led straight into the main living space, which was quite open, despite the age of the home. He could see a fireplace to his right, unlit since the last time the weather was cold, and surrounded by a comfortable looking couch and sofa. The built-in bookshelves all around were filled with books. To his left was the kitchen, separated from the living room by a large island, which had two bags of fresh groceries on it.

"Don't worry about the dogs," Winston said. "They didn't bother me. I'm sure they could probably smell Buster on me anyways."

"Oh yeah, I was meaning to ask you about Buster the next time I saw you!" So, she planned on seeing me again, Winston thought and smiled. "How is he doing? Does he like his new home?"

"Actually," Winston said. "Buster is going to be staying at the shop with Earl, until I figure out some things in the city." He could see the reaction on her face when she heard Earl's name, and silently hoped she wouldn't react the same way she did at lunch the other day.

"Oh" is all she said, in a nonchalant sort of way.

"He seems to really have taken to Earl. In fact, I think he sort of thinks he is Earl's dog at this point." Emma didn't really react, so he continued. "We built him a really nice doghouse today before I saw you walking your bike. You should see it. There's even a little porch on the front, just like you have here." Winston now realized why Earl made such a big deal about the front porch. Every house should have a nice front porch… makes it feel like home. He missed this place. Or at least he missed his life when he was here.

"Yeah, that sounds really nice." There was little sincerity in Emma's voice, and Winston could tell she wanted to change the subject. "Want me to take that?" She held her hand out and he gave her the bottle of wine. "Thanks for bringing this. I haven't had wine in ages. I don't drink much." She walked towards the kitchen and he remembered how she felt about alcohol. For a moment, Winston wondered if bringing it was a good idea, until she looked at the label and spoke again. "I've had this kind before somewhere. I'm not sure where, but I remember really liking it. Good choice."

"No problem. How about a quick tour of the place? I'd like to see more. So far your house seems to be cozy and lovely."

"Thanks, I'm glad you like it. I guess I can show you around. Follow me." She proceeded to lead him through the entire first floor, recapping the living room and kitchen, as well as the dining room, the office, the bathroom, and her bedroom (which she only allowed him to quickly glance into).

Walking around, with the dogs following them from room to room, he couldn't help but picture her living there with Earl and her mother, and what it must have been like. He pictured Earl sitting in the recliner or tending to the fire in the winter months, and Emma reading a book on the couch as her mother cooked in the kitchen.

In the hallway, she passed over one door rather quickly, only saying it was another bedroom upstairs that she doesn't ever use anymore and that it's not worth seeing. Winston guessed that it was her parents' room at one time, and that it hadn't changed since her mother died. He also guessed that she still slept in the same room she grew up in as a child.

Eventually, they made it to the kitchen, and he looked out the window. "What's in that old barn out there?"

"Oh nothing," Emma said sheepishly. "Just a bunch of old junk." Winston looked again and pictured her mom's car gathering dust just behind the wooden doors.

He pulled out all the fresh groceries from the bags. "I can hardly wait," Winston said. "Asiago chicken pasta with a caper cream sauce and sun dried tomatoes! It just sounds delicious!"

"I've only made it once, so I hope you like it," Emma said. "Can you start cutting the chicken and I'll go grab my apron?"

"Sure."

"The knives are in the top drawer in the middle."

Winston found a knife and began slicing the chicken, as the dogs watched him carefully for any piece that might fall to the floor. When Emma returned, she was wearing a bright yellow apron. Winston looked up. He was shocked to see Caroline walking towards him. She seemed to be walking in slow motion towards him, as they looked deep into each other's eyes. He looked around, and noticed he was back in his old house, in his own kitchen. He and Caroline were about to cook their first meal together.

"Ouch!" Winston yelped, as he nicked his finger with the knife.

"Are you ok?" Emma said, as she ran over to him.

Winston snapped out of it when he heard her voice. "Yeah, I'm… I'm sorry. It's not that bad. I'll be fine. I just must have dozed off for a second there." Winston knew his mind was fighting for Caroline. He was reminded more and more about her and his search for the other driver, and the constant tugging at his thoughts was becoming a problem. But at the same time, he wanted to believe Emma was more to him than a distraction. I want to be here with her. She is more than that. Yet his heart was still Caroline's. I'm sorry Caroline. I haven't forgotten about you. He felt the wrenching in his heart. He knew there was no room for Emma there while it was still holding on to Caroline. It was as if his heart was a balloon and he was overfilling it with air, but he didn't know how to stop it. Sooner or later he knew it would burst. He rubbed his finger where the ring used to be, and unwelcomed questions entered his mind. What if Caroline was watching me now? Should I be in the city searching, instead of here with Emma?

"Come over here," Emma said as she eased him over to the sink. Emma's grace and beauty overpowered the vision of Caroline, and the sound of her voice made the questions in his mind disappear. Emma held his hand under the water and rinsed the blood off. Then she grabbed a paper towel and pressed it on the small cut. "Hold this tight, I'll be right back." Her voice was sweet and warm. She ran to the bathroom and grabbed a bandage from the medicine cabinet. When she returned, she removed the paper towel and gently placed the bandage on his finger. "I'm sorry if this hurts." He watched her tend to him with care, and felt her touch. It was soft and gentle, and as she leaned in to him, he could smell the wonderful scent of her skin and her hair. In that moment, Winston thought of only Emma. He wanted more than anything in the world to pull her close, but he couldn't. What if she pulls away? I can't chance it.

They finished preparing the meal without another incident or injury. The conversation was small, but the electricity Winston felt flying between them was not. There was a struggle going on inside both of them tonight, and battles raged on between the emotions that filled them. Winston had his past with Caroline, his present with Emma, and the entirety of his falling-apart life swirling around in his head. Emma had her struggle to allow someone in, her desire to be close with someone, her abandonment issues, and her closed off emotions. Several times they made lengthy eye contact during dinner, which always led to smiles on both ends. It was as if they knew they needed each other, yet were both unwilling to let go and let it happen.

After dinner, Winston helped her clean the table and put away the unused groceries. They stood at the sink and cleaned the dishes together, and when the last dish was done, they both sifted through the soapy water for more, and their hands met underwater. After a slight pull back, Winston slid his fingers on top of hers and caressed her silky skin. Time paused, and she looked at him with big innocent eyes filled with both fear and desire. He could see the struggle within her, debating whether to push him away or let him pull her closer.

"How's your finger?" she said nervously, to break the tension, and let go of his hand.

He pulled his hand out of the water and grabbed a dry dishtowel for them to dry their hands. "I think I'll live," he said with a little laugh that made her smile.

They locked eyes for several seconds, motionless, and he felt as if he was falling into them. They were as deep as the oceans. He could feel the tension between them. It pulled them closer like an unstoppable magnet. When they were only an inch apart, she pulled away.

"I'm sorry," she said.

"What's wrong?"

"I'm just… not used to this. I don't really date… or have people over for dinner. I've never…"

"It's ok." Winston cut her off. "I understand."

"Thank you." She looked at him nervously. He could tell she was insecure and scared, but also that she wished she wasn't. She wanted to be close to him too. She just didn't know how. He looked into her eyes again.

"Emma," he said. "You have the most beautiful eyes."

His words seemed to ease her nerves. She touched his hand again. Before long, they were drawing closer and closer again. Emma's eyes never left Winston's. They paused again when they were only an inch apart, hovering for a few seconds. Winston closed his eyes, and was surprised when Emma's lips rushed forward to meet his. She closed her eyes and pressed against him with force. Winston didn't know it, but it was her first kiss, and it sent a rush of cascading electricity all down her body. Winston was lost in another world, a dream reality, a version of life that he knew he didn't deserve. How could I be here? How could this be happening after all I've been through?

When Winston opened his eyes slowly, once again he saw Caroline. Her face was young and vibrant, and she smiled at him. Every curve of her face was just as he remembered on the night he proposed. He looked down and saw the sand under his feet and felt the ring in his pocket. Her hair billowed in the breeze. Then suddenly he was back in his car again. Caroline was once again standing on the side of the road with a white dress on. He saw the black car heading towards her. He wanted to shout at her to move, to save herself. He knew he was helpless.

Winston stumbled backwards against the fridge behind him with a clank. The jolt cleared the fog from his mind and the daydream from his eyes. He shook his head and blinked. Then he saw the look of shock on Emma's face.

"What was that all about?" she said. Her eyes were wide.

"I'm sorry, I must have slipped again." He reached for her but this time she backed away slightly.

"I don't know what's going on with you," she said. "But I get the feeling you are somewhere else in your head."

He stepped towards her and put his hand on her arm. She reluctantly let him. "Emma, I haven't felt like this in a really long time. I guess I don't know what I'm doing anymore. Sometimes I feel like I'm in a dream when I'm with you." He let go and looked at the floor. "I'm sorry if I keep messing it up. Please forgive me."

She stood there for a second and watched him. She could tell he wasn't' lying. She felt the same way sometimes. "It's fine," she said. "It's been a long time for me too. I get it, actually."

"Thanks," he said. "Can we just go have a drink and talk for a while?"

She nodded and grabbed the bottle of wine and two glasses from a cabinet. "Grab the corkscrew from the top drawer, would you?"

He took a deep breath and felt relieved.

They filled the glasses with the deep red wine and sat on the couch. The dogs followed and curled up on the floor. Winston stared at Emma almost continuously, and marveled at how beautiful she was. He couldn't take his eyes off her. They both sort of reset their emotions, and began chatting about her job at the animal clinic, the diner, her daily routine, and other items of small talk until the bottle of wine was three quarters of the way empty. They felt at ease again.

He told her about today being his last day at the shop, and that his deal with Doc would be done. "I get my stitches out tomorrow I think. I'm not sure when." She asked what his plans were now that he didn't have to come to Salima Falls anymore, but he struggled to answer her. "To be honest, I have no idea. I'm just going to figure it out as it comes, I guess." Part of him wanted a second chance at kissing her, but he couldn't stop thinking about his talk with Earl. He wanted to talk to her about everything he knew, but feared her reaction. He knew he couldn't hold it in forever.

"Emma, I have to tell you something." Winston's tone changed and he sounded more serious. He put his wine glass on the table. She looked scared at what was to come next. "I found out some things," he continued. "And I thought I should tell you so it's not weird."

"What kind of things?"

"Well," he began slowly. "For instance, I know about your mom's accident."

"Who told you that?"

"Earl did. I just wanted to say that I'm sorry about all that, and if you…"

"My life is none of his business!" she interjected, cutting him off. It was the loudest he ever heard her speak. "He has no right to tell you anything about me."

Winston reached into his shirt pocket. He pulled out the picture he found of her on Earl's lap at the birthday party, and handed it to her. He had swiped it when he was changing in Earl's room after his shower.

"Where did you get this?"

"After our lunch the other day, when I said those awful things to you and you left, I went back to Earl's shop, and Buster sort of knocked over some papers, and there it was. I had no idea up until then that he was your dad, but now I know why everything I said was so stupid. Earl told me the whole story, and I don't want to pretend I don't know anymore."

She stared at the picture and a tear formed in her eye. Winston wasn't quite sure what the look on her face meant. It seemed to contain all sort of emotions, from anger to sadness to reminiscence.

"I know you two don't talk anymore, and I know he blames himself."

Emma got a look in her eye that Winston had never seen before. "Well good, serves him right!"

"He's your dad," Winston said, with a hint of judgment in his voice.

"Not anymore, I don't have a dad! I don't need him!"

"I'm sorry," he said. "I didn't want to upset you. I just thought maybe we could talk about it."

"No," she said immediately, without looking up. "I don't want to talk about him or any of it. Is that why you came over here? Did he ask you to?" Emma stood up from the couch. "If so, then you can leave."

"Emma, of course that's not why I came! I wanted to see you. I wanted to get to know you."

"Well it sounds like you know just about everything, don't you?" She walked towards the kitchen and sat her glass on the counter a bit too hard and it shattered. The dogs stood and ran to her. They could tell she was upset, as she mumbled to herself. "This is why I keep to myself. This is why I'm better off alone."

"Look," Winston said. "I just wanted to be honest with you."

"Honest?" Emma glared at him. "You think you're being honest?" She walked towards him. "You are always thinking about something or someone else. You freaked out twice tonight, about cut your finger off, and then nearly fell when we kissed."

"I'm sorry," Winston said. "I don't know what you want me to tell you."

She came up to him and grabbed his left hand. "How about this!" She grabbed his hand and lifted his ring finger up to his face. "Have you been honest about that? Have you told me about that? You are keeping something from me too. The first day I saw you at Doc's house you were wearing a wedding ring. Then a few days later you weren't. You still have the tan lines and indentations. It must have been on recently, and yet you've never even mentioned her to me."

Winston pulled his hand away and looked down at his finger. He rubbed the spot where the ring left a mark. "I can explain…"

"Don't," she said quickly and forcefully. "I want to be alone, so please just leave."

"But Emma…"

"Just go."

He looked her in the eye and he knew he blew it again. He knew it was lost for good this time. There would be no other chance. He exhaled deeply and lowered his head as he walked to the door. The dogs watched curiously from behind Emma. Winston paused when his hand touched the handle. He wanted to turn around, but he didn't. He knew there was nothing he could do. He simply opened the door and walked down the steps to the bike, which was still leaning against the tree. He heard the door shut behind him. The sky was dark and the night air was crisp on his face as he pedaled away.

Emma sat on the couch and noticed the picture Winston handed her earlier was face down on the floor. In his quick exit, it had fallen. She picked it up and laid on her side on the couch. Harley and Charlie curled up on the floor next to her. She stared at the image for a long time, and as Winston pulled into Earl's shop, a tear fell from her eyes and ran down her cheek.

CHAPTER THIRTY-TWO

A Wall of Corn

As Winston neared the parking lot of Earl's shop, he saw Carter's cab idling near the entrance with the lights on. It was late and the night sky was completely dark. He just realized Carter didn't know he was going to Emma's tonight. He leaned the bike up against the shop wall and slowly plodded over to the driver door, where Carter had the window open.

"Well, well," Carter said with a chuckle. "Don't you have a face like a wet weekend!"

Winston raised his head. He had never heard that phrase before but was in no mood to question it. "I'm sorry I didn't tell you I'd be late today. I hope you didn't wait here for me this whole time."

"Oh, of course not," Carter said. "I was just heading back from an errand when I happen to catch a glimpse of you heading up the road on that bike. Thought I'd see if you needed a ride, since I'm headed back to the city. Guess our timing worked out after all." Carter flashed his usual smile.

"I guess so." Winston looked skeptical, especially after all coincidental things Carter had said earlier. Carter only smiled at Winston, who just now realized he hadn't yet thought about what he would do when he left Emma's tonight. He looked back at the shop and didn't like the prospect of waking Earl to ask if he could spend the night on the couch. His own bed sounded much nicer. "I guess I got lucky."

"Now hop in," Carter said. "And tell me why you look like you just got a fly in your soup." Winston heard Carter chuckle again as he walked around the car and opened the front passenger door.

As they were driving back, Winston told Carter about his date with Emma tonight, and how disastrous it was. He gave him a quick rundown of what happened, although in the back of his mind he felt like Carter already knew somehow. He didn't mention the visions of Caroline. He just kept saying he drifted off and was thinking about something else.

"Sounds like you have a transmission problem," Carter said, when he finally spoke. Winston shot him a baffling look. "Yes sir, a transmission problem."

"I don't understand," Winston said.

"Hehe," Carter chuckled again. "Well, from the sound of things, you're having trouble going forward. Yep, you've either been driving in reverse for too long, or you are stuck in neutral. Maybe your gears are broken and you need a push. Or maybe you just need to clean the windshield off so you can see what's ahead instead of what's behind."

Strangely, this actually made sense to Winston, and once again he was amazed at the way Carter's advice always seemed prevalent. Does he know about Caroline? "I see what you are getting at," he said. "Somehow."

He stared out the window for a long time thinking about what Carter said. He knew he was right, but no matter what he tried, he couldn't forget what happened to Caroline. The anger he held inside for the other driver wasn't going away. The rest of the ride back to his apartment was quiet. When Carter pulled up to the sidewalk, Winston thanked him for the ride and got out. He slowly walked up the steps to his apartment, and when he got to the building, he noticed the glow of a light on in his apartment. He stopped and heard faded voices somewhere inside. Gently, he turned the door handle and pushed open the door a fraction of an inch. The glow from the television cast a blue hue on the walls, and the sound echoed around the room. Guess I left it on… He opened the door and was shocked to see someone sitting on his couch.

The door creaked, and the person turned and looked at Winston.

"Oh shit," Winston said when he saw Marlow's face looking back at him. "What are you doing here this late? Scared me half to death."

"You should lock your door, and I should ask you the same thing," Marlow said.

"Can't lock the door," Winston replied. "Only house key was with my car keys that got stolen. And what do you mean you should ask me the same thing? I can come back whenever I want."

"What do I mean?" Marlow got up from the couch and walked over to Winston. "I don't believe this. You have no idea, do you?"

"No idea about what?"

"You made me look like a fool today, that's what!" Marlow wasn't even blinking. He was just staring at Winston with fury in his eyes. "You blew off the meeting I set up with my boss!"

Winston suddenly remembered, and the look on his face broadcasted it. He shook his head. "Oh man, I'm sorry. I didn't realize today was the day, I swear."

"Friday? Five o'clock? My office? Any of that ring a bell?" Marlow began pacing. "You know, I stick my neck out for you and this is how you repay me?"

"I'm sorry man, I had something to do, and it slipped my mind."

"I hadn't heard from you, so I figured you got another ride or something. So, I sat there with my boss, waiting and waiting, like a fool. After I vouched for you! I told him you just needed a chance, and you wouldn't let him down, even if I was starting to not believe it myself!"

Winston opened his mouth to retort, but Marlow wasn't in the mood for excuses. "And don't stand there and tell me you had something to do. Like I'm an idiot or something. I know exactly what you were out doing. You were chasing ghosts again, and I'm sick of it! I thought when I got here and saw you had cleaned up the place, that you were making progress. But I was wrong!" He shook his head back and forth and lowered his voice. "Look man, I'm done trying to help you move on with your life. This was the last time."

"Hey, I wasn't out looking for the car," Winston said. "I swear! I was in…" He hesitated because he knew Marlow didn't want to hear what he was about to say. "…Salima Falls."

Marlow shot bullets at him with his eyes when he heard those words again. "Oh my god, not again! You are legitimately losing it."

"I'm not, I swear," Winston pleaded.

Marlow looked up at the ceiling in disbelief, and began talking to himself. "I'm going to have to commit my best friend, I can't believe it." He focused back on Winston. "Let me guess, the magical cab picked you up and took you to the mystery town again? Well, guess what, I did some research. I found nothing on Salima Falls or this doctor or this cab company. None of it is real." He stared hard at Winston, waiting for a better explanation, but Winston only stared back at him. "This is ridiculous! I'm trying to be your friend, man!"

"I'm not lying, Marlow. I swear."

Marlow stepped closer to Winston and lowered his voice. "That's the thing, Winston." He spoke calmly and coldly. "I don't think you are lying to me anymore. I think you actually believe the nonsense that comes out of your mouth. You live in a fantasy world. You don't even understand where you're at half the time, or what you're doing anymore… and it wouldn't be the first time, either." He turned his back on Winston and walked to the door. "I'm out of here." He opened the door.

"Wait," Winston shouted. Marlow stopped in his tracks. "I'll take you there."

Marlow held the door open, motionless for a few seconds, before turning back to Winston.

"You'll take me to Salima Falls?" He sounded as if he were calling Winston's bluff, and he had a calculating look in his eye. Winston just nodded. "Okay then, let's go." The look on Marlow's face told Winston that he still didn't believe Salima Falls was real. He was only going to prove his point, and prove Winston wrong.

Of course it's real. I've spent a week there! Earl's shop… Carter's cab… Emma… Buster... I'm not crazy. I'll show him.

Winston walked to the door and followed Marlow to his car.

"I'll drive, you give the directions," Marlow said.

"No problem," Winston replied. I've been watching the turns. I can get there on my own now. I'll recognize the roads when I see them. I know it.

They wound their way through the city and eventually out of it, until the buildings were lost in the night behind them. Winston called out the lefts and the rights along the way, through field after field, on one small road after another. I'm on the right track so far. I know it. Almost there.

"We are getting closer," he told Marlow. "Just a few more turns."

Marlow looked out the window in the night. He saw nothing that would lead him to believe there was a town nearby. "We are in the middle of nowhere man. We've been driving for forty minutes already. There's nothing out here."

"It's closer than you think," Winston said. "There are no signs or anything, you just have to know the way. It's hard to get there without someone leading the way, but I know it by now. Turn left here."

Marlow did as instructed without argument. He did however, have doubt in his eyes. But he knew he didn't need to say anything else to Winston. The time for convincing with words was over. He knew by the end of this trip that one of them would have nothing more to argue. "I hope you are prepared for what we find when we get there."

Winston ignored his skepticism. "Okay, there's a little road just over this hill. Take that to the right." Please be there, Winston thought to himself. It was as if suddenly he needed to convince himself too. Marlow had allowed the slightest bit of doubt to enter his mind. As they topped the hill slowly, Winston saw the little road off to the right. I knew it. Almost there.

Marlow turned onto the small road and he could see in his headlights up ahead that the road teed with another paved road that went left and right. "Left or right ahead?" he asked Winston. Winston looked ahead. He saw the familiar place that he and Carter had been every day this week. I knew it.

"It only appears from a distance to be a tee. When you get closer you will see that you can go straight. There is a very small road that goes directly through that cornfield ahead. Salima Falls is on the other side. He sat back in his seat and smiled. He was about to prove to Marlow that he wasn't lying. That he was in fact, perfectly sane. He closed his eyes and remembered his date with Emma. He wondered if it was possible to fix it this time. He felt the car slow to a stop and opened his eyes.

Marlow was staring ahead, as was Winston. In front of them was a wall of corn, about twenty feet off the road, and higher than the top of the car. In between was nothing but grass, illuminated by their headlights.

CHAPTER THIRTY-THREE

Metallic Bitterness

Marlow squinted, but could see no signs of a road leading through the corn, or a town that might exist beyond the field. He closed his eyes and exhaled deeply, as if a large weight has just been lifted. This was the moment he had waited for most of the last year since Caroline's accident. There could be no arguing now. Winston had to see he was right. The answer was looking back at him.

Winston's eyes grew large, and the light of the moon glinted in them through the windshield. The shock on his face was evident, as Marlow watched him stare ahead at the wall of corn. There was no opening. There was no small road that led up to and into the field. There was nothing. Winston slowly opened the car door and stepped outside. His eyes never left the corn. He was certain, beyond all doubt, that this was where Carter brought him each morning. It's here. I know it. It has to be here.

Marlow stayed in the car, as Winston walked into the grass, still staring at the corn, almost trying to will it to open with his eyes. From his driver's seat, he saw Winston fall to his knees in the grass and lower his head. He wondered if it was time. He reached into the glove compartment and grabbed something. He slipped it into his pocket as he got out of the car.

Winston appeared to be under spotlights, lit both from the moon above and the car's headlights behind, which cast his large kneeling shadow onto the corn in front of him. Marlow stepped closer.

"I'm sorry man." He put his hand on Winston's shoulder. "I hope you can let it go now. I hope you can just move on with your life."

After a pause, Winston spoke in a defeated, helpless voice. "What life?"

"You'll get through it man," Marlow answered.

Winston stood with anger and tears mixing in his eyes. "What life do I have?" He turned to Marlow and the headlights lit up the emotion in his eyes. Marlow thought he almost looked scary. "My life was Caroline… and she was taken from me. She's dead, and my life died with her." His eyes were filling more and more with anger.

"It doesn't have to be that way," Marlow said boldly. "You have a long life ahead of you. You can move on and find something else to make you happy."

Winston looked back at the wall of corn. "I thought I had."

"I can help you through this. Caroline wouldn't want to see you like this man. She would want you to be happy. She would want you to move on."

Winston remembered his failures with Emma. He knew he couldn't move on until Caroline's death was avenged.

That much was certain to him. He looked directly into Marlow's eyes. "The only way I can move on is if I find the man responsible for all of this.

Marlow looked up at the sky with disgust. "I beg you to stop this."

"What Caroline would want…," Winston continued. "…is justice."

Marlow pulled on his own hair in frustration. "Oh, would you STOP this obsession with finding the other car already!" He raised his voice in exasperation. "I'm so sick of it! Can't you see what's it's doing to you?" He walked past Winston and pointed at the wall of corn in front of them. "Look! Would you look! There's nothing here! It's all in your mind! You're losing it! You can't stand there and tell me it's not making you crazy! Just forget about the accident and move on!"

Winston's eyes filled with rage. "Forget?" he said calmly. "Forget!" he screamed. "I'll NEVER FORGET! NEVER!"

Marlow raised his arms. "Alright, then don't forget. Always remember Caroline. But don't let her accident ruin the rest of your life! Yeah, life dealt you a shitty hand, I know. Lots of people get shitty hands, Winston. And you know what they do? They move on. They take their lumps and move on. It's been a year! Maybe it's time to forgive. Have you considered that?"

"Forgive? I'll never forgive him for taking my Caroline!"

Marlow's lips were pursed and full of tension. He wondered if it was now or never. He walked forward, until he was face to face with Winston. "Tell me," he said. "What exactly would you do if you found the man responsible for the wreck that night?"

Winston stared into Marlow's cold eyes and matched the stare with fire in his own eyes. "Honestly, I don't know. But I'll remember those eyes. And I'll know what to do when I'm staring directly into them." Flashes of that dreadful night once again filled his mind. He saw the man staring at him in the rear-view mirror, like he had a thousand times since. He saw those raging green eyes again, looking into his own. He saw Caroline standing on the sidewalk with the flower in her hair. He saw the black car slide off the road in slow motion towards her.

"NO!" he screamed to clear the vision from his eyes, and backed up. "Stop it!" he screamed at Marlow. "Why are you doing this to me! Just take me back home!" He started walking back to the car.

"I'm doing this because I'm trying to help," Marlow said to his back. "The time has come."

Winston kept walking with his back to Marlow.

"I'm done living this charade with you Winston. I thought by now you would snap out of it, but it's only getting worse. And I'm done pretending to help you find this other driver."

Winston turned to face Marlow again. "I don't need you then, I can find him on my own! Take me back to the city where I belong!"

"It's a wild good chase, man." Marlow was certain the time had come now. There was no way out of it.

"I will find him! And I will face him!" Winston shouted at him from next to the passenger door. "Now let's go!"

Marlow walked straight at Winston. "You want to face him?" he said.

"Of course I do!"

Marlow kept walking, straight at Winston. "You want to face him?" he shouted again.

"Yes!" Winston shouted back at him.

"YOU WANT TO FACE HIM?!?!" Marlow's patience was over. The time was now.

"YESSSSSSSSSSS!" Winston screamed with a year's worth of pent up rage right into Marlow's face, as Marlow reached his arms out for him. He grabbed Winston violently, and turned him towards the passenger window. The moon was bright above, and both of their reflections were clearly visible in the glass. "Well there he is! Take a good look at him!" Marlow's screams matched the volume and ferocity of Winston's. He pointed directly at Winston's own reflection. "There's the man responsible for Caroline's death. What are you going to do now?"

Winston turned to Marlow. "You son-of-a-bitch," he said in a low and evil voice. He pushed Marlow with a heavy blow to his chest, and Marlow stumbled backwards.

When Marlow recovered, he looked into Winston's eyes. They raged with more fury than ever. They seemed to be on fire with hate. "Look again," he said to Winston.

"What did you say to me?" Winston stepped towards Marlow.

"I said look again, at the man who killed Caroline."

As soon as the words hit Winston's ears, he swung his fist as hard as he could at Marlow's face. With a thundering pop, the punch landed, and Marlow fell backwards onto his back. He hit the road with a thud. Winston stepped forward and looked down on him. His eyes still raged. "Now I know what I'll do when I find him. Only I might not stop there."

Marlow managed to get to his elbows and look up at Winston. He touched his fingers to his lips and felt the blood. His lips were busted open and he tasted the metallic bitterness of his own blood as it dripped down from his mouth onto his chin. After a long look into Winston's eyes, he spoke.

"What other car?"

The world seemed to fall into silence when Winston heard these words. He looked at Marlow in disbelief, but somehow it seemed to hit home. He took a step back and looked away from Marlow.

Marlow reached into his pocket. The worst had come. There was no reason to hold back anymore. It was time to do what he came here to do. He pulled out the item from his pocket.

Winston heard something rustle and looked back at Marlow, who was holding something in his hand. Marlow threw some papers at Winston's feet. His bloody fingerprints had stained them. "Read carefully," he said calmly, speaking like a friend again.

Winston reached down and picked up the papers, as Marlow spit some blood from his mouth. He opened the roll of papers and looked closely at the top one. At the top, it read "POLICE DEPARTMENT" in big bold letters. Under that was written "VEHICLE ACCIDENT REPORT" only slightly smaller. He could see from the date that it was from the night of Caroline's death. He flipped through the other pages.

Marlow sat up but stayed seated on the ground. "Eye-witness accounts from that night, statements from bystanders, even from you yourself, plus a transcript from your only therapy session. It's all there."

Winston stepped backwards and leaned against the car. He was completely immersed in what he was reading. Single car veered off the road… charcoal-colored BMW… driven by the husband… distraught and inconsolable… disbelieves the facts… ruled an accident… husband cleared of all charges… judge requests psychological evaluation and therapy… husband

still assigns blame to 'other' driver… disillusionment…
augmented reality…

CHAPTER THIRTY-FOUR
Just a Spectator

After Winston read all that he could read, he rolled the papers back up, and dropped them to the ground. There seemed to be a change in the air, and a slight breeze wafted his hair in the night. He looked up at the moonlight that shined down onto his face, and closed his eyes. He slid his back down the car, and fell to the pavement. He sat on the road, leaning against the car, and pictured that dreadful night again.

OVER ONE YEAR AGO

Eight, Zero, Eight, Three... Winston dialed the number to the restaurant from his desk at work. He was a software salesman, who hated his job. But he loved his wife, and the sun was shining today, both in his office, and on his life. Tonight was her birthday. Tonight, he would treat her to sushi and a twenty-dollar bottle of wine. And on top of that, he planned on surprising her. He had booked and paid for a weekend away in the mountains with her, and she had no idea. They would spend two nights in a warm and cozy log cabin that overlooked five hundred acres of the most pristine wildlife within a day's drive of Dunsport. Tonight, after dinner, they would share a glass of their favorite wine, and he would tell her to pack a bag.

Everything was ready to go. The plans were made. The only problem was that a last-minute call from a client of his had pushed back his plans a little. He changed the reservation over the phone and knew he would be cutting it close to get there on time. He would have to swing by home quickly and pick up Caroline if they were to make the reservation. The best laid plans… he thought.

Just as Winston was about to leave, his boss walked by his office.

"Winston. How come I haven't seen the details on that Booker upgrade proposal yet?" His tone was harsh and his gaze was penetrating. Winston hated him, and he was sure the feeling was mutual. He didn't have time for this.

"The numbers are crunched, I just have to put some final touches on the last page. I can have it printed and in your mailbox first thing Monday morn…." The last syllable was still in his throat when he was cut off.

"Monday is no good!" his boss said. "I want to look it over this weekend. Have it in my mailbox before you leave. Don't disappoint me, Winston."

Eleven minutes later he was angrily shoving the paperwork in his boss's mailbox, mumbling something under his breath about an ungrateful bastard. He dodged the usual chatterboxes on the way to the elevator. Winston turned the corner after the last cubicle and took a right towards the hallway. He saw two women enter an open elevator door ahead of him.

"I'm coming. Hold on." He was still holding the wine bottle in one hand and the flowers in the other, and neither woman seemed to notice him. "Hey! Hold the elevator!" The doors touched each other just as he reached them. He elbowed the button frantically, but it was too late. He kicked the elevator door in frustration and darted for the stairs instead. He looked at his watch. He knew if they were more than a few minutes late they would give away his table. He raced down the stairwell, taking steps two at a time, until he reached the ground floor, sweating and even more ticked off. It seemed some unseen force was trying to ruin his perfect plan.

He zipped through the lobby quickly, avoiding all conversations, and made it to his car in the parking lot at the rear of the building. He tossed the wine bottle and the flowers in the seat next to him and sped out of the parking lot.

In the car, he called Caroline. He had no idea this was the last time he would talk to her. Her beautifully sweet voice answered the phone for the last time. He wished he could have recorded it.

"Hey there, are you almost home? I'm ready to go. Just sitting here by the window, enjoying the sunlight. Isn't it beautiful outside?" She closed her eyes and Winston could sense she was smiling on the other end, as he braked for the red light in front of him.

"It would be nicer if I didn't get stopped by every damn light in the city!"

He told her he would be there in five minutes to pick her up, and she agreed to wait outside by the sidewalk so he could just stop quickly and they would be on their way.

"I can't wait to see you!" she said. Remembering her words tore at his heart.

"Me neither," he replied. "I lo…"

Just as he started the words, another car shot out from a side road and cut Winston off. Winston had to slam on his brakes and skid to avoid hitting it. His phone flew from his hands and hit the floorboard. The tires locked up and slid on the pavement, leaving long black streaks in the sunlight, as smoke drifted up from the melted rubber.

Anger and rage that had been building for the last hour filled Winston. Everything that could go wrong was going wrong today, and he had reached the limit to his patience. He stuck his arm out of the window and thrust his middle finger high in the air to the other driver. He then slammed on the gas and sped up. His car moaned like an injured lion, ignoring the pain for one final chase. One final hunt. He flew up to the other car again with fury, and moved into the passing lane, passing the other car and yelling at him as he went by. Winston swerved in front of the other driver and cut him off. He hit the brakes hard to make his point, and the wine bottle in the seat next to him flew from the seat and landed on the passenger floor mat. The other car barely avoided a collision with him.

As Winston was looking in the rear-view mirror, he leaned in and caught a glimpse of his own eyes, glaring back at him, ferocious and penetrating, filled with anger and purpose. The sunlight seemed to focus on them and they shined a bright boiling green, as they focused back on Winston. It was if he was looking at someone else. He barely recognized himself.

Winston swerved back and forth, not letting the other car by as he approached his house. The wine bottle rolled back and forth on the floorboard, glimmering in the sunlight. The other car, apparently fearful of Winston's actions, honked and slowed down. It turned on the next road, but Winston didn't notice as he was battling the glare from the sun off the wine bottle on the floor, shining directly into his raging green eyes.

Winston raised a hand to shield the sun and leaned over into the passenger floorboard to retrieve the bottle. He took his eyes off the road for merely a second or two, but that was all it took to change his life forever. He grabbed the bottle and sat it once again in the seat next to him, as he felt the rumble of his tires leave the pavement and hit the loose gravel on the side of the road. What happened next happened in utter slow motion for Winston. Time seemed to slow all energy and motion to a crawl, but had no effect on thought or agony. He was helpless to watch machine and metal, dust and rock, flying through the air and skidding along the ground. Helpless to change the direction of force and inevitability, as his car continued to slide farther off the road.

In the endless and torturous stop motion of that moment, Winston blinked and turned his eyes toward the white object ahead. As the seconds ticked by, each felt like a minute, but this new sight changed everything. It made those minutes turn into hours, or years. The white object was about thirty feet away and standing erect just off the sidewalk. It was Caroline. She was standing with her eyes closed, silent and happy in her own world of joy. A world which consisted only of the white dogwoods that lined the street, along with the beautiful green grass under her feet, and the warm rays of sunlight that touched her. She was wearing a beautiful white summer dress that billowed slightly in the breeze. Winston could only watch as the sun held her in its embrace, lifting her up in majesty like a shiny pearl among dark waters. In her hand, she held a small bundle of the flowers she had pulled from the tree, and she held them up to her nose to take in the wonderful smells of early summer. She had one of these flowers in her hair, which gleamed like silk in the sunlight.

The best moments of their relationship flashed in Winston's mind. He felt all at once the thousand days of happiness he had shared with Caroline between the flickering flames of the fire the night they first met and the screeching bellows of tires in this instant. He felt the taste of their first kiss. The softness of the first time he touched her skin. The look on her face when he took her to see the new baby elephant at the zoo last year. He saw the tears in her eyes the night he got on one knee on the beach in Costa Rica. He felt the wonderful ache in his heart when he walked down the aisle towards her. He felt the excitement of their first night in their new house. And he wanted more than anything to go back.

He wanted to relive those moments again all the way up to this day, only with more appreciation this time. And he wanted to go back to the office today. Back when he watched the sunlight pour through his window, and to try again. Caroline was more important than it all, and he knew in this moment what he would do. This time he would leave the phone ringing and his client waiting. He would leave an hour earlier and not be there when his boss stopped by his office.

He would smile into the sunlight as he drove home. He would open his window and take a deep breath of summer air. He wasn't sure how he got to this precise moment in time, but he would go back and forget the other driver for cutting him off and all the rage and anger he was responsible for. He would appreciate all that life had given him. Caroline was more important than it all.

But the sad truth is that moments and seconds and minutes all come in order, one after another. Winston knew that he couldn't go back. He knew only the seconds ahead of him were malleable. Only the minutes and hours he had yet to encounter could be forged into something new. The ones behind him were gone, and the one staring him in the face has long been written by the actions leading up to it. He was just a spectator now. And he could only watch the cruel story of these seconds unfold before him. All Winston could do is close his eyes and slam on the brake, as he screamed her name one syllable at a time. "CAR…O….LINE!"

The wine bottle flew off the seat again and shattered on the dash as Winston slammed his foot on the brake. When his car hit Caroline, it threw her to the grass. He jumped out, ran over to her, and held her in his arms. He wept uncontrollably and apologized over and over.

CHAPTER THIRTY-FIVE
Universe Urging

When Winston opened his eyes, he was still sitting on the pavement and leaning against the car, with the moonlight overhead and the papers at his feet. Everything seemed different now. He felt truly awake for the first time since Caroline's death. The world seemed real to him again, as if he had just woken from a bad dream. The breeze was crisper, the road was more tangible, the moon was brighter, and his heartbeat was stronger, letting him know just how alive he was.

He stood and turned around to look at his reflection in the passenger window again. He leaned in and stared deeply into his own eyes, and saw for a brief moment, those same raging eyes that had haunted his dreams for the last year. *They were my eyes*, he thought to himself, before speaking aloud.

"It was me the whole time." The world seemed to go silent to accept these words into the air. They were meant more for himself than for Marlow, who was still sitting on the ground a few yards away, still bleeding from the punch Winston delivered just a few minutes ago.

As Winston stared into his own eyes, a calm swept over him like a cool breeze in the afternoon. He could see the hate and anger drain from them, getting washed away in the deluge of tears that fell to the pavement below. He felt like a pot of boiling water that had been on the stove for too long, and someone finally turned off the heat. He could feel the bubbles slowly stop and the waters inside him return to smooth.

He stared at his reflection for several seconds, until he recognized himself again. The last year, he had felt like someone else entirely, but that person faded away into the moonlight. He could see the man he was before the accident, appearing slowly before him. He remembered everything.

Marlow could see the change in Winston almost immediately, and could feel his old friend returning to him, as he watched from his seated position on the pavement. Winston looked over to him. Marlow saw only regret in his eyes now, and a hint of embarrassment. The anger and animosity from before were all gone. Winston reached down and picked up the papers at his feet. After rolling them up tight, he put them in his back pocket and walked over to Marlow. He couldn't believe that a few minutes earlier, he had struck his best friend with violent aggression. The look in Winston's eyes said he was sorry, even if he couldn't muster the words. To cement the idea, he extended his hand to Marlow and helped him to his feet.

Marlow wiped the blood from his lips with the back of his hands and brushed them on his jeans. He patted Winston on the shoulder and walked around the car to the driver's side door.

"What do you say we get off this road and head home?" he said to Winston. He spoke as if nothing had happened, as if tonight they had simply gone on an uneventful late-night drive. Winston nodded in agreement and opened the passenger door.

"I'm sorry I hit you," he finally said to Marlow, as the car's engine roared to life again.

"And I'm sorry I said what I did, and that I had to push you over the edge like that. I didn't know any other way." Marlow did a tight loop and turned the car back towards the city. There was a glow in the sky that told them they were pointed in the right direction. The rest of the ride back to the city was done in silence. As men, they didn't need to talk about what happened. They both understood, and Marlow knew Winston probably needed time to process things. The only sound was the constant hum of the tires on the winding roads beneath them.

Winston stared out the window, lost in his thoughts about the last year and all the events that led him to this point. He relived Marlow's words. There's nothing here! It's all in your mind! He had trouble believing those words were true. He thought about Emma and Salima Falls. How could it not be there? He thought about Earl and the shop. About Carter and the cab. Even Buster and the doc. But he was unsure what to believe anymore. How could something so real exist only in my head? I don't understand. Where have I been if I haven't been in Salima Falls?

He couldn't explain any of it, and wished the answer was simple. Perhaps he had picked the wrong road tonight. Did I lead Marlow to the wrong cornfield? Was Emma out there somewhere? Was she at home with Harley and Charlie, thinking about me right now? Or was she just a dream? He had no answers, only questions.

Marlow had pulled up the car next to the sidewalk outside of his apartment before Winston even noticed they were back in the city. "We're here," Marlow said after a few seconds.

Winston looked up and realized where they were. He pulled the handle and opened the door slightly before he paused and looked back at Marlow. "Um, thanks… and I'm sorry… for everything."

"I understand, it's ok," Marlow said. "Just glad to have you back, that's all. I'd have taken a punch for that any day." Winston managed the slightest of unnoticeable smiles. "Keep your head up man, it's all up hill from here. Any idea what you're going to do now?"

Winston just shook his head. "Not really." He took a deep breath, and thought about Caroline again. "There's one thing I have to do." He got out of his seat and stepped outside. "I guess I'll just figure the rest out later."

"Hey Winston," Marlow said. Winston leaned down and looked at him. "I'll swing by tomorrow at some point, ok?" Winston just nodded in agreement and shut the door. He watched Marlow drive away. When the car was out of sight, Winston started walking down the sidewalk, away from his apartment. He knew what he had to do, and he didn't want to waste any more time. Only ten blocks up and four blocks over, he thought to himself. Surprisingly, tonight was both dry and warm in the city, and he could use a good walk and some fresh air, as fresh as Dunsport air could be.

As he stepped along the concrete, he began to notice all the little things in the city that he had looked past before: the halos of light around the street lamps that cascaded orange glows onto the sidewalks below, the patterns hidden among the seemingly random array of lighted rooms in the high-rise buildings, the hum of the cars that could be heard constantly all around but only seen peeking into view here and there between the buildings and the parked cars lining the streets. The city also contained a myriad of smells that invaded the nose with every breath. He smelled the steam rising through the grates from the maze of piping below the streets. He smelled the food from closing time at a hundred restaurants that ended up in dumpsters and trashcans. All of it seemed to meld together and surround Winston with a sense of place, which was something he hadn't felt in a long time. It was like he was meeting the city again for the first time.

When he arrived at his destination, he walked through the gated archway leading into the cemetery. Wisteria vines had crawled up the sides of the metal arch and woven themselves tightly among the letters. Purple flowers hung like clusters of grapes all along it. He walked along one of the small roads that wound endlessly through the enormous cemetery. It was past visiting hours, but there was no guard on duty that he could see, and even if there were, he wouldn't have cared. He didn't know how long it had been since he had been here, but he still knew the way to her stone. It was nestled in a corner at the far end of the huge lot, under the shadow of a giant poplar tree that reminded him of the one holding a tire swing in Emma's front yard. From somewhere off in the distance, he could smell the aroma of a Juniper tree wafting towards him.

Winston walked up slowly, and stopped in front of the memorial, which was intricately carved in the shape of an angel, whose stone wings were draped around the edges of the rest of the stone. She was weeping and holding it tightly, as her wings framed the words before him.

MY BELOVED CAROLINE
may time hold you until I get the chance again…

He reached out his hand and ran his fingers along the angel's wing and up to her hair. The hair was longer than Caroline's ever was, and reminded him more of Emma's than of hers. He looked at the sad face on the angel and again was reminded how sad Emma looked the day he first saw her in the diner. Her face flashed in his eyes as he touched the stone angel's cheek, and for an instant, he was standing in her kitchen about to kiss her again. He immediately jerked his hand back as if he had just touched a hot stove, and fell to his knees in front of the stone. He buried his face in his hands and spoke aloud through the tears.

"I'm so sorry Caroline. I know I haven't been here for you. I've been lost." He pulled his hands away from his face. "I know I've been thinking of someone else lately. I can't seem to stop it." He read the words again to himself. My beloved Caroline. "And I know I promised you I would find the man responsible for putting you here." He wept loudly into the night.

"Well, I found him. After all this time, I found him." He pulled his hands from his face. The tears glistened in the moonlight. "And he's sitting here and talking to you right now." His tears fell to the ground between his knees. "I hope more than anything that you can forgive him..." Marlow's words sounded in his memory. You need to forgive whoever was responsible. It won't bring her back. It will just ruin the life you have remaining. "...and I hope I can forgive myself."

He wiped the tears from his face and closed his eyes. He saw her standing there on the sidewalk again, with a flower in her hair. She looked so peaceful. I wish I could go back... I'm sorry... I'm so sorry. He knew somehow, that she heard him. A breeze fluttered through the leaves in the trees above. He imagined it was her reply, trying to tell him it was ok, that she forgives him. He knew inside somehow, that it was true.

I miss you so much.

More of Marlow's words entered his head. "She would want you to move on," he said. But how? Winston wondered if it were true. Do you really want me to move on? How can I force myself to stop thinking about you? What am I supposed to do with the life I have left? How can I move on?

He wished Caroline would give him a sign. He wished she could help him. It was then, for some reason, that he glanced beyond the stone angel's wings and through the trees at the back of the cemetery. He could just faintly make out the front porch of a small house outside the cemetery, lit by the street lamps. As the trees along the perimeter swayed, the front porch of the house popped in and out of view. He could see a wooden swing hanging by chains, and he thought of the front porch at Emma's house. He pictured sitting in the swing, overlooking the fields, with Emma next to him. He could smell the Juniper trees across the field again, and the breeze cooling his face. He looked into Emma's eyes and smiled.

For a moment, he felt guilty thinking of Emma while sitting at Caroline's grave, but then he knew the image of her didn't come by accident. He could feel his mind being directed by some unseen force. He looked to the sky and smiled, knowing something greater was in control now, and he only had to open his mind and let the answers to his questions come to him. He looked back at the porch swing. You're right, he thought. Emma has been the only thing that has taken my mind off Caroline. He looked up at the angel and pictured Emma. She has been the light in my darkness. She has made me feel again. She is how I will move on. But how? How can I find her? How can I know she is real? How can I be at peace with Caroline?

He closed his eyes and was suddenly taken back to a memory of Caroline. They were driving on a warm summer day and listening to the radio. The sun was glistening in her hair. A favorite song of hers came on the radio and she quickly turned the volume up. He could hear the words in his head, as if the singer was describing him.

> Seems like I was walking in the wrong direction
> I barely recognize my own reflection
> Scared of love… scared of life…
> It's time for me to let it go

He looked to the passenger seat on his right, and watched Caroline's hair blowing gently in the wind. He could hear her voice as she smiled at him and sang into his eyes.

> "Just when we think that love will never find you
> You runaway but still it's right behind you"

He loved how happy she looked. She had played this song many times before, and he knew the words that came next. He sang back to her. "I'm ready to feel now… I guess I'm ready to love again."

The memory of Caroline in the car vanished, and suddenly he was with Emma on the swing again. He was looking in her eyes as before. They were a beautiful deep brown. The air smelled of Juniper trees, and the sun glistened in her hair. She smiled at him and stared into his eyes. She looked at him the same way Caroline had, and then began to sing to him as well. Her sweet voice sounded the final words to the song.

> "So, come and find me
> I'll be waiting up for you"

When the vision passed, he opened his eyes, and stared at the stone monument before him. He didn't know what he was looking for when he walked here tonight, but he felt like he had found it. It was as if Caroline was talking to him tonight, through the trees and through his thoughts. She was telling him that it was ok to let go. That she forgave him. That he could now forgive himself. And that it was ok for him to move on. He knew Caroline would always be in his heart, but that if he was going to continue to live, he had to make room for someone else. He had to find a light bright enough to cut through the darkness.

Winston knew Emma was the light. He felt destiny urging him. He was supposed to be in Salima Falls with her. But how? More questions flooded his mind. Was she really out there somewhere? Was she really waiting up for him? Could he really find her? But where? I tried to get to her. I tried to go to Salima Falls. Is it real? Is she real? Then how can I find her again? How can I get back to Salima Falls?

He looked to the sky again and tried to clear his thoughts. He heard Carter's words echo in his head. "If you belong somewhere, and you are supposed to be there, then the world just has a way of getting you there. You just have to have faith that the universe knows what it's doing." He smiled when Carter's face popped into his memory. Could he be right? Could it be that simple? He closed his eyes and tried hard to just let fate tell him where he was supposed to be. OK? Where do I belong? If I'm supposed to be in Salima Falls, then tell me. Tell me where I need to be. Give me a sign…

Just then he heard a dog bark somewhere a short distance away. He opened his eyes and stood. His knees ached from kneeling for so long. He looked around him, but he couldn't see any dog in the darkness. He heard it again and spun around. It was closer this time. He squinted his eyes and then spotted a little white dog racing along the cemetery lane towards him. It ran right up to his feet and jumped on him.

"Hey there little buddy," Winston said as he reached down to calm the excited puppy. It ran in circles and jumped up to lick his hands. He knelt to the dog and patted it on the back. It brought with it memories of Buster. "What are you doing out here in the cemetery at night? Don't you have a home?" He rubbed his hands along the collar and found a dog tag. In the light of the moon and city he could barely make out the image. It was a laurel wreath, overlaid with gold letters. Apollo. He said the word aloud to himself. "Apollo. Where have I seen that before?" Then he remembered Carter's cab. This was the same logo as on the side of it. He smiled. He knew this was the sign he was looking for. *The universe knows what it's doing...*, he thought. He was supposed to be in Salima Falls. He knew it now.

"Okay then, Carter," he said aloud. "I believe." He rubbed the dog behind the ears. "Now what?"

Just then, both he and the dog turned, as a light came racing over the hill towards where the dog came from. He held the dog's collar and watched closely in the direction of the growing light. Soon, a car came into view, slowly driving towards them. *Apollo!* Winston knew it must be Carter, coming to take him back to Salima Falls. *I just sort of go where I'm needed,* he could hear Carter saying.

He had a large smile on his face when the car pulled up and stopped about twenty feet from Caroline's stone. A bright light from the driver's window aimed at his face and blinded him. He held his hand up to his face to block the light. The dog's collar slipped from his fingers and he raced off into the night.

"Hey! You there! What are you doing?" Winston didn't recognize the voice behind the light. "You can't be in here after midnight!" Winston walked towards the light, shielding his eyes and trying to see the face behind it. When he got closer, the security guard lowered his flashlight, as Winston approached the window.

Winston stood and stared in disbelief at the small security car before him. He was so certain that it was Carter coming over the hill towards him. He looked behind him and the dog was nowhere to be seen.

"I said what are you doing in here?" the guard barked at him again.

"I'm… uh, I'm sorry, I didn't realize it was so late."

The guard shined his light on Winston's face again. He could see he had been crying. He saw the dirt on his knees and knew he had been kneeling in front of a grave. The guard sighed and Winston sensed he recognized him. His tone changed.

"Well, I suppose I understand. Hop in and I'll take you out of here."

Winston, still in disbelief, wondered if his mind was flirting with reality again. He lowered his head and slowly made his way to the passenger door in silence.

The guard looked at him with pity. "Where to?"

Winston just stared ahead. "How about ten blocks down and four blocks over?"

"Yes sir," the guard said. Winston watched the stones go by out his window, as they headed for the exit.

CHAPTER THIRTY-SIX

Winston woke the next morning still swimming in dreams of
Salima Falls. It was the best sleep he had in a year. He
thought about the events in the cemetery the night before, and
wondered what was real and what was in his head. He
contemplated his own sanity and was deep in thoughts of
Emma, when he was interrupted by the sound of someone
knocking at his apartment door. He shook his head to make
sure it was real, and then distinctly heard the loud knocks
again.

He stood, still wearing his clothes from the night
before, and walked to the living room. He remembered
Marlow saying he was going to be stopping by today. He
looked at the clock on the wall and saw the small hand
hovering near the seven. What is he doing here so early? Loud
bangs on the door rattled his head again. "Alright, alright! I'm
coming! No need to break the damned door down!" He
stomped to the door and swung it open. "Marlow, knock it off

before I…" He cut his sentence off when he saw the police officer standing in front of him.

"Are you Winston Novak?" The officer's voice was deep and authoritative.

"Yes." Winston wondered if this had anything to do with the cemetery last night.

"Do you own a black BMW?"

Winston looked confused for a second before realizing what this was about. "Well, it's really more of a charcoal color, but yeah I guess so. It was reported stolen about a week ago."

"Well, good news. We found it," the officer said with little enthusiasm. "It's at the police impound down town."

"That is good news," Winston said.

The officer was holding a small package in his hand. He handed it to Winston. "And this was outside your door here."

Winston opened the package and pulled out his wallet. It was no longer wet, but appeared to be untouched, otherwise. He opened it and saw his driver's license and credit cards. Everything seemed to be there. "I guess it's my lucky day," he said.

"I guess so. Do you need a ride to pick up your car? I'm on my way downtown now."

Winston put the wallet in his pocket and threw the empty package inside his door. He stepped outside and shut the door behind him. "Yeah sure," he said. "Can I ask where you found the car?"

"It was abandoned at an old run down body shop near a cemetery not too far from here. Someone probably planned on chopping it up for parts. But luckily, we got to it first, I guess." Winston just nodded and followed the officer to his car.

On the way back from pickup up his car, he rolled the window down and let the wind blow his through his hair. He forgot how free he felt behind the wheel. He remembered his conversation with Carter about his car getting stolen.

"It will make its way back to you in due time," Carter said. "Things just seem to turn up when we need them the most."

"And when do you suppose that is?" Winston said with a little attitude.

"When you are ready I suppose," Carter said.

He wondered what Carter had meant that day, and he wondered again now. Carter's words seemed to have a way of coming into light later. When I'm ready for what exactly? As he drove home, he let his thoughts drift to Salima Falls again. Could it be real? Could Emma be out there waiting for me? But I've already tried to go on my own…

Inside, he believed that his car and wallet both showing up on the same day was more than a coincidence. Especially after last night in the cemetery. But what did it mean? Why now? More of the conversation with Carter came to him.

"I tend to think everything happens in the order it is supposed to," Carter said. "Right now, you don't have a car, so you ride with me. When you get it back, I suppose you can drive yourself."

"That's it," Winston said to himself aloud. "When you get it back… you can drive yourself." Marlow was driving. The rest of the way home Winston had a smile on his face. He knew where he belonged, or more importantly, where he didn't. Dunsport wasn't for him anymore. He belonged somewhere else. It was only his guilt for Caroline, and his search for closure, that tied him to this city. Neither held him back anymore. He could feel the ache inside him. It was an emptiness that needed filled. The darkness that was in him was gone, and he longed for something else to take its place. For someone else. For Emma.

I have to try to go back. Even if I can't find it. Even if Salima Falls isn't there when I reach the tee in the road. I will just turn and keep driving. I'm not going to stop. Emma is out there somewhere, waiting for me. Maybe in Salima Falls, maybe somewhere else. But I have to try.

When he got back to his apartment, he went inside with a mission. There was a new determination in his steps. He went to the bedroom and found the suitcases buried under his bed. He opened them up, threw them on his bed, and started dumping clothes from the closet and dresser drawers haphazardly into them. He grabbed his favorites, and the rest went in garbage bags. After both suitcases and several garbage bags were filled to the max, he set them by the door. He emptied out all the cabinets and the closets, filling several more bags.

When the place was mostly empty, he stepped back and looked all around him. He had spent the last year of his life here, or more accurately, the worst year of his life here. Part of him still couldn't believe how delusional he had been. But it was all over now, and he knew no matter what lay ahead, it would be far better than the darkness he lived in while here. He saw the magnet on the fridge that he and Caroline had bought on their first trip together. The colorful beach scene struck his eye from across the room. He went over to the fridge and pulled the magnet off, and rubbed the image with his thumb. He smiled at the memory, just as he heard a familiar voice behind him.

"Hey buddy! What's going on here?" It was Marlow, who opened the door and walked straight into the suitcases by the door. "You going somewhere?"

Winston stuck the magnet in his pocket and walked over to Marlow. "I think it's about time I get a change of scenery. Besides, the eviction notice said ten days. That was five days ago. So, the clock was ticking anyway. I figured I'd just get it over with. No sense hanging around. New beginnings, right?"

"New beginnings…," Marlow repeated. "I like the sound of that." Marlow's face grew a big smile. "I think that's a great idea man. Sounds like exactly what you need." He patted Winston on the shoulder. "I see you got your car back too. Right on time too, huh?"

"Yeah," Winston said. "Right when I needed it most."

"Funny how things work out like that."

Winston agreed with a nod. "Funny."

Marlow looked him up and down, and seemed to be surprised by how Winston looked. "You look good man. Sober. Rested. Determined. I'm glad to see some clarity in your eyes again."

"Look, about last night…" Winston began, before being cut off immediately.

"Hey, forget about it. No hard feelings, ok? I had been dreading that night for months. It was bound to happen sooner or later. I'm just glad it's over. We're past it now, ok? Don't beat yourself up over it." He rubbed his cheek again. "And don't beat me up either." They both smiled and knew that everything was going to be fine between them. It didn't have to be mentioned again.

"Want to give me a hand with these bags?" Winston asked. They loaded his car and hauled the rest to the dumpster around the corner, before walking back inside. Winston sat on a wooden chair and swung one around for Marlow too.

"You know, Winston, I'm happy for you. And I think you are right. A change will do you good. Any idea where you are going to go?"

Winston looked out the window. He knew where he planned on going first. He pictured the street that ran right down the middle of Salima Falls. He could almost smell the scents of the town. But something inside him held that part back. "I'm not sure really. I just know I need a fresh start somewhere. I need to get out of this city and go someplace… quieter. Someplace where I can breathe."

"What about work?"

"I guess I'll figure that part out when I get there."

"Well, you know how to get a hold of me if you need me," Marlow said.

Winston pulled the key to the apartment off his key ring and sat it on the empty table. They both stood and pushed their chairs in. "When I get settled, I'll give you a ring, I promise."

They walked towards the door and Marlow stopped. "What about your TV?"

"Winston didn't break his pace. "It's yours if you want it."

Soon after, Winston was winding his way out of the city, with the windows down and the wind in his hair, never once looking in the rear-view mirror. He left the main road and found himself staring out at the familiar fields he had passed so many times before. The dented front bumper hadn't even crossed his mind. Turn after turn came, with each new field and each new road looking more and more like the one he just left. Yet he smiled as the sun crashed through the window on his face. He knew he wasn't lost. He could feel it. He would find Salima Falls. He wouldn't fail. He couldn't. He only had to let his heart guide him.

After a while, he looked ahead and saw the hill where the little road branched off to the right. His heart raced as he approached the top and made the right turn. Ahead, he could see the spot where Marlow and he had their confrontation the night before. Yet it felt different this time. It's there, I know it. He slowed to a stop when he reached the tee in the road. Left and right, the paved road led off into the distance. Straight ahead was the same wall of corn Marlow pointed at in the moonlight.

Winston stared ahead and felt the hairs on the back of his neck prickle. He didn't need to see the path to know it was there. He idled forward and eased the car off the road, through the tee and into the grass. When his bumper was only fifteen feet or so from the corn, he slowed to a stop and held his foot on the brake. He stared ahead of him at the wall of green and listened to Carter's words replaying over and over in his head. "The universe will get you where you are supposed to be… You just have to believe…"

He felt the engine rumble as he held his foot on the brake and revved it up. The sound reverberated in his ears and the sun gleamed in his eye. You just have to believe… He closed his eyes and pictured Emma, sitting on her porch waiting for him. I believe. He didn't know if she hated him or missed him, or even thought of him. He didn't know if he could find her again, but he didn't care. I believe. He had to try. He had to go to Salima Falls. I believe. He had to look into those eyes again…

He opened his eyes and stared one more time at the corn in front of him.

"I believe," he said. Then he closed his eyes and slammed his foot on the gas.

CHAPTER THIRTY-SEVEN

Just... Push

When Winston opened his eyes, he couldn't believe what he saw. I knew it! The corn stalks seemed to be parting magically in front of his car, revealing a small road no wider than his car. He stared ahead at the sea of green as he kept his foot on the gas. The stalks whipped past his windows as he laughed out loud. I believe! The sun above was bright and warm as it crashed through his windshield.

He looked behind him and saw the stalks folding together again behind his car, concealing his path, and he laughed aloud once more. The thought of Emma somewhere on the other side of this field filled his mind, and his heart raced in his chest.

A few minutes later, the stalks opened a bit further, and he could see beyond them into the town ahead. He slowed down as he approached the field's end and quietly drove onto the main street with ease. All around him, the familiar sights and smells overwhelmed him. He saw the row of poplars that marked the edge of the field and formed a wall. He smelled the honeysuckle that grew at their bases.

Up ahead, he noticed the two large magnolia trees that grew at the edge of the street near the doc's house. They were covered in clumps of purple flowers. Winston slowed down and stopped his car next to the sidewalk outside of the doc's house. He recognized the orange flowers that lined that walkway up to the doc's door.

Suddenly, he remembered the stitches in his head. He ran his fingers over the now-healed wound under his hair. He had almost forgotten it was there. That's right. He got out of his car and walked up to the doc's door, taking in the scenery of the street and town, just as he did the first time he was here. He reached down and touched the flowers, as if to prove to himself they were really there. The door opened in front of him.

"Winston!" The doc stepped out into the sunlight. "How very nice to see you, my good man. How have you been?"

Winston smiled at him and stood up. He had no idea where to begin telling him everything that had happened since he saw him last. But something told him there was no need. "I suppose I'm all right."

"Well, you sure look a lot better. I hope this week treated you well, and you had sufficient time to heal." There was a twinkle in his eye, and Winston wondered if the stitches were all he was referring to. He reached up and rubbed them again.

"I think so."

"Well, I was hoping I was going to see you today. I hadn't seen you all week and I was wondering how you and Earl were getting along. I hope he didn't put you through more than you could handle."

Winston thought about the shop and how much he had enjoyed his time there. "It wasn't bad at all, actually. I even would say I enjoyed it."

"Well, that's just wonderful to hear." He looked past Winston to the street. "I see you drove here this morning. I'll have to tell Carter that you won't be needing a ride anymore. So how was the trip? I hope you found your way without too much trouble."

"It wasn't easy, but I got here."

"I knew you'd find your way. Just needed to be shown, that's all."

Winston held his gaze, and the doc cracked a wry smile.

"Well, don't think I forgot our deal," he said. "Come on inside and we'll see about those stitches."

Winston nodded and followed him inside.

"Have a seat at the kitchen table Winston," the doc said as he walked to the fridge. "Can I interest you in some more of Greta's famous orange juice?"

"Sure," Winston said. "Don't we have to go to your office or hospital or something to do this?"

Doc sat a glass of deliciously bright orange juice on the table in front of Winston. He chuckled a little. "Oh, there's no need for that here."

"You mean in Salima Falls?" Winston asked.

The doc smiled. "I meant here today. It's only stitches. Now let me take a look and see how well you have healed." Winston took a sip of the juice as the doc pulled back his hair and examined his handiwork from a week ago.

"So, Winston," he said. "Tell me, what is next on the horizon for you, now that our little arrangement is nearly complete."

"Nearly?" Winston said. "What do you mean? I thought it was complete yesterday. Do I still have something I'm supposed to do?"

"Ahhhh, fair question Winston. But only you can know if you have unfinished business in Salima Falls. I only meant nearly complete because I haven't finished my end of the bargain yet. I still have some very important work to do with you. Now sit here while I grab my instrument bag. I'll be right back."

Winston drank his juice and looked out the window at the wonderful colors of Salima Falls. He always loved how this town looked like a painting, like the type of painting where the colors are so bold and bright it lacked realism. He agreed, it was beautiful here, but surreal as well. The window was lifted a few inches, and Winston closed his eyes and took a deep breath. The wonderful scents of town filled his nose.

The doc came back holding a regal leather bag and unfolded it on the table. There were numerous medical instruments, and several that looked viscous and scary. Winston's eyes focused on one particularly torturous-looking device. "Hopefully, we won't be needing that," he said, to the delight of the doc.

"Don't worry," Doc said as he pulled a small pair of tweezers and the tiniest of scissors from his bag. "You can relax. These should do the trick just fine." He showed them to Winston, who then leaned back and relaxed, as the doc began to work.

"So, tell me Winston, did you enjoy your first week here in Salima Falls?"

Winston quickly replayed most of the week in his mind, and it was filled with visions of Earl, Carter, and Buster, but mostly Emma. Thoughts of her brought a smile to his face. "I did actually."

The doc matched his smile. "I'm glad to hear it. I am very proud of Salima Falls, although I might be a little biased if I do say so myself. But I do think this place is just about perfect."

Winston thought of Emma's beautiful eyes again. "Yes, it is."

"It is a beautiful place, Salima Falls," the doc continued. "It has everything a person could possibly want or need."

"Yeah," Winston agreed. "Everyone here does seem to be very… happy." The doc remained silent and slowly pulled out another stitch or two and laid them on the table. Winston thought about Emma and Earl. They seemed to be the only people in town that didn't fit that description. "Well… almost everyone I guess."

The doc smiled and nodded. He seemed to have been waiting for Winston's words. "I suppose there might be a person or two in town that has yet to find everything they are looking for here."

"I thought you said Salima Falls has everything a person could possibly want?" Winston said.

"Ahhh yes," he said. "But you have to be willing to find it. You see, I believe everyone has the potential to achieve perfect happiness in their lives, no matter where they are. They have the power to find that exact thing they are missing. Unfortunately, sometimes the answer is right in front of them, and they can't see it. Some simply miss it because they aren't looking. Others because they see it and are afraid to reach for it."

Winston thought about his own life and the last year he spent looking for something that couldn't be found. "What if they don't know what they are looking for?"

This brought an even bigger smile to the doc's face.

"Well, I tend to believe that in time, the world will reveal it to them, when they are ready to see it. When they are ready to fill in the missing piece and be whole again."

Winston knew exactly what the doc meant. He had been missing something himself. He had been missing the truth, and he wasn't ready for it for a long time. Thoughts of his confrontation last night in the road with Marlow came to him. He knew Marlow had done the right thing. It had been time for him to know the truth. It had been time for him to hit the bottom, so he could begin his rise again.

"Sometimes people need a push I think," Winston said. Even if it meant going through pain, it was worth it for him. It was time to feel whole again. Whole again. He said the words over and over to himself in his head. He wanted to feel whole again and knew what was missing for him now. Emma. He wondered what it was that she needed. What would make her whole? "What do I do then?" he asked, as the doc pulled out the last stitch and put it on the table.

The doc paused and looked at Winston. "Well then," he said with a smile and a wink. "I suppose you just… push." He put his tools back in his bag and returned it to the hall closet, leaving Winston to wonder what it is he could do to help Emma. She was the light that he so desperately needed, and he wanted to be that for her too. But he always seemed to make it worse. He always seemed to screw it up. How could it be different this time? He didn't know what she needed. He didn't know how to help her. How am I supposed to push?

When Doc came back, he put the empty glass in the sink and turned back to Winston, who stood from his chair. "Well, it looks like you are good as new again." He patted Winston on the shoulder and started for the door. "I'm sorry you had to come all the way out here on a Saturday," the doc said. "But at least it was a nice day outside for a drive."

"Yeah, it was quite nice outside."

"I bet it feels good to be back behind the wheel again. There's something about driving your own car on a sunny day that seems to just mend the soul."

Winston agreed. He remembered driving here with the windows down. The wind was blowing through his hair and the sunshine was warm on his face. His eyes were filled with the promise of a new beginning in front of him. "It was… glorious," he said. "It was like…"

"Like all the worries in life will just pass by," the doc said. "And get swept away in the breeze."

They stepped outside into the sunlight. Winston just nodded and smiled.

"Thanks again, Doc."

"No problem Winston, I'll be sure to wave when I see you around."

"I hope so. I appreciate all you've done."

They exchanged smiles and Winston walked towards his car.

CHAPTER THIRTY-EIGHT

The Right Car

As Winston drove through Salima Falls, he wondered what he was going to do about Emma. He had no idea how to win her back, and feared he had messed up too badly this time. Yet the smile on his face grew and grew as he passed the familiar spots along the way. He felt at home here in this mysterious town, and drove towards the only place he could think of.

As he pulled into Earl's shop, he felt a warmth fall over him again. He parked his car and stood outside, taking in the scenery around him. He looked around at the cars parked all around the lot, and looked up at the big bold letters on the front part of the building that read "EARL'S AUTO SERVICE & GASOLINE". He actually missed this place. He remembered the first time Carter dropped him off here. It felt so long ago.

He realized Earl had no idea he was going to be coming here today, and so he walked into the shop quietly and rang the unattended bell on the counter, which he knew Earl hated. He heard the rumble of music from the garage beyond the wall, and after a few more loud bangs on the bell, he heard the music stop suddenly. He hit the bell again. The grumpy growl of an old man could be heard this time, and he whacked the bell again, even harder. The growls and retorts got louder as Earl approached the door, and Winston smacked the bell again, enjoying himself considerably.

"Would you knock that off!" Earl said as he burst through the door. "What's the big idea anyways? Are you trying to…" He stopped his words when he saw that it was Winston, who was smiling widely and enjoying Earl's anger immensely. Winston burst out laughing with pride.

"I'm just messing with you, Earl. No need to pop a vein in your head."

"I'm throwing that bell out, I swear," Earl said, as his face slowly changed into a smile. They both shared a laugh together.

"Didn't think I'd see your ugly mug for a while," Earl said. "I thought you had plans in the city or something?"

"Well," Winston said. "Let's just say I found what I was looking for earlier than expected."

Earl just looked at him curiously. "So, what brings you back to town so soon? You come to pick up Buster already?"

Winston just realized that Buster hadn't come running for him this time. "Where is the little guy anyways?"

"Oh, he's probably out back playing in those tires or burying something again. Couldn't find my three-eighths wrench earlier until I saw him run by with it." Earl turned to the open door to the back. "BUSTER!" he yelled loudly and deep. In a matter of seconds, Buster came flying through the door and jumped all over Winston. His paws were covered in dirt.

"There you are!" Winston knelt and wrestled with him a bit. "How have you been little buddy?" He noticed the dirt on his paws and turned to Earl. "Might want to do inventory when you get back out there." He turned back to Buster. "So how was your first night in your new house?" Knowing he couldn't answer, Winston looked up at Earl for the answer.

Earl shook his head from side to side. "He wanted in here with me as soon as I came in and shut the door. I heard him whining, so I gave in. Slept at the foot of the bed like he always does. I guess that house we built is more of a daytime retreat or something. He was sitting in there earlier while I was in the garage under a car."

"Look, now that you mention Buster," Winston said. "I was thinking. He has really taken to you, and I know you won't admit it, but I think you have a soft spot for him too. Plus, there is so much here for him to run around and play with. So, I was thinking…"

"Come on, spit it out," Earl said.

"I was thinking Buster could stay here permanently. That is, if you want him."

Winston could see Earl's eyes light up for an instant, as Earl tried to hide his excitement.

"Well I guess that would be ok," Earl said in his deepest manly voice.

"He's yours then," Winston said. He looked down at Buster again, who immediately grew bored of their talking and ran back outside to continue his mischievous project. "I think he's ok with it."

"So where are you headed now?" Earl said. "Just passing through?"

"Actually, I had to see the doc this morning to get my stitches out. And now I'm thinking of staying in town a bit longer." Earl gave him a questioning look. "I have something I need to do." Earl just stared at him. "I don't know where I'm going to stay yet. I suppose I should have asked the doc when I was there this morning if he knew any places."

"Well," Earl said. "You can stay here at the shop until you find someplace to your liking?"

Winston smiled. "Alright, I think I can handle that, if it's not too much trouble."

"Nonsense," Earl replied. "I have a couch we can drag out here for a few days. You should be comfortable on that."

"And while I'm here," Winston said. "If you need any help around the shop, I'd be glad to help out. It's the least I can do if I'm staying here." A thought suddenly popped into his head. "And when I get my own place…" he seemed nervous to ask. "If you have the work, I might be interested in a… job. Part time of course, at first."

Earl seemed to be leery of the idea. "I've… never had an employee before. Nothing more than a kid helping in the summer, anyway. I'm not sure…"

"I remember you said someday you might start using the paint shed again… start painting cars again like your old man did." Earl raised his eyebrows. "I don't know nothin' about painting cars, but if you need a guy, you could teach me I suppose. And there are plenty of old beat up cars around here to practice on."

Earl seemed to enjoy the idea. His eyes wandered off for a bit, and Winston could tell he was picturing it. "Tell you what," Earl said. "I'll think about it." Winston smiled. He knew that was Earl's way of saying yes.

Earl looked out the window behind Winston's head and noticed the BMW sitting outside. "Is that your ride out there?"

"Yeah," Winston answered, as Earl walked past him and headed outside.

　　　"Why are you running around in this foreign-made piece of junk, anyways? You should be driving American made!"

　　　"What's wrong with a BMW?" Winston asked in an insulted tone.

　　　"What's wrong with it?" Earl said in an annoyed voice. "I'll tell you what's wrong with it. These foreign cars don't even sound like real cars. They are so quiet. They sound like hot wheels. The front end is all busted up too, I see."

　　　Winston looked at the dented front bumper. Surprisingly, there was no sting in Earl's words. He thought about telling Earl everything, but he didn't. "Well, it's fun to drive," is all he said.

　　　"Well of course it's fun to drive," Earl sounded annoyed. "It's a car, ain't it? It's just not as fun as it could be. You are driving the wrong kind, that's all. You want a car that rumbles under your seat when you press the pedal down." Winston could see a fire in Earl's eyes when he spoke. He looked off into the distance, down the dirt road leading towards Emma's house, as Earl continued. "You want a car that you can hear and feel, as the wind blows in your hair and the sun's warmth hits you in the face." He looked down at Winston's car again. "This is a car, but it's not the right car, I tell you. And the right car has the power to change a person."

　　　Winston stopped listening to Earl. He kept staring down the dirt road towards Emma's house.

　　　The power to change a person. "That's it!" he said calmly.

　　　Earl stopped talking. "What's what?" he said.

　　　"That's the answer!" Winston said.

　　　Earl laughed. "See, I knew you would agree with me about this foreign…"

"No," Winston interrupted. "I mean, that's what I have to do. That's what WE have to do. That's the missing thing. I see it now." He remembered Doc's words from this morning.

"Sometimes the answer is right in front of them and they can't see it…"

"Could it be so simple?"

"…all the worries in life will just pass by… and get swept away in the breeze…."

A smile formed on Winston's face as he stared down the dirt road.

"…behind the wheel again…"

"That's it."

"…there's something about driving your own car on a sunny day that seems to just mend the soul."

"I'm certain of it."

"What are you talking about?" Earl said.

Winston blinked and looked at Earl. "We have to fix Emma's car."

Earl stared at him with an incredulous expression on his face. "We have to do what?"

Winston smiled. "We have to fix Emma's car!" He seemed excited and full of enterprise. "We have to go to her house and get it out of the barn and bring it back here." His eyes got wide. "And we have to get it running again."

"Now why in the world do we need to do that?" Earl said.

"You said it yourself," Winston exclaimed. "The right car has the power to change a person. And Doc said it too. He said a car can mend the soul. It all makes sense now. We just have to fix the car!"

"I don't see what that's going to accomplish. Plus, that car hasn't ran in years," Earl said. "How are we going to get it back here?"

"Can't we tow it or something?" Winston asked.

"Do you see a tow truck laying around?" Earl said.

"Can't we call someone?"

"Stan Adams is the only one around here who tows," Earl said. "And he don't work on the weekend. Plus, I don't think he would be too willing to help us steal a car."

"Well, there has to be a way to get it here," Winston said.

"You tell me, then."

Earl stood there, staring into Winston's face, waiting for an answer. Winston looked off into the distance, and then got the most curious smile on his face, like he just remembered something. He replayed parts of his earlier conversation with Doc in his mind.

"What do I do then?" he asked, as the doc pulled out the last stitch and put it on the table.

The doc paused and looked at Winston.

"Well then," he said with a smile and a wink.

Winston finished the rest aloud for Earl.

"I suppose we just… push."

CHAPTER THIRTY-NINE
Semi-Flat Tires

Later that evening, Winston went over the plan for Emma's car in his head again and again, as he and Earl fiddled around the shop, discussing the paint shed and how they would eventually put it back to use. He had spent most of the day waiting for the sun to go down, and trying to convince Earl that they could do it, and that it needed to be done. Earl didn't understand exactly what Winston was hoping to accomplish, but Winston could tell that on some level, Earl was just happy for a change of pace. There was a sense of adventure in his eyes that Winston detected. However, Earl made considerable effort to hide this fact.

"I'm too old to be pushing a car through a field and a mile down the road," he said again and again. "In the middle of the night no less!"

"Oh, quit your whining Earl, you'll be fine," Winston retorted. "It's downhill most of the way here. Once we get it out on the road and get it moving, it will be easy."

"Easy?" Earl shook his head back and forth. "Probably never get the thing out of the barn if I had to bet on it."

Something told Winston Earl was wrong. He could feel that this was what needed to be done. He had faith in the universe again and was calm about it. "We can do it, I know it."

"Well how can you be so sure?"

"I just am," Winston said. There was no point in trying to convince him. And Winston knew from his dealings with Marlow that speaking about cryptic signs, coincidental statements, and gut feelings were not the best ways to do it.

They spent the remaining time until the sun went down clearing out a place for the car, in the event they did indeed return to the shop with it. The conversation remained much the same, yet Winston could tell as the sun got lower and lower in the sky and the time neared, Earl's skepticism seemed to be turning slowly into anticipation.

Earl hadn't seen the car in years, but described every detail of it to Winston with fondness in his eyes. He told him the story of the first day he brought it home to his wife Rebecca, and the day they brought Emma home in it from the hospital, and the first time he had to fix a dent in the fender from when Rebecca backed into the poplar in the front yard. Like Emma, Earl had plenty of his own memories tied to that car. But unlike her, he chose to only remember those memories which made him smile. And Winston wondered if perhaps this was his motivation. He missed Emma, and even though he knew it was unlikely for her to ever give him another chance, he wanted to reconnect in some way with his past, even if it was through a car.

When the clock struck eleven and Earl had exhausted his pile of photos on Winston, Winston walked to the window and looked out. "Are you ready for this Earl?"

Earl had a determined look in his eyes. He carried Buster to the back bedroom and set him on the bed. "Sorry buddy," he said. "Can't have you following us all the way there, barking at Harley and Charlie." He shut the door and looked at Winston. "Ready as I can be."

When they stepped outside, the night air was crisp, but still warm. They walked the mile and half down the road towards Earl's old home mostly in silence, listening to the crickets and the breeze in the trees. When they got within a hundred yards, they stopped.

"All the lights are off," Winston whispered. "You were right."

"Emma was always early to bed," Earl said as quietly as he could. "Heavy sleeper too. I guess that comes from being around a lot of cars and power tools as a child. So as long as we don't alert the dogs, I think we should be good."

They cut through the field at the same place they planned to bring the car, and came around the back of the barn. They wanted to keep as much distance between them and the house as possible. When they got to the barn, Winston snuck around front to see if he could slip the doors open, as Earl made his way through a side door to the inside. Winston tried to slide the heavy barn doors open, and as he did, a latch fell with a clang. He froze in his tracks and looked up at the house, holding his breath.

After he was certain no one heard him, he slid open the door about a foot and squeezed inside, where he saw Earl shining a flashlight on a large tarp that was obviously concealing a car. He could see the front bumper sticking out from under the tarp, aiming right at him. A large dent could be seen in the glimmer of Earl's light.

"Grab that end," Earl said. Together they pulled back the tarp and revealed the car. "She's a beauty, isn't she?"

Winston raised his eyebrows and looked at the dented and dusty heap before him with an incredulous look on his face. It looked nothing like it did in the picture. He couldn't even tell what color the car was under all the filth.

"If you say so."

Earl scoffed. "Ahhh, you just don't know what you're looking at. Too young to appreciate a classic. You'll see when she's all cleaned up."

"What was it called again? A V...."

"Nineteen seventy-two Chevy Vega," Earl said. "She was the best car I ever owned. Now hop in and see if you can get her into neutral, while I clear out some room behind it to push."

Winston hopped in and stared at the shifter knob in the middle. After an embarrassingly long amount of time, Earl finished moving the boxes and came to the driver door.

"Well, did you get it?" he whispered.

"Ummm…" Winston looked confused. "I don't see an N on here."

Earl just shook his head back and forth. "You mean to tell me you can work a computer but you can't even drive a stick?" Winston just grinned. "Kids these days, I swear," Earl said, while shaking his head. "Push down the clutch and put the gear between first and second." Winston still looked confused. Earl knew he didn't know where the clutch was. "The left pedal," he said in an insulting tone. "Goodness. Now, let's see if we can get that door open wide enough for the car without waking the whole town."

After managing to slide the door open, they got behind the car and pushed until it was safely outside. They gently eased the doors of the barn shut again, and made sure there was no commotion up at the house. Then they pushed the car slowly and steadily through the grass back the way they came, along the edge of the field. They strained mightily on semi-flat tires. Once they were far enough away from the house, they paused at the spot they were going to cut left and get the car onto the road. Earl stepped away from the car and stretched his back.

"I told you I was too old for this," he said, finally able to talk above a whisper.

Winston smiled at him. "Oh, you love this, I can tell. Anyway, it got you out of the shop, didn't it?"

Earl took a deep breath of the night air and looked around him. He seemed younger today to Winston. There was more life in him than normal, and more vigor in his demeanor. "I suppose so."

"You know, I was thinking," Winston said.

"Maybe someday you can take me to those good fishing spots you mentioned to me earlier, over by Cobb's Creek."

Earl smiled back at Winston. "That sounds like a great idea." He looked back at the house again, and seemed to reminisce for several seconds.

"You know, Winston, you're the first man that ever seemed to really care about my baby girl, and I really appreciate that."

Winston raised his eyebrows. "She's the most beautiful person I've ever met, I don't see how that's possible. And she's smart, caring, hard-working, kind, I could go on."

"See that's the thing," Earl said. "Anyone else would have stopped at beautiful. Especially after they tried to talk to her. But you didn't. From the first time you mentioned her, I could tell. You saw more in her. You kept trying to break down the wall. You wouldn't let her shut you out."

"Well, thanks, but I'm afraid she's shut me out pretty hard right now. The wall is high this time. I seem to mess everything up every time I see her. I'm not sure she even wants to see me again."

"Sure she does," Earl said. "She's been lonely her whole life." Earl felt shame as he said the words. He knew his not having a relationship with her was part of it. "She needs you, Winston. She needs you to break the wall down. To show her there's more to life."

"I don't know how I'm supposed to do that," Winston said.

"Well," Earl replied. "You're here now, aren't you? You came back for her. I knew you would. And if this plan doesn't work, I'm sure you will come up with another one. That's what we do when we fall in love, don't we? We'll do anything to get the girl."

"In love?" Winston's eyes widened.

Earl looked at Winston and shook his head with a grin. "It's as plain as day. I know, cause I've been there. I once hung over the edge of the bridge over Cobb's Creek by just my feet to write Rebecca's name on it. Seems silly now, but that's what we did back in my day when we were in love. Anyway, I just wanted to tell you thanks." Earl patted Winston on the back. "Now come on, it's after midnight. Let's get this baby rolling again."

It took them almost two hours before they were finally pushing the car off the road and into Earl's lot.

CHAPTER FORTY
A Blur of Grease

Earl woke the next morning to the sound of a vacuum running somewhere out in the shop. Buster was missing from the foot of his bed. He turned his head towards the small window to his left. It was still quite dark outside. He rubbed his eyes and looked at the small digital clock next to his bed. "Four forty-five?"

He slowly got to his feet and stretched. His back was still sore from the adventure just a few hours ago. He threw on some clothes and shoes, and made his way to the main garage. Winston saw him and killed the power to the vacuum.

"Hey Earl. Good morning."

Earl squinted under the lights above, and gave him a grumpy look. Buster ran over to him and demanded a good morning rub. "If the sun ain't up, it ain't morning," Earl said. He walked closer to the car in between him and Winston. "What are you doing anyway?"

"I couldn't sleep," Winston said. "So, I figured I'd get a jump start out here. She was a mess. Had years of barn dust and field dirt in every nook and cranny. I already wiped her down from head to toe and I'm about done vacuuming. Been at it an hour already and I think she's cleaning up real nice."

Earl smiled and looked the car over from left to right several times. Winston could tell he was picturing it as it was long ago, when both he and the car were much younger and more vibrant. "I told you she was a beauty," he said. "I'll put on some coffee while you finish up vacuuming."

About an hour later, after a few cups of coffee and a rehashing of last night's adventure, they both were standing next to the car again. "Alright," Earl said after thinking for several seconds. "Let's start with the guts. Cars are a lot like people. If they just sit around doing nothing for years, everything starts to rot on the inside. So, the first thing we have to do is get all the old fluids out. I'll let you crawl under there and drain the oil and gas, and I'll have a look under the hood."

From under the car, Winston could hear Earl taking inventory of the things they would have to do to get it back on the road. "Rubber's all dry rotted... gonna need all new hoses, fuel lines, timing belt, spark plugs, filters…. battery looks shot too. Carburetor and throttle body need a good cleaning." He stepped back and looked at the front of the car as Winston crawled out from under it.

"Tires need air and a good cleaning too," Winston said. He walked to the front of the car and joined Earl. They stared at the heavily dented front bumper together. It was a vivid reminder for each of them of the worst day they had lived through.

"And one dent needs…" Earl paused, with his eyes never leaving the bumper. "…brought back to life." His tone and careful choice of words told Winston he was talking about more than the bumper. "Yes, that will be the last piece," he added. Winston saw a strange look in his eye, as if Earl thought somehow pushing back the clock on this car would do the same for him too. Winston turned his head and looked out the door to the outside. He could just barely see the dented front bumper of his own car peeking around the corner. "Make that two bumpers," he added.

Earl turned to Winston and they gave each other a look of determination. "Let's kick on some tunes and get to work then, what do you say?" Without saying anything, Winston walked to the stereo and hit the power button. He turned the volume knob loud and the lyrics echoed throughout the garage.

> And as we wind on down the road…
> Our shadows taller than our soul…
> There walks a lady we all know…

Their eyes lit up. "A classic," Earl shouted.

> Who shines white light and wants to show…

This song happened to be a favorite song of Winston's too, and he sang the next line out loud. "How everything still turns to gold…" He strummed his air guitar perfectly with the next riff, which brought a look of mild surprise and respect to Earl's face. They shouted the next three lines together, both strumming their fictional electric guitars in unison.

> "And if you listen very hard…
> The tune will come to you at last…
> When all are one and one is all…"

Even though they were both running on only a few hours of sleep and several cups of coffee, they danced around the shop like fools, to the excitement of Buster.

The next three days were a blur of grease, motor oil, beer, classic rock, and very little sleep. They toiled day and night on the car repairs, working usually from sunup to well after sundown, taking breaks only to eat, or to head into town for a part.

On the second day, they fired up the engine for the first time. It roared in the garage, bringing a smile to Earl's face. "Now that's what a car should sound like," he told Winston.

On the third day, the final piece was installed and the newly smooth bumpers were bolted into place. They stood back to admire their work. The shop smelled of sweat, grease, glass cleaner, and tire shine. The Chevy Vega sparkled from bumper to bumper and looked nearly new again. It was white with a hatchback in the rear and white round headlights in the front that looked like eyes.

"You were right, Earl," Winston said. "She IS a beauty." He looked over at Earl, who appeared to be lost in his own thoughts. He was staring at the car with a glazed smile on his face, and his eyes were glistening. Winston knew he was in a memory somewhere, probably with the windows down and the radio turned up. Then he saw a tear form in Earl's eye.

"You gonna be ok, Earl?"

Earl kept staring at the car. He wiped his eye. "I miss her, Winston."

"Well, she's not in the barn anymore," Winston replied. "She's right here."

Earl snickered and looked at Winston. "I'm not talking about the car." He looked back at the shiny Vega. "Although it's good to have her back." He took a deep breath and sighed. "I miss my wife, Winston. And I miss my daughter."

Winston just nodded, not knowing what to say. He missed Emma too, and was in the same boat as Earl. He wondered if Emma would ever talk to him again.

"Thanks again Winston," Earl said.

"For what?"

"Well, for helping out here at the shop, and for asking questions I didn't want to be asked, and for listening to memories I didn't want to think about. As much as I might have hated it, it was good to… to remember again. Suppose I just needed to hear the story again."

"You're welcome, I guess. I'm not sure I really did anything though. Just got in the way most likely."

"Well," Earl said. "Thanks anyways. For stirring the pot. For trying to change things around here."

"I'm not sure I changed anything for the better, actually."

"Well, this car would have just rotted away forever in that barn if it weren't for you. Forgotten and wasting away. And I might have too. Now look at her. She's alive again."

A few hours later, after a much-needed break and a call to the animal shelter, Earl walked in with Buster in his arms.

"You are certain she isn't home?" Earl said.

"Yes," Winston answered. He was looking out the window towards the road to Emma's.

Earl put Buster in the bedroom and shut the door. "I just want to make sure you heard right."

Winston turned around. "For the last time. They said she was there and that she worked until six o'clock. They were calling her name out loud to come and pick up the phone when I hung up."

Earl nodded and paced nervously back and forth.

"You have everything ready?" Winston asked. Earl nodded again. "Okay then, let's go."

CHAPTER FORTY-ONE
New Memories

When Emma left the animal shelter that evening, she had no idea what was waiting for her at home. She hopped on her bike and took a deep breath of the wonderful Salima Falls air, as she did every evening. The sun was getting lower in the sky, and she liked to be home before dark to let the dogs out.

As she pedaled through town towards home, she thought about Winston, as she had done several times since he left her house a few nights ago. She kept replaying the events of that night over and over in her head, and her mind seemed to always go back to the kiss. Even when she thought about the look on his face when he pulled away, or when she thought about the other woman that was playing an unknown part in Winston's life, she always came back to the kiss, and it made her insides flutter.

It was different now, as she approached the road that led to her house near the entrance to Earl's shop. For years, she would just turn her head and avoid any possibility of seeing him. Yet now she found herself looking as she went by, wondering if he was there, and what he was doing. The picture of her and Earl that Winston left at her house was pinned to the basket on the front of her bike. She often looked at it when she was on the road and thought about Winston's words that night on the couch. "He's your dad… he blames himself."

She rounded the corner and headed down the last mile and a half towards her house. In either direction, the fields seemed to go on forever. She could already smell the juniper trees somewhere off in the distance. She wondered where Winston was, and if he would ever come back to Salima Falls. She was sure he said something about coming back for Buster, but she wasn't sure. She wondered if she would ever see him again.

When she got within sight of her house, she noticed a shiny white car sitting out front in her yard, next to the large poplar tree. It had been so long since she had seen it, that she didn't even recognize the car. Who could that be? Why are they here?

When she turned into her driveway, she looked at the car as she passed. No one was inside, so she headed straight for her front porch. She hopped off the bike, leaned it against the railing, and ran up to the door. "Hello," she yelled as she opened the door. Harley and Charlie barreled out, almost knocking her over. They ran to the car to inspect it. Emma did a quick lap around her house. "Is anyone here?" No one answered and her eyes were drawn to the barn out the back window. Was the door slightly open? She ran back out to the front porch, and a feeling starting to sink into her stomach.

She walked down the steps towards the car, taking her steps slowly. About halfway there, it hit her. This is my mother's car. A memory flashed in her head like lightening of her mom passing out in the car, and drifting off the road. It knocked Emma to her knees like she had been kicked in the stomach. She hadn't seen it first person, but she could always picture the accident as if she had. She tried to fight the memory. She tried to put up the wall like she had done so many times before and close off all feelings about her mother's death, but she was unable to this time. The car in front of her was like a beacon, shining light on the worst of her memories and thoughts. She saw her mom's eyes close as she slumped in the seat.

"Mom!" she screamed to the sky in a long, drawn-out syllable. Tears poured down her face.

Who could have done this? Who would do this to me?

She looked at the car again, which glistened in the fading sunlight. She lowered her head and cried for several minutes into her hands and hair.

"I miss you so much," she moaned. "I want you back. Why did you leave me? Why?" The tears soaked her face and the ground beneath her knees. Several minutes and a thousand tears passed, as she sat on her knees in the grass. When her eyes finally went dry, and could leak no more, she looked back to the car.

A calm suddenly came over her. She wiped her face and stared at the shining beauty before her. The car looked like it did when Earl first brought it home. It was like it went back in time to when she first saw it, and suddenly she couldn't remember it any other way. It was beautiful, and it reminded her of her mother's beauty. Before the accident. Before the divorce. For the first time since her mom's death, Emma truly remembered her, as she was when everything was perfect. "When time was endless, when life was free." She remembered her mom smiling and happy. She remembered Christmases and birthdays and picnics in the park. She remembered all the good times and had trouble remembering anything else. The car wouldn't let her. It was if it stared back at her with those round eyes and told her that things could change. That something old and dusty could be shiny and new again. That something broken could be fixed.

A smile formed on her lips. She stood and stepped closer to the car. A focus came over her. It was all becoming clear to her now. "I'm sorry mom," she said aloud. She knew now that pretending her past didn't exist wasn't going to change it. It wasn't going to rewrite history. She knew it was no way to live. It was no way to remember her. She had let the memory of her mother disintegrate. She let it crumble to dust like the car, a prisoner in the barn. "I'm so sorry."

The sunlight glistened off the car. It was perfect again. It came back to life. She stepped to the door, wondering if there might be hope for her too. She ran her hand along the polished metal and looked inside. She remembered riding in the back seat for the first time as a child. She touched the door handle and hesitated, then opened the door. She sat behind the wheel and gripped it for the first time. She hadn't driven since she was in high school.

She looked down and saw a note folded neatly in the consol. Her name was written on the outside. She opened it and began to read.

Emma,

The first thing I want to say is that I am sorry. I know now I have been a fool. All I can think about is how badly I have screwed things up, and how desperately I wished

I hadn't. I'm not sure you will forgive me for not being totally honest with you, but I plan to start, beginning with this letter.

You were right about so many things. There was another woman in my life. Like you, I too lost someone dear to me. And like you, I've let it have too much control over my life. But I'm seeing things more clearly now. I have put the past behind me and I'm focusing on what's to come. I know what's done is done, and there's nothing I can do to change it. But I know I can change everything that lies ahead. And most importantly, I know where I belong now. I belong in Salima Falls. And I belong with you. I know now that I love you.

This might sound crazy, but I believe it is meant to be. I believe the universe itself wants us to be together. It has found ways to tell me, and ways to lead me here to you.

I am sorry again. And I'm sorry if this car brought back memories and emotions you have long forgotten about. I know that it can be rough, and I didn't mean to cause you any pain. If you don't want to see me again, I understand. But I miss you and hope that is not the case.

So, I hope this car finds you well. Perhaps it will be a light in your darkness, as you have been for me.

> *P.S. The keys are in the*
> *glove compartment.*

Emma opened the glove compartment and saw the key, which was taped to a small note. Tears hit the paper as she read the words.

> *To my baby girl Emma,*
> *you have no idea how*
> *much I miss you. I hope*
> *someday I can make it up*
> *to you.*
>
> *P.S. I think it's time for*
> *you to make some new*
> *memories in this car. ~*
> *Love Dad*

CHAPTER FORTY-TWO

Abyss of Happiness

The next morning, Winston seemed to be relaxed, but Earl didn't know what to do with himself. He tried to keep busy cleaning up the shop, but inside he couldn't stop wondering what Emma's reaction to the car was. Was it back in the barn already? Was all their hard work for nothing? Did she curse their names and rip up the letters without even reading them? As the hours trickled by, he became antsy and paced around nervously.

"Calm down Earl," Winston finally said. "You're driving me nuts." He wasn't nervous, but he did wonder if Emma was forced to face her past the way he had done himself a few nights before. He wondered if his little push had pushed her in the right direction.

"I told you it was a stupid plan," Earl said.

"Wow, you sure changed your mind quickly."

"I just don't like all this not knowing. I'm a simple man, Winston. I don't like a lot of fuss and confusion in life."

"Well, go change a tire or something. Just stay busy."

Just then, they heard a vehicle pull into the lot in the front of the shop. Winston could hear the tires on the gravel and a car door open. "Good, there's a customer," he said to Earl. "Maybe that will give you something to do for a while. I'll go see what they need. Since I work here and all now."

He smiled at Earl and turned towards the door. He swung it open and stepped out into the sunlight. He took two steps towards the car and used his hand to shield the sun. He stopped in his tracks immediately. It was Emma, standing there in front of him.

Several seconds passed as they stared into each other's eyes. Winston was uncertain what motivation or emotion was racing through her mind. He wanted to run to her. He wanted to lift her high in the air and twirl her around. He wanted to hold her in the sunlight and pull her close. But he didn't move. He was frozen, unsure still what she was feeling. He saw the car behind her. He opened his mouth, wanting to speak, to break the silence, to break the tension, but he didn't know what to say.

A tear rolled down her cheek, and he saw that her eyes were wet. He hesitated, and just then she leapt towards him. She ran over to him and jumped into his arms. She threw her arms around his neck and their lips met in a fury of kisses. He held her in the air and kissed her as they twirled around and around in the early afternoon sunlight.

In the middle of their kiss, Earl burst through the door. "Oh, alright Buster, quit your yap…" His words faded out when he saw them kissing. Buster came bolting around the corner behind him and ran up to their feet. Emma's feet touched the ground again, and Buster jumped all over her, licking her wildly. Earl looked towards the ground awkwardly.

"I'm sorry, I didn't mean to… I'll just…" He turned to go back inside.

"Wait," Emma's voice stopped him again. He turned towards her, but could barely look her in the eye. She walked towards him, and he fidgeted in place. She stopped in front of him and he nervously looked up. They made eye contact, and both of them slowly began to get tears. Emma put her arms around his neck and hugged him, as they cried together.

"Emma," Earl said through his tears. "My baby girl. I missed you so much."

"I know," she said. "I missed you too, I just didn't know it."

Winston walked to the car to give them some space. He ran his fingers along the metal and felt the warmth of the sun overhead on his skin. He closed his eyes and smiled and let everything wash over him. He knew it would all work out now. He looked up into the sky and marveled at the colors. Off in the distance somewhere, he could smell a juniper tree, and could hear the birds happily singing. How do you thank the universe, he thought.

"Hey Winston," get over here. He turned and walked towards them, at total peace.

"What do you say the three of us go down to the diner and get a cup of coffee?" Earl was beaming larger than Winston had ever seen him. Emma was smiling at him too. He closed his eyes slowly and opened them again to be sure this moment was really happening.

"Sounds wonderful."

Emma walked past him to the car, as Earl picked up Buster and took him back inside. "Well, hop in if you're coming," she said.

Winston climbed in the back seat as he had done so many times in Carter's cab. He watched out the window as the familiar shops and sights passed. He could barely hear the conversation happening in the front seat. It sounded sweet, was all he thought. He was lost in his own world, a world that seemed to be created just for him, until finally he heard his name again.

"Winston!"

"Oh, sorry, I was daydreaming again."

"Did you hear that?" Earl said. "Emma says she is thinking about renaming the diner."

"Oh yeah," Winston replied. "To what?"

Earl and Emma spoke in unison. "Rebecca's"

Winston smiled in agreement. "Great choice." He continued in his daze as they arrived at the diner and found a table. It was the same booth Winston sat in that first time he laid eyes on Emma. It seemed like a year ago. He let himself fall into the abyss of happiness that surrounded him. He had trusted his heart, and it had shown him the way. He could see it all now. He knew he would stay here in Salima Falls forever. He knew he and Emma would fall in Love and never part again. He knew he would live with her in the farmhouse. He knew he would work at Earl's shop and learn to paint cars. He knew they would walk the dogs in the park, and Buster would run around Harley and Charlie in the yard when Earl visited. He knew this was the first of endless meals with Earl and Emma at the diner. He knew he and Emma would share coffee in the mornings on the porch. He could almost smell the Juniper trees as he thought about it. He could see his entire future. The rest of his life played out before him like a movie as he closed his eyes.

⁜

Back in the city, Marlow parked his car in front of the cemetery arches. He supposed now was as good a time as any to make his final visit. He had only been to Caroline's grave once, but had a general idea where it was. He walked along the path holding flowers in his hand, towards the back-right corner of the lot, remembering the promise he made to Caroline after her death. He promised he would help Winston get through it, and he felt he finally had. He pulled out his cell phone and checked for any word from Winston. There was nothing. He wondered if he had found his peace as he walked past stones with every name he could think of, and some he had never heard before. He mumbled to himself as he placed his steps.

Outside the diner, Carter and Doc were enjoying a midday stroll through Salima Falls together. They walked down the sidewalk on the opposite side of the street from the diner, enjoying the predictably perfect weather.

"Nice day out, isn't it Doc?"

The doc just nodded his head and ambled on.

"Might be the best day Salima Falls has ever seen," Carter said.

"Might be," the doc replied.

Carter looked across the street and noticed Earl, Emma, and Winston through the far diner window. They were laughing and smiling together as Earl recounted a story, most likely the one of Winston's return from his lunch date, and just how silly he looked. The three of them seemed perfectly happy. Carter and Doc noticed too. They paused their walk for a few seconds to have a look.

Marlow walked along the far fence of the cemetery. He couldn't seem to find the spot in which he stood over a year ago. He passed a stack of old tires, and a random pile of sticks that didn't seem to belong. He read off the names on the stones to himself as he passed. There was a cross that reached high in the sky. Dr. Evan James. There was an obelisk that looked like a miniature Washington monument. Greta Davis. There were rows and rows of smaller square stones. Pearl Masterson… Betty Lewis... Dave Shumpert, Eleanor Powell, Lenny Stephens, James P. Callahan, Gladys Cobb, Gayle Gardner, Susie Laciak. Marlow walked past a simple-looking stone with a carving of a snake that appeared to be eating his own tail. Joseph Burgess. There were some stones with quotes, others with bible verses. Ryan Templeton. Jessica Willow. Norah Jenkins. He came to a large stone angel standing almost as tall as he did. Emmanual Salvadore. Finally, he looked up and recognized the tree from when he was here at the funeral a year ago and walked over near it. After a few quick glances, he saw Caroline's stone. He walked over to it and laid the flowers at the base.

Carter and Doc watched, as Winston, Emma, and Earl laughed and smiled together across the street in the diner. The three of them seemed to fit right in with the rest of the happy people in Salima Falls. Carter and Doc looked at each other with pride in their eyes, and Doc gave Carter a wink. They both nodded simultaneously, and formed identical smiles on their faces.

"Another perfect day in Salima Falls."

The doc smiled and nodded, and looked up at the clear blue sky.

"Yes sir," Carter added. "Perfect."

He pat Doc on the back as they continued their stroll.

"So, what now?" Carter asked.

"Now?" Doc said.

"Just wondering if we're done. Where do we go from here? What's next?"

"Ah yes," the doc said. "The eternal questions." He took a deep breath and raised his head to the sunlight, letting it warm his face as he closed his eyes. "Onward and upward," he said, as he opened them. "But I say let's not concern ourselves with tomorrow just yet," he continued. He turned his head to the right and looked once more at the diner. Then he and Carter turned the corner and walked out of sight.

"Today is perfect enough, and there is still more of it left."

The End